THE BODY IN THE GREENHOUSE

Caprice quickly searched through the first floor, then called up the wide stairway, "Louise?"

She received no answer.

Louise had said she was going to putter in her greenhouse this morning. Caprice gardened and her mom gardened even more. She knew how easy it was to become distracted by watering, examining, sorting. Maybe Louise was still in the greenhouse and was unmindful of the time.

"I'll check the greenhouse," she told Nikki as she passed her in the kitchen, her head deep in the refrigerator.

Caprice hurried to the greenhouse and saw the door was almost closed, but not completely. She pushed it open, calling, "Louise?"

There was no answer.

When she stepped inside—

She spotted Louise crumpled on the floor. She let out a loud "No," ran toward the older woman, and stopped at her prone form, aghast at what she saw.

She was *dead*.

Books by Karen Rose Smith

STAGED TO DEATH

DEADLY DÉCOR

GILT BY ASSOCIATION

Published by Kensington Publishing Corporation

Gilt by Association

Karen Rose Smith

KENSINGTON PUBLISHING CORP.

http://www.kensingtonbooks.com

KENSINGTON BOOKS are published by

Kensington Publishing Corp.
119 West 40th Street
New York, NY 10018

All Kensington Titles, Imprints, and Distributed Lines are available at special quantity discounts for bulk purchases for sales promotions, premiums, fund-raising, and educational or institutional use. Special book excerpts or customized printings can also be created to fit specific needs. For details, write or phone the office of the Kensington special sales manager: Kensington Publishing Corp., 119 West 40th Street, New York, NY 10018, attn: Special Sales Department, Phone: 1-800-221-2647.

Kensington and the K logo Reg. U.S. Pat & TM Off.

ISBN-13: 978-0-7582-8488-4
ISBN-10: 0-7582-8488-8
First Kensington Mass Market Edition: February 2015

eISBN-13: 978-0-7582-8489-1
eISBN-10: 0-7582-8489-6
First Kensington Electronic Edition: February 2015

10 9 8 7 6 5 4 3 2 1

Printed in the United States of America

*I dedicate this mystery to my husband, Steve—
my Valentine of 43 years.*

Acknowledgments

I would like to thank Officer Greg Berry and Officer Patrick Heron, my law enforcement consultants.

Thanks also to chemist Kenneth Smith, Ph.D., for helping me understand plant-based substances and their effects.

Chapter One

If her sister could run away, she probably would!

At least that's what Caprice De Luca thought after glancing at the expression on Bella's face, as well as the total disarray in Bella and Joe Santini's home.

This kind of chaos probably wasn't unusual for a mom with a three-week-old baby because *everything* changed when a baby entered a house. A baby . . . or a pup.

Caprice patted her hip to bring her dog, Lady, to her side. But Lady's head swung back and forth between Caprice and the newborn infant in Bella's arms who began to wail again.

Caprice wished she had more time to stay and help her sister, but shortly she was due at an appointment with a client. During February in Kismet, Pennsylvania, houses sold slowly. On the other hand, if a house hunter was looking at this time of year, the prospective buyer was usually serious. When Louise Downing, her mom's best friend, hired Caprice to stage her house, Caprice was more than ready with a Valentine's Day idea. An open house in conjunction with the popular holiday would be different than anything she'd done before. Louise's home already was all about hearts and flowers so that would be the underlying home-staging theme.

All at once, Bella's son Timmy yelled at his sister Megan, "You don't know how to play hide-and-seek." At eight, he was an expert.

Although Megan was only six, she still knew the rules. "You didn't count. You cheated."

Their squabbling was born out of restlessness and change. The letdown after the holidays had segued into welcoming their new brother into their home. Caprice supposed that they'd expected a newborn baby to be more fun. Since their mom had to give most of her attention to little Benedict, they were antsy and looking for trouble. That's where Aunt Caprice had come in. But she wasn't sure she'd done a very good job this Saturday afternoon. Bella was sleep-deprived and cranky, even though she loved her baby to bits. Trying to help out, Caprice had decided to keep them all company, do a little cooking and laundry.

Suddenly the front door to the modest ranch-style house opened. Cold winter wind blew in with Bella's husband, who'd been shoveling melting slush from the driveway so it wouldn't freeze. He looked as if he wanted to turn around and return to shoveling when Benny wailed again.

Suddenly Megan squeaked, "Oh, no," just as Lady squatted under the table and . . .

She'd obviously been trying to tell them she needed to go out and no one had listened.

Caprice sighed. No, babies and pups weren't that different sometimes.

She rushed over to Lady. "Eh-eh," she said in a non-threatening but even tone. Then she patted her hip, said, "Come," and headed for the door.

Joe called from the middle of the living room as he unzipped his coat. "She's not going to want to go out there any more than you will. There's snow in the air again."

"She knows we have to make this quick. I'll clean up when we're done," she assured him, grabbing her sixties-style pea coat from a kitchen chair along with a paper towel and a plastic bag from the counter.

After pushing her straight, long, dark brown hair over her shoulder, Caprice dropped the paper towel on the puddle, grabbed Lady's leash, and headed onto the back porch, patting her hip so her dog would follow her.

Caprice's bangs blew in the wind and she knew that she should be wearing her hat, but it was in her van. She attached Lady's leash and had to laugh as the cocker romped in the snow patches and turned around to look at Caprice as if asking her if she wanted to play. After all, she *was* wearing boots. She ran to the edge of the yard with her, said, "Go potty," and waited as Lady did her business. She praised her while she did.

After Caprice cleaned up, she followed the five-and-a-half-month-old pup back inside. Lady shook herself, leaving sparkles of water on the kitchen floor.

"I'll get it," she told anyone in the vicinity. She wasn't going to cause any extra work here today.

Taking care of a newborn wasn't easy in the best of households. Joe had seemed to form a new cooperation with Bella since little Benedict was born, but you never knew when that could end.

While Caprice cleaned up the kitchen floor, she saw Joe had taken the baby from his wife and was walking him.

Bella held up a bottle. "He just won't take it from me. And he has to or I'll never get any sleep."

Her sister had been breastfeeding but was trying to transition her newborn to a bottle so Joe could handle some of the feedings . . . or a babysitter could.

Joe assured her, "Maybe he's just not hungry."

"He's a baby. He *has* to be hungry," Bella insisted.

Lady whined at the anxiousness in Bella's tone.

Focusing on the situation at hand, Caprice realized the best thing she could do for her sister was to take her older kids out of the house, maybe ice skating, sometime soon.

"I thought Lady would entertain the kids," she said. "But we're adding to the commotion."

"And you didn't want to leave your dog home alone too much," Joe added, as if he'd heard it all before. "She's a pup. She can't be alone all the time, or she'll develop bad habits. I've got three kids. I know all about bad habits."

His expression was even, and Caprice couldn't really tell what he was thinking. Actually, she used to be able to tell better. Not that she could ever read his mind. But he'd turned over a new leaf last summer, and now it was hard to tell exactly what he was feeling . . . or thinking.

She crossed to Bella who looked close to tears. "Bee, you just fed Benny not so long ago."

Bella shook her head and her black curls flew. "But he's crying again."

Caprice was at a loss. Pups and kittens she understood. Babies, not so much. "Maybe he just needs a little walk or something."

Bella glanced around her house. "It's not as if we have that far to walk, and I don't want to take him outside when it's this cold. I just wish the snow and sleet would stop and the sun would come out."

Bella had deep blue smudges under her eyes. Her hair didn't look as if it had been washed today. Her slacks and sweatshirt weren't anything a recent fashion magazine would advertise. Caprice wondered if Joe had been helping at night or if—

As if Bella could read her thoughts, she assured Caprice, "Joe's been getting up with me at night. He's been great." She smiled up at him.

Caprice had noticed that Joe had been kind and attentive soon after he and Bella had started counseling with Father Gregory last summer. He'd been by her side during every minute of her labor and delivery. He really *had* seemed to change from the arrogant man he'd once been. Caprice wondered, though, if he had changed for good, or if he'd changed for Father Gregory's approval . . . or the De Luca family's approval, for that matter. Eight months ago her sister's marriage had almost fallen apart when Bella had found out she was pregnant again . . . and soon after when both she and Joe had become suspects in a murder investigation.

Now Caprice and her family just weren't sure what to think about the couple. Hope for the best and prepare for the worst, she thought. Wasn't that the Italian Catholic motto?

Joe jiggled his youngest son and repositioned him on his shoulder. "It's really okay if you leave, Caprice."

She should. Leaving was better for them and better for her. As it was, she might be a few minutes late for her meeting with her sister Nikki—who was catering the Hearts and Flowers open house—and Louise Downing.

"I made a mac and cheese casserole," she explained to Joe. "With Mom's creamy cheese sauce you like so much. Put it in the oven, ten minutes later shove in the chicken fingers, and everything should get done about half an hour after that. I even steamed broccoli and all you have to do is warm that up in the microwave. It's a semi-healthy meal. I brought along some new cookies I whipped up for Valentine's Day, too. Give them a taste and let me know if you like them."

"What's in them?" Joe asked suspiciously.

"White chocolate, dried cranberries, orange zest, and a secret ingredient," Caprice answered jovially, learning that was the best way with Joe.

The infant had quieted now and Joe said to Caprice, "I'll walk you out. Can you get the dog okay?"

In no time at all, Caprice had buttoned her jacket, rounded up Lady, and clipped on her leash once more. After giving the kids and Bella kisses and hugs, she walked to the door.

In a low voice, Joe thanked her. "I appreciate everything you're doing. Don't think I'll forget it."

"We're family, Joe. We stick together, good times and bad. You and Bella have had enough of the bad." She added, "Just remember, she could still be going through some postpartum baby blues—"

"You have to meddle, don't you?" he asked in a resigned, almost amused tone. "But I guess I can accept that now because I know it's for her own good . . . and mine. I'm making sure she does something for herself each day, even if it's just to take a bubble bath."

Perhaps Joe really had changed.

Lady was dancing around, keeping near to Caprice's legs.

Caprice squeezed her brother-in-law's arm affectionately. "Thanks for taking care of my sister. I'll see you soon."

Once outside, Caprice opened her van. Because Lady was still a pup, Caprice enclosed her in a crate in the back. She used this one solely in the van and when they traveled. That kept her safe. Fortunately Louise and her husband, Chet, liked animals. They especially liked Lady, so she'd been a welcome guest at their house as they'd talked over strategies for staging their house to sell.

Caprice tossed a treat into the crate and Lady went in after it. When she turned around again, Caprice made a fuss, praising her, saying "Good dog" over and over. She gave her another treat from her pocket and closed the door. They'd worked on crate training early on. Lady didn't mind being closed inside because they went to fun places and had new adventures.

Snow was falling softly as Caprice climbed in the driver's side of her vehicle. She always smiled when she saw the swirling turquoise, fuchsia, and lime psychedelic colors painted on the side along with a few large flowers and turquoise lettering that read CAPRICE DE LUCA—REDESIGN AND HOME-STAGING. She loved the sixties and it showed in her fashions, in her home-stagings, and especially in her home-decorating. No matter who she was decorating or staging for, she chose colors because of the emotions they evoked. Sixties colors made *her* happy.

She switched on her windshield wipers but didn't really need them. The flurries were teeny dots that didn't even leave wet spots. She hoped the snow wouldn't fall heavier until much later. Then neither she nor Nikki would have to worry about driving in it.

With her own catering business, her older sister Nikki always helped with Caprice's home-stagings, and together they made them events. This was a busy time of year for both of them. They'd be helping with Kismet's Give-from-the-Heart Day food and clothing drive, as well as the Valentine's Day dance. The next two weeks would be nonstop activity.

Dusk was wrapping itself around the town as Caprice drove her van down slush-filled streets. The temperature hovered around thirty-two.

Crossing White Rose Way—the main street arrowing through the center of town—she headed for the outskirts of Kismet and the Downings' neighborhood. The streets hadn't been cleaned as well in this section where snow-banks lined the road. Expensive houses stretched along Middlebrook Drive where Louise lived. These homes weren't quite mansions, but they sprawled across acre lots. Many of them were older, unlike the new estates in the Reservoir Heights area. Country club patrons inhabited the homes on Middlebrook and had lived in them for more than one generation.

Louise and Chet Downing's property was elegant and pleasing to the eye. The house covered about forty-eight hundred square feet. Caprice knew almost every square foot since she was in the process of staging it. She drove around the front of the property, whose boundary was delineated by an intricate brick and stone wall. Sturdy brick pillars stood at ten-foot intervals. A broad lawn, now mostly snow-covered, led up to the front entrance with the floor-to-ceiling unique window treatments, arches, and multipaned glass. A four-story sycamore, its branches still prettily snow-covered, draped over the front lawn. Multilevel roofs and gables lent character to the house, and evergreen shrubs gave color to what could have been a drab winter landscape.

Louise was quite the gardener and had a hand in the landscaping. Come spring, color would overflow from every planter, border, and manicured garden surrounding the house. Since she enjoyed dabbling in a greenhouse of her own out back, every January she started plants from seeds—impatiens, geraniums, and petunias.

Caprice drove toward the garage side of the house and the greenhouse, entering the driveway in the rear of the property. She appreciated the architecture of the back of the house almost as much as the front. French doors on the first and second floors provided panoramic views of the gardens. Now, however, she parked her van, exited, and released Lady from her crate. After attaching the leash, she watched the pup jump from the van onto the snow-cleared driveway. Every day, Caprice spent time training Lady with gentle, reward-earning incentives. They were working on "heel" and Lady was learning how to walk on a loose leash beside her. Together they ambled up the flagstone path to the kitchen entrance. This is where friends and family usually entered.

Louise's maid, Rachel Cosgrove, answered the melodic chime of the back door. She was about Caprice's age, thirty-two, with honey-blond hair she kept restrained in a low ponytail. "C'mon in. Nikki and Mrs. Downing have been chatting. It's surely cold out there, isn't it? I'll take your coat."

Caprice could hear voices coming from the breakfast nook. When Caprice removed Lady's leash, the cocker raced to the women, wiggling around their feet.

After Caprice shrugged out of her jacket, she handed it to Rachel as Louise smiled and made an attempt to pet Lady. But her smile seemed a little forced.

Nikki patted the chair seat next to her. The burgundy and green flowered chairs on wheels suited their staging theme, so Caprice hadn't suggested Louise change them. Glancing at Nikki again, Caprice realized her sister must have had her hair highlighted recently because golden strands in the midst of dark brown glowed under the shiny brass chandelier. She looked gorgeous.

Louise told Rachel, "Bring Caprice's usual—a cup of coffee with cream and sugar." Her tone was a bit absent, even a little condescending.

Caprice took the chair Nikki offered, wondering if Louise was worried about this open house . . . or something else.

Staging the house had been easy. Louise's home was

all about "pretty" mixed with "elegant." Lace curtains at the windows and gilt-edged mirrors added a touch of old world feel. Heart-shaped pillows trimmed with ecru lace decorated the love seat by the small fireplace in the kitchen, as well as the rose and green damask-covered sofa in the living room. Caprice had de-cluttered a bit for the home-staging but, for the most part, had just rearranged the expensive furnishings and valuable antiques Louise had chosen over the years.

After greetings all around, Nikki nodded to the tablet computer in front of her. "We're brainstorming what to serve at the open house. I know your theme is hearts and flowers, but how over-the-top Valentine's Day do you want to make it?"

"There's no over-the-top for Valentine's Day," Louise maintained, possibly a little too firmly to be believable. "After all, Chet and I fell in love at first sight at The Pretzel Party's Valentine Day shindig all those years ago."

Louise almost sounded as if she was trying to convince herself as well as them, and Caprice wondered why. She knew Louise's story well because Louise and her mom had become fast friends when they'd met at Saint Francis of Assisi Catholic Church soon after Louise first arrived in Kismet. Back then, she'd been a secretary at The Pretzel Party, Chet Downing's snack company. She'd caught his eye, and they'd gotten married over thirty years ago. Theirs had been one of those Cinderella stories that had become a legend in Kismet.

But something about Louise's attitude tonight made Caprice wonder if Louise and Chet had argued about something. Obviously Louise loved lace and gold leaf, flowers and hearts. Her house reflected that. However, now she and Chet wanted to downsize to travel more. This home-staging and open house was supposedly going to sell the Downing estate faster. Hearts and flowers had been the obvious theme, especially with Valentine's Day right around the corner.

"Do you really think Chet's going to be happy selling The Pretzel Party?" Caprice asked Louise now, guessing the man of the house was in his den down the hall away from their planning session.

"He's always wanted to travel more," Louise answered. "With no restrictions on our time, we can choose places we *both* want to see." She hesitated, then added, a bit thin-lipped, "By the way, he's staying overnight in Philadelphia tonight for a late meeting. At least he won't be on the road in this weather."

So Chet wasn't down the hall. Maybe he and Louise had disagreed about him going to Philly this weekend?

As Rachel set a porcelain cup and saucer before Caprice, Louise scolded not for the first time, saying, "You really should switch to herbal tea, Caprice, or at least decaffeinated coffee. I had a latté at the Koffee Klatch just a few weeks ago. After I drank half of it, my heart skipped beats. The barista had used caffeinated coffee instead of decaffeinated. I could have gotten her fired but she was young and in a hurry."

Because her mom and Louise were friends, Caprice knew Louise had suffered with atrial fibrillation and tachycardia since she was young. The arrhythmia didn't act up often, but caffeine could activate the problem.

"I drink tea with Nana. I'll keep in mind your advice and try to cut down on caffeine," she assured Louise, knowing if she didn't, the older woman would try more thoroughly to convince her. Louise's opinions were usually unshakeable.

Moving their meeting forward, Caprice asked Nikki, "So what did you have in mind for food for the open house?"

Lady had settled at Caprice's feet and her tail wagged against the floor in a thump-thump-thump rhythm. Some people found that thumping bothersome, but Caprice found it soothing.

Nikki glanced at Caprice, then read from her list on her e-tablet. "We talked about hors d'oeuvres. They're easy—heart-shaped bruschetta, kiwi slices with tiny cream cheese hearts in the centers. I also have access to soup bowls shaped like hearts that would be great for tomato bisque. I can use red rose petals to decorate the plates, and carnations are edible, too. They can taste spicy, peppery, even clovelike. Chrysanthemums have a more bitter taste so I could use some of their petals in the salads."

Nikki paused and thought about that. "Some people have allergies to flowers in food, though, so it might be better just to decorate the buffet with them rather than use them in the dishes. We wouldn't want anyone to have an allergic attack."

"Goodness, no," Louise said, her hand covering her heart. "No flowers in the food. Nevertheless, red rose petals on a white tablecloth would look fabulous."

"Not everything has to be heart-shaped," Caprice

reminded them. "I just made a batch of white chocolate and cranberry cookies. They'd be a great Valentine treat with chamomile tea, hot chocolate, or coffee."

"Not to mention strawberry cheesecake, and cherries with meringue," Nikki suggested with a lift of one brow. "The choices are endless with this kind of theme."

"I spoke with Jamie Bergman at Garden Glory," Louise informed them. "I placed an order for peace lilies, grafted hibiscus trees and, of course, palms. Jamie had the terrific idea of planting flowers in the base of the palms. She's going to look into exactly what varieties are available and get back to me."

Louise was one of those clients who liked control over the home-staging. Since she knew plants and flowers well, Caprice had let her handle that, though she or her assistant would actually place them.

Caprice tapped Nikki's electronic tablet. "What about our main dishes? When guests come to one of my stagings, they expect substantial food, too."

Nikki nodded. "I was thinking of prosciutto-wrapped stuffed chicken. Sliced correctly, the slices could look like heart shapes. Fettuccini would go well with it. Shrimp scampi is another possibility. I also thought about using those heart-shaped bowls for individual casseroles of shepherd's pie with lamb and pork. This time of year, with this weather, that kind of food can warm your heart."

"That sounds wonderful," Louise agreed. "But back to incidentals . . . Let's not forget chocolate-covered peanut butter creams. They're my favorite candy." Her eyes seemed to grow a little misty as she added, "Chet and I shared a few of those the first night we met."

Louise and Chet had been married for thirty years. Caprice's mom and dad had been married thirty-seven years. So the idea of a lifelong union wasn't foreign. Yet Caprice could hardly imagine being married to someone for that long. Still she wanted that kind of committed, all-in-for-life marriage. If it was happy. Was Louise still happy? Was Chet?

Back to the subject at hand, Caprice said, "We'll make sure we have your favorite peanut butter creams." In fact, her mom had mentioned she might send Louise a box for Valentine's Day.

Rachel approached the table, her expression worried. "I don't mean to interrupt, Mrs. Downing, but the snow is falling rather heavily again."

The blinds in the nook were closed. Louise looked toward them and nodded. "Thank you for telling us."

"I think we're ready," Caprice announced. "The house is staged exactly the way we want it except for the plants, and Garden Glory will deliver them the day before the open house. The menu sounds perfect. By next weekend, we'll be all set."

A few minutes later after Rachel procured their coats and they hugged and said their good-byes, Caprice walked Lady to her van.

She happened to glance at the frosting of snow on the driveway and caught the glare of headlights as a truck sped away from the driveway's entrance. A visitor who decided not to come in? A wrong turn on a snowy night?

Caprice gave herself a mental shake. She was just paranoid because she'd been followed once before . . . and almost killed.

Nothing was going to happen tonight.

Lady dashed into her crate. Caprice lavished her with praise and another tiny piece of doggie cookie. After she climbed in, buckled up, and started the van, she followed Nikki's car out of the driveway.

Her sister's car had just turned off onto a side street when the snow swirled in almost-blizzard proportions with a howl of wind. Recently, snow squalls seemed to become more prevalent in the Pennsylvania winter weather patterns. She was glad Lady was safely enclosed in her crate.

Caprice was carefully slowing for a stop sign when her cell phone played the Beatles' "Good Day Sunshine" from her cup holder. She thought about not taking the call, but then her curiosity, as usual, got the best of her.

Checking the caller ID, she saw that the caller was Grant Weatherford, her brother's law partner. She listened to a few more notes of the music and took a deep breath. Lately, Grant's voice made her feel both excited and nervous. They'd been getting along better since he'd adopted Patches, Lady's brother. They discussed training techniques and used similar strategies, comparing notes. But there was still so much tension between them.

She swiped her finger across the face of her phone and picked it up. "Hey, Grant, what's up?"

"I think we have a problem," he warned her.

She started off again across the intersection, wishing

she still had taillights in front of her to follow. "And what might that be?" she asked.

"I think your brother is in love with Roz Winslow. What are we going to do about it?"

The question so startled Caprice and broke her concentration that she hit a patch of ice and slid sideways into a snowbank by the side of the road.

Chapter Two

Grant must have heard Lady barking at Caprice's sudden jerking stop. He also must have heard Caprice's low groan of disapproval as the passenger side wheel seemed to stick in the snowbank.

"Where are you?" he asked.

"I'm driving home from the Downings." She'd told him about this open house last week when they'd spoken at a puppy training and socialization session at Furry Friends Veterinary Clinic.

"Are you all right?" Grant wanted to know. "It's snowing pretty heavily out there."

"We're fine," she muttered with almost gritted teeth, hoping she could back out of the snowbank, hoping even more that she didn't need any help.

While she spun her wheels, she thought about Vince and what Grant had said. Her brother was in love with Roz? Her brother was a serial dater, and he seemed to be a confirmed bachelor. Her friend Roz had been widowed less than a year. Just what was Grant basing his theory on?

"Why do you think Vince is in love with Roz?" The van's engine vroomed as she gained a small amount of traction.

"Because he wants to handle all her paperwork."

Caprice scoffed and rocked the van back and forth as her dad had taught her. "That's not proof."

She couldn't see much with a blizzard whiting out her front and back windshields.

Lady barked again.

Caprice gave up the rocking motion for the moment so she could have this conversation with Grant. She carried a bucket of cat litter in the back of the van and she could use that to gain traction under her wheels.

"He told me this afternoon he's going to ask Roz to the Valentine's Day dance," Grant explained. "Vince had a twinkle in his eye, and he asked me about corsages. This is your brother, Caprice. He doesn't think about corsages."

Grant was right about that. He and Vince had gone through law school together and been roommates so he knew Vince almost better than anyone.

"I don't think we have to worry about one dance. And what would be so bad if they did hook up?" Roz needed to start socializing again with someone who could appreciate her intelligence as well as her beauty. And Vince?

Silence met her posed question as the snow squall swirled around the van and everything else in Kismet.

"What would be so bad?" Grant repeated with some annoyance. "You try to protect your friends, don't you? You tried to protect Roz from a murder charge."

"Vince and a murder charge aren't exactly the same thing."

"No, Vince could be worse. He could date her once, twice, maybe even three times and then decide he's no longer interested. That's your brother, Caprice."

Yes, that *was* her brother. "Did you talk to him?"

"He didn't want to hear what I had to say. He claimed he was too busy to talk. Do you think Roz will listen to *you*?"

"I'm not sure what I'm supposed to say. Don't date my brother, he might drop you? Don't date my brother though he's debonair and a good dancer and could give you a good time?"

"Caprice . . ." There was that warning note in Grant's voice that she'd heard many times before. Her windshield wipers swept across the windshield, but they were impeded by too much powder too fast.

After a few moments, Grant asked, "Are you almost home?"

She looked around, knowing she was only a few streets away from her neighborhood. He didn't have to know every detail . . . like the incidental detail that she was stuck.

She agreed, "Almost."

"You wouldn't be going to the dance, would you?"

The snow squall and her surroundings seemed to fade away. Was he asking her to go with him?

"I'm involved in organizing the food drive and decorating the hall earlier in the day, so I'll definitely be at the dance. What about you?" she asked as casually as she could.

"It's for a good cause. I was going to stop in."

Caprice couldn't help but feel a little trip in her heart that Grant was going to be there, too. But as silence stretched between them, reality sunk in and stripped the smile from her face. He obviously wasn't going to ask her to accompany him. No matter what had happened between them last summer, he still didn't seem ready for much more than a surface relationship.

And she had to escape this snowbank's hold and drive home. "Grant, I've got to go and keep my mind on what I'm doing."

"I know. This weather's tough. You *are* wearing boots, aren't you?"

"Sort of. They're suede and have fringes. I'm good."

"Your retro styles aren't going to keep your feet from freezing in this weather."

"It wasn't snowing when I left home." She couldn't keep herself from asking, "You're still going to Marcus's puppy socialization class Monday night, aren't you?"

"Wouldn't miss it. We'll have to see who does better, Patches or Lady."

"It's not a competition."

"Life is always a competition."

Different. They were very different. Still . . .

"I'll let you go," he said. "I'll see you Monday unless Marcus cancels because of the weather. Don't forget to wear decent boots if it's snowing."

As always, when he took that authoritarian tone with her, she hung up on him.

With a sigh, she climbed out of her van into the snow, went to the back for the bucket of cat litter, dumped it in behind her front right wheel . . . and hoped it would provide enough traction to get her out of this mess.

✥ ✥ ✥

As Caprice watched Marcus Reed on Monday evening, she was glad she could call him a friend as well as her pets' veterinarian. He was tall and husky. African-American, he kept his hair trimmed short and usually wore a broad smile. He owned Furry Friends Veterinary Clinic and was an excellent dog trainer as well as a veterinarian. The puppies in this class were all five to six months old. Besides learning to socialize with a few other dogs, and teaching them how to make friends instead of enemies, Marcus was focusing on basic commands, too—down, sit, stand, come. And then there were leash manners and the heel command.

Caprice glanced at Grant who was working beside her since their pups already knew each other.

Marcus stopped between them. "Are you still treating all your walks as training sessions, keeping them short?"

"Patches behaves better when he's had a walk and play session before we start the day," Grant conceded.

Marcus eyed Caprice. "You *are* making Lady spend private time, aren't you? She's not with you all the time?"

"She naps in her puppy apartment sometimes while I work in my office. But she does want to be with me." Caprice and Grant both had purchased "puppy apartments"—large crates with both a sleep area and a bathroom area. Caprice had taught Lady the "go potty" command by utilizing the crate with its special pads. When she had to leave Lady at the house alone, she attached puppy gates at the doorways to her kitchen. That way Lady had her bed and bathroom area as well as the kitchen to play in.

"And you want to be with her," Marcus said with a raised brow. "That's just the way you are. But raising a puppy is different from taking in a stray adult dog. You don't want problems with separation anxiety later on."

"I know, and her chewing's getting better. As long as I keep her supplied with different toys, she stays away from my slippers and the table legs."

Grant shook his head. "Patches ruined one of my best pair of loafers. I learned to rotate toys, too, so he doesn't get bored with any of them."

Marcus laughed a big hearty laugh. "I don't need to worry about *you* two. After all, anyone who sees their pups born is invested." He gave a wink.

Last summer, Caprice had taken in a cocker spaniel she'd found in her mom's backyard. She'd dubbed her Shasta since she was the color of the Shasta daisies in her garden and soon after discovered the cocker was pregnant. One evening late in the cocker's pregnancy, she and Grant had run into each other at a party and he'd followed her home. Shasta had been in labor and they'd delivered her pups together. That had seemed to form a special bond between them—especially when Grant had adopted the last pup in the litter and named him Patches. Where Lady was a golden buff color, Grant's dog was cream-colored with brown ears, brown circles around his eyes and nose, as well as brown patches on his back and flank.

Marcus suddenly called across the room, "Don't keep walking when your pup pulls. You don't want to reinforce bad behavior. Walk the other way and she'll learn she won't get any farther. Give her a treat and praise for staying in that space beside you."

Grant and Caprice, their dogs on a loose leash hold beside them, followed a course delineated by blue tape on the floor. As Marcus watched, Patches and Lady both walked to the left of them without pulling on their leashes.

He nodded approvingly. "You two have confidence and patience. That's what some of these dog owners are lacking. Your dogs can tell."

When Marcus moved across the room to give more specific instructions to a woman who was having problems encouraging her dog to heel, Caprice took a sneak peek at Grant. His thick black hair was crisply parted and brushed to one side. His gray eyes were as intense as ever. She admired his casual look tonight. The chambray shirt seemed to make his shoulders look broader. His jeans fit like jeans should fit a man. She was much more used to seeing him in a shirt and tie and suit coat. Before she tore her gaze away from him—of course she was simply studying the way he handled Patches—her phone vibrated in the pocket of her tapestry blazer. A second later, she heard the muffled tones of "Good Day Sunshine." She'd set her phone on vibrate, too, in case she couldn't hear it with puppies yapping, and their owners talking.

"Sit," she said to Lady, also giving her a hand signal, and sit Lady did. She gave her an affectionate pat under the chin and "good girl" animated praise. That positive reinforcement was all-important.

Bella's picture stared at her from the surface of her

phone so she answered the call. "I'm at puppy training class," she told Bella.

"I know, but I can't get hold of Nikki, and I didn't want to bother Mom because she's grading exams and it's cold out—"

"What do you need?"

Grant looked toward her with a questioning eye because he could obviously hear her. She just shrugged.

"Joe's not here," Bella said. "He took Megan and Timmy to the movies, so they'd have some fun time together. But Benny has a fever of one hundred, and he's stuffy. I called the doctor and she said to watch his fever, but she also said a cool mist humidifier would help. The one I had for Megan when she was little stopped running and I ditched it. Can you possibly go the drugstore and pick one up for me? He's so little to have a stuffy nose and I'm worried."

Of course, Bella was worried. What mother wouldn't be? And she was trying to juggle everyone and everything in her life. Bella wasn't good at juggling. She liked things in order, unlike Caprice who was much more used to accepting the lemons life threw at her. So that's what she did now.

"I'll leave right now, but I'll have to bring Lady along. Are you okay with that?"

Bella believed animals were nothing but more work and trouble. She didn't see them the same way Caprice did.

"It's fine," her sister said with a resigned sigh. "I just need the humidifier."

When Caprice ended the call, Grant moved closer to her, Patches by his side. "Problem?"

"How do you know I wasn't just talking to an old friend?" she asked.

"Because the corners of your lips were turned down. When you talk to an old friend, you smile," he said acerbically.

Relenting, she told him, "It was Bella. Benny's sick, and she needs a cool mist humidifier. I'm going to leave and get her one."

"Lady will miss the second half of the class."

"Can't be helped."

"Actually, it can be. The next part of the session is mostly socializing with the other dogs. I've watched Patches and Lady in the dog park when you see somebody you know. I can handle them both."

She considered leaving Lady here with Patches. Patches was basically a middle pack dog. He was friendly and easygoing, and usually compliant. She knew Lady bordered on a lower pack dog. She liked to keep close by and quickly responded to rewards and corrections. She avoided conflict with Caprice's cat, Sophia, though she did enjoy a good chase. Caprice knew Grant would be good with her pup and watch out for her.

"Are you sure you don't mind?"

"No, I don't mind. I'll take Lady home with me. You can pick her up when you're through at Bella's. Let's go get her crate so I'll have that, too."

Since Grant had adopted Patches, he mostly worked from home. He'd insisted that once Patches was less exuberant, he'd work out of his office in Vince's law business downtown and take Patches to work with him.

But for now, this arrangement seemed to suit him. She realized the qualities she admired in him when dealing with Patches were qualities he'd probably gained as a dad. Only, he never talked about that because being a father had ended in tragedy. Losing a child had led to his divorce. However, that divorce and a change in lifestyle had also encouraged him to set up practice with Vince in Kismet.

Yes, she could entrust Lady's care to Grant. She was sure of it.

Forty-five minutes later, Caprice held Benny while Bella set up the cool mist humidifier in the master bedroom. That's where they'd placed his crib for now.

Caprice lowered her lips to the baby's head and smelled baby shampoo. His warm little body in her arms, she felt protective as she walked him around the room, crooning to him, rocking him a little. A twinge of something that didn't often nudge her felt almost painful now. What was that? A desire to be a mother? Was that why she took in strays? Because she had the need to nurture? Nevertheless, being a mother meant more than nurturing. She was aware of *that*.

Unbidden, she thought of Seth Randolph—the doctor she'd dated last summer and now e-mailed with more infrequency than she'd like—in the role of husband and father. Next, her focus switched to thoughts of Grant. Neither man was ready for married life or babies, but that didn't mean *she* wasn't. If she reached a certain age and still wasn't married, she could consider adopting a baby. Marriage was complicated. Two people had to compromise. They should be real partners, had to have the same values, even think alike most of the time. Maybe raising a child would be better if she did it on her own.

After Bella set up the humidifier and it was running, she took little Benedict from Caprice's arms. Caprice felt that wistful longing still remained.

"I'm going to change him and see if I can get him to fall asleep. He likes the swing you and Nikki gave him. Maybe he'll fall asleep in that."

"So he likes motion."

"He always falls asleep in the car, but with it so cold and icy out, I don't want to take him for a drive."

"I can understand that."

Bella glanced at her. "You're good with him."

"You sound surprised."

"You weren't that interested when Megan and Timmy were little."

"Maybe I'm older and wiser."

Bella laughed. "Aren't we all."

Bella was two years younger than Caprice, Nikki two years older. But since Bella had married when she was young, sometimes *she* seemed like the big sister. She was certainly always ready to give advice, not so ready to take it. But that was Isabella Santini.

Expertly fastening the diaper, she said, "Joe went online and registered a domain name for me."

"Really? What did you get?"

"CostumesByBella.com. What else?"

Bella sewed Halloween costumes for kids and had

sold a few to friends, as well as to parents at Megan and Timmy's school. Now she was going to go at it in a more businesslike way.

She went on. "Joe found this place we could set up a free Web site, but it will serve our purposes for now."

"Our?"

Bella shrugged. "I don't know if Joe's going to want to have much to do with my business or not. He sees how tired I am at the end of the day and he's being helpful. Dana at the Cupcake House wants me to make a bunny costume for one of the employees for Easter. I said I would."

"You could have a real specialty business."

"I don't know about that, but the extra income would be nice, at least until I go back to work at Roz's boutique. Joe's not too thrilled with that idea."

Caprice hoped they could figure it out and Bella's working wouldn't cause dissention in their marriage.

"So you have an open house this coming weekend?" Bella asked as she settled Benny in the swing and wound up the mechanism.

"I do. At Chet and Louise Downing's."

"Louise and Mom have been friends forever," Bella acknowledged, watching her son with a mother's affectionate eye.

"I'm just hoping the weather cooperates." That was Caprice's main concern. "I don't need a blizzard on Saturday."

"Have you checked the extended forecast?"

"So far, so good. But you know how that goes. Maybe weathermen have better tools than they used to

have, but one inch of snow could turn into six, and rain
could change to sleet if the temperature drops just a
degree."

So Caprice wouldn't take a relaxed breath until Saturday morning came with no precipitation or sign of it.

Suddenly there was the sound of voices in the
living room. Bella and Joe's bedroom was located at
the back of the house, so they hadn't heard the garage
door go up. Seconds later, Joe was in the doorway, his
coat still on.

After a look at Benny and the humidifier, he asked,
"What's wrong?"

"A fever and a stuffy nose. I'm trying to make him
more comfortable," Bella told him. "Caprice stopped for
the humidifier for me."

"I'll pay you," Joe said.

"You don't have to," Caprice started but then stopped.
Joe was a proud man, and he and Bella were trying to
get their finances back in order after a big upheaval last
summer.

"If you want, you can. I have the receipt in my purse."

Joe called to Timmy and Megan, "Climb into your
pj's, kids, then you can have a cookie and say good-
night to your mom and Aunt Caprice."

"I'll get that receipt," Caprice said as she headed for
the living room. She passed the kids in the hall and
gave both of them hugs, asked them about the movie,
and listened while they chattered for a few minutes.
She noticed Joe was watching her, and she wondered if
he was eager for her to leave.

After Megan and Timmy went to their rooms, she
headed for the living room. To her surprise, Joe followed.

Out of earshot of the bedroom, he said, "I've got to make this quick so Bella doesn't suspect anything."

Puzzled, Caprice asked, "Make what quick?"

"I want to do something special for Bella for Valentine's Day. I can't afford expensive jewelry, and do you know what a dozen roses cost right now?"

Caprice had to smile. "I do, because I order them for home-stagings."

He shook his head. "One rose in a vase looks feeble. I want to do more than that. Do you have any suggestions?"

Joe asking for suggestions from her had to be a first. She gave it serious thought.

"My guess is, right now Bella might like something that makes her feel good rather than something she could hold in her hand. I mean, I'm sure she'd appreciate a romantic card, but I was thinking along the lines of a gift certificate to get her hair done at Curls R Us, or maybe a massage at Green Tea Spa."

"Green Tea Spa. Your doctor got your mom a spa day there for her birthday, didn't he? That place is pretty expensive."

Seth had indeed gifted her mother with a spa day at Green Tea. He was thoughtful that way, just as he'd been thoughtful when he'd sent her a dozen roses after their first date.

Pushing that thought aside, she said, "You can buy a gift certificate for just a massage. They even run coupons in the *Kismet Crier*. You can check their site online."

"That sounds like a good idea."

"I do have them once in a while," she kidded him.

But Joe's expression turned serious. "Bella and I have talked about putting the house up for sale now that the market's picking up. I'm looking for a bigger house. Now might be a good time to clinch a deal. There are bargains out there, I've heard. You'd know about that, wouldn't you?"

She mostly signed on high-end clients now, but she did, of course, have contacts in the real estate business. "I can keep an ear out if you tell me what you're looking for."

"The big thing is four bedrooms, and maybe a basement we can make into a playroom. We're bursting at the seams here. We've talked to Father Gregory about it and he thinks we all need a little more room, a little privacy. I mean, the baby's in *our* room."

Again Caprice had to smile. That certainly didn't lend to a couple's intimacy.

"Bella's on the alert with every breath he takes. That's another reason she's not getting enough sleep."

So Joe wasn't only concerned about himself and his needs. He was concerned about Bella. Maybe, just maybe, this couple was going to have a happy Valentine's Day this year.

Fifteen minutes later, Grant answered the door with a serious expression on his face after Caprice rang his doorbell.

"Is everything all right?" she asked before stepping inside.

The corner of Grant's lip quirked a little. "Lady didn't even miss you."

He pointed inside his living room where a sports channel was playing. Both dogs lay side by side with the requisite chew toys tossed haphazardly nearby. They didn't even look up when Caprice walked in.

"A sports channel. Not even HGTV!" she said with mock outrage.

"I'm raising a male."

"And I'm raising a female to go beyond her gender boundaries. She's heard of the Ravens and the Orioles."

"What about the Pirates and the Steelers?" he countered.

Caprice waved her hand in front of her. "Too many sports teams will just confuse her."

Grant gave a chuckle, then sobered. "How did it go with your sister?"

"I don't think she's going to get much sleep tonight. Joe either. It's that way with a sick baby."

She said it thinking about Grant's life now, not his life as it used to be. These days, he seemed like a bachelor with no cares besides work . . . and Patches. When she gazed into his eyes, though, there was still pain there.

"I remember how it was with a baby," he said evenly.

His child had drowned in a pool, and nothing had been the same after that. Maybe sometime he'd talk to her about it. She had the feeling that until he did, they'd never really get close.

Is close what she wanted, when Seth Randolph was still on the fringes of her mind?

Moving closer to the dogs, he said, "I can switch channels if you want a beer. No wine in the house. Vince hasn't brought any over lately."

Her brother thought of himself as a wine connoisseur

of sorts. When they had their family dinners once a month, she and Bella and Nikki, her mom and nana, even her dad sometimes, cooked and Vince usually brought the wine. But that was okay. Everyone contributed something.

She hadn't been in Grant's town house before. Usually they met at her place or the dog park. His living room was furnished in black leather and gray suede. Somehow, sitting here with him in his dim living room with the dogs lazily resting close by, just didn't seem like a good idea. Maybe *she* was the one who was skittish. Maybe *she* was the one who wasn't sure of what she wanted. At age thirty-two, she certainly should be sure. But her experiences since last May—meeting Seth, solving two murders—had shaken up her life a bit.

"I'd better get going," she murmured.

But Grant was never easy. He never let anything just pass by. "Come to think of it, I don't know if I've ever seen you drink a beer."

"Of course, I drink beer. I'm not a wine snob. You know Rolling Rock? I like Rolling Rock."

He laughed out loud. "Well, if you know Rolling Rock, then you really must know beer."

"Actually, it's what my grandpop used to drink."

"Nana Celia's husband?"

"Yep. He'd slip me a quarter of an inch in a glass when no one was looking."

While there was still peace between them, and still an easy atmosphere, Caprice went to pick up Lady's leash, fuchsia in color, which was lying over the coffee table.

She'd just looped it over her arm, ready to wake Lady, when her cell phone vibrated, then played.

The caller couldn't be Bella. She'd just left there. Taking it from her blazer pocket, she saw it was her mom.

She held the phone to her ear. "Hi, Mom."

"Something awful has happened," her mother said, sounding close to tears. "Louise was taken to the hospital."

Chapter Three

Caprice felt as if she'd had the air knocked out of her. "What happened? Louise was perfectly fine on Saturday. Did she catch the flu? Was she in an accident?"

Louise and her mom were best friends, so she could only imagine what her mother was feeling.

"No one's exactly sure what happened," her mom explained. "Rachel was out. When she came home, she found her. It was some kind of stomach upset and then her heart condition factored in, so Rachel called nine-one-one and that's all I know. Chet called me, beside himself. He's pacing the emergency room while they do tests on her. He thinks they're going to admit her. I asked if he wanted me to come down there and he said that would be useless tonight. But if they do admit her, of course, she'd want me to visit tomorrow. I'd take a personal day, but we have midterm exams."

Louise was one of those mavens of Kismet who had tons of friends. She belonged to the Garden Club and was involved in a multitude of charities. But how many *close* friends did she have? She and her mom went way back and that made a difference in friendship.

Caprice thought about Roz Winslow, the high school friend who'd gotten caught up in a murder investigation. She and Caprice had reinvigorated their friendship, and now were almost as close as sisters again. Good friends were so important.

"Mom, I know you want to be with Louise, but it might be useless to take the day off without knowing her condition, and how long she'll be there. I'll call the hospital in the morning and if I can, I'll go in and visit."

"I'd go during lunch if I could, but I wouldn't have enough time to make it to York and back."

Kismet wasn't large enough to have its own hospital. They had doctors and an urgent care center where Seth had worked. But for a hospital, Kismet residents had to travel to York, about twenty minutes away.

"If Louise is there and can have visitors, I'll tell her you'll be there as soon as school dismisses."

"I don't want to let her down," her mother said. "There were many times she backed me up when I needed someone to stay with you kids. Remember when Nikki was in that biking accident when she was sixteen? Your father was on a job site and I couldn't reach him. Louise was with me when I got the call, and she didn't hesitate to drive me to the hospital and stay with me and Nikki until she was taken care of . . . until your father arrived. I haven't seen her as much as I'd like over the past few years. She seemed to grow a little distant. But we're still good friends, and friends help each other in the rough times."

"I understand, Mom, I really do. I'll check things out

and text you or leave a message on your phone. Then you'll know how she is, and when she's going to be discharged. They don't keep anyone in the hospital very long anymore. She could be sent home before you even think about visiting her. Nikki was going to come over tomorrow morning. We have a couple more open houses to plan for. Maybe she can stay with Lady, and I can keep Louise company as long as she needs me there."

"Thank you, honey. I really appreciate this."

Lady and Patches were now awake and had decided a bit of romping was a good idea. Grant was standing by, ready to referee if he had to, but suddenly Patches barked and Lady barked back.

Her mother asked, "Are you at home?"

Caprice hesitated, then finally responded, "No, I'm at Grant's. Bella called me while I was at puppy training class. She needed a cool mist humidifier because Benny is sick."

"How sick?"

"He had a temperature of a hundred and a stuffy nose, but Joe was there when I left, and they'll be fine. Really."

"And you and Grant?"

Her mother often asked her this question, and Caprice didn't particularly like the probing. However, she answered patiently, "He brought Lady home so she wouldn't miss the rest of the class."

"Are you staying a while?" Her mother's voice sounded as if it had a bit of hope in it.

"No. I still have work to do tonight."

"Caprice."

Caprice knew what was coming. "Mom, don't."

"I wouldn't be your mother, a mother who loves you very much, if I didn't remind you, you have to try to forget about Seth and move on."

"Mom, I can't have this conversation now."

"No, I suppose not, but you know it's true."

Caprice wasn't sure it *was* true. Where men were concerned, she wasn't sure about anything.

"In between classes in the morning, watch for texts," Caprice reminded her. "And try not to worry about Louise."

"Try not to worry about Louise?" her mom asked rhetorically. "That's like saying your father shouldn't worry about his brother Dominic who he has loaned money to more than once."

"So Dad's talked to him recently?"

Her uncle Dominic lived near Baltimore. She remembered a tall, thin man who'd swept her up in his arms when she was little. But she also remembered raised voices between him and her father, between Dominic and Nana Celia and her grandpa when she'd been home from college. After that, they didn't see him very much. Her father checked in with him now and then, and sometimes drove down to Baltimore on his own to visit. But no one talked about those visits. No one brought up her uncle's name very much anymore.

Caprice and her brother and sisters, raised in a Catholic family, going to parochial schools, had been taught to respect their elders. Although their family was fairly open as families go, they all had sensitivity as to what made each other uncomfortable. The subject of Uncle Dominic made everyone uncomfortable.

Maybe sometime she'd talk to Nana Celia about it, but the time had to be just right.

"Your father visited your uncle," her mother responded to her question. "In spite of that new snow, he drove down there yesterday. But Maryland's roads are always better than ours."

"Was the visit . . . worthwhile?"

"Your father didn't say a lot about it, just that since his divorce, Dominic might not be able to hold on to the house, and that's not to spread around."

"Of course not."

"It's probably better if you don't say anything to your brother and sisters about your dad's visit to Dom. It just sort of slipped out when I got upset."

"I understand, Mom."

Her mother sighed. "I know you don't keep secrets from Nikki. Just forget about what I said. If you want to tell her, that's fine."

"Are you and Dad thinking about helping Uncle Dominic?"

"That could be a bone of contention with Nana Celia. It's all very complicated."

Caprice and her brother and sisters had understood that. Maybe that's why they'd never asked questions about it.

"Try to get a good night's sleep, Mom."

After saying good-bye, she ended the call.

Grant was eyeing her speculatively. "Not that I meant to listen in, but it sounds as if a lot's going on."

That was the understatement of the night.

* * *

The following morning, Caprice parked in the multilevel parking garage at York Hospital. Then she made her way to the main entrance. She already had the information she needed—Louise was in one of the rooms on the cardiac floor. Since she was still here, Caprice guessed they were watching her carefully. All she could get from the nurses' desk was her room number. HIPAA laws, and all that. Doctors and hospitals were becoming more paranoid about privacy, yet there were multiple systems of computer networks within the healthcare system, and none of those seemed to talk to each other. You could go for a lab test at one facility that would be hooked into the specialist's computer. But if you went to your family doctor, she might not be able to even access those records. Caprice had the feeling that a good hacker could get anybody's medical records if he wanted and no one would even know.

She realized she was distracting herself with those thoughts because she was concerned about Louise. Nikki had assured her she'd take Lady for a walk even in this cold weather, give her lots of praise when she succeeded at a doggie task, and she wouldn't forget to give Sophia half a dropperful of omega-3 fatty acids with wild anchovy and sardine oil in her lunch. As long as Sophia didn't know she was eating something good for her, she was fine with it. Again, not so different from humans.

Caprice passed the gift shop where she'd often found unique presents for friends and members of her family. Then she wended her way to the elevator.

It didn't take her long to find Louise's room. She peeked in the door and saw that Louise had company.

Jamie Bergman was there. Caprice noted the plant on
the windowsill, greenery mixed with mums. It stood
beside a bouquet of tulips and daisies that was probably
from Chet.

Louise caught sight of Caprice right away. She was
looking pale and weak, but she was wearing a smile.
"Come here, my dear. Chet will be back in a minute. He
just went to check with the nurse about something."

Caprice hugged Louise and saw that the monitor
above her bed was recording her heart rhythms and
pulse rate. As Chet had said, she was still being moni-
tored carefully.

After she leaned away from Louise, she nodded at
Jamie. "It's good to see you again, only not under these
circumstances."

"I'll say not," Jamie agreed.

Jamie Bergman might be in her fifties, with no gray
showing in her hair. But that didn't mean much these
days. A good hairdresser could take care of that. A
brunette, Jamie had dark brows, a long nose, and dark
rimmed glasses that she often wore on top of her head.
Caprice was about ten pounds overweight, and she
guessed Jamie was probably twenty pounds overweight. She was wearing jeans that were more snug
than Caprice would wear them, and a short striped
sweater, with the stripes going the wrong way for a
person who might be trying to look thinner. But that was
really none of Caprice's concern. Jamie knew her
plants, and over the past year had been a big help when
Caprice needed greenery to enhance a home-staging.

"Do the doctors know yet what caused this?" Caprice
asked Louise.

Chet answered her from the doorway. "The doctors don't know. But this stomach flu, or whatever it was, disrupted her heart's rhythm. Even her usual medication couldn't control it. The cardiologist adjusted it and now she seems to be more stable. But I think we should cancel the open house on Saturday."

"Saturday is five days away," Louise protested. "I don't want to cancel it. If I'm not feeling well, I don't have to be there for it. I can visit with a friend for the afternoon. I'm not going to let a little stomach episode throw off our schedule or Caprice's."

Often, when someone thought they had the stomach flu or a virus, it was really food poisoning. Maybe Louise had eaten some bad fish or something. The cause really didn't matter as long as Louise was okay.

Jamie motioned to Chet's flowers. "The bouquet you gave Louise is beautiful, even if it did come from Posies rather than Garden Glory."

Posies and Garden Glory weren't exactly rival businesses. Posies' main product was a bouquet like Chet had bought. They were known for their unique flower arrangements and their gift baskets. Garden Glory, on the other hand, was a nursery that specialized in landscaping plants, yet they also arranged planters for gifts and decorated them with flowers.

"When Jamie called the house this morning to arrange the delivery of the plants for the open house," Chet explained, "I told her Louise was in the hospital and that I'd already put my order in to Posies."

"I'm just teasing," Jamie said amiably. She picked up her tote bag purse. "I'd better be going now. I don't want to be late for my shift."

After there were good-byes all around and Jamie left, Caprice sat by Louise's bed and patted her hand. "My mom's worried about you."

"So you came to check up on me by proxy?" Louise asked.

Caprice chuckled. "Something like that. I'm supposed to text her or call and give her a full report. She'll be here as soon as she can get away from school."

"Your mother has been a good friend. Even with her life as busy as it always has been, she's made time for me."

"You make time for *her,* too."

"Oh, my dear, it's not the same. I've never had children and a job to juggle. Yes, I have commitments, charity work, the Garden Club, friends I play bridge with. But that's not at all the same as teaching teenagers English like your mom does, and taking care of all of you at the same time."

Caprice thought about Bella, how tired she looked, how sleep-deprived she was. She considered her own mother being a young mom, a wife, and a teacher, and handling all of it. Maybe kids never gave their parents enough credit. Maybe she could find a present down in the gift shop for her mom for Valentine's Day, just to show her appreciation. Sometimes a card just wasn't quite enough. She was sure her dad would send her mom flowers. Nikki might cook her something special.

Bella? Well, her mom would understand if Bella kind of skipped over Valentine's Day this year. And then there was Vince. Maybe Caprice should give him a call anyway to find out what was going on with him and Roz. Maybe she should call Roz. She'd probably get a lot more information that way. Of course, then she couldn't nudge her brother to do something nice for their mom.

Louise studied Caprice. "Is something wrong, dear? We *are* ready for Saturday, aren't we?"

"I'll certainly be ready if you want to go through with the open house."

"Chet's already looking at other properties. He was showing me pictures this morning. There's a house out on Lake Road that looks especially nice. The only problem is there are no housekeeper quarters, and we'd have to decide what to do about Rachel. I'm not sure she wants to move back home with her parents."

Chet approached Louise on the other side of the bed and patted her arm. "Maybe we shouldn't take Rachel with us. But I'll keep looking. Now that the housing market's picking up, more homes are for sale. Actually, we might even be able to find a bargain or a place that's gone into foreclosure. It could take a little while to sell ours in spite of the open house. I don't want you worrying about it."

"You've always taken care of me," Louise said to her husband.

In some ways, Louise and Chet reminded Caprice of her own parents. They'd been married a long time. They were a team. They seemed to navigate the marital waters without dissension. Her own parents argued sometimes and those arguments could get very loud. But they always made up. Louise and Chet, however, didn't seem as connected as her own parents did. Could that be because they didn't have children?

There was suddenly a noise that came from the phone

in the holster on Chet's belt. It was a vibration as if he had the ring tone turned off.

"I'm expecting an important text about negotiations. If you'll excuse me, I'll go outside and take care of it."

He stepped outside the door into the hall.

Louise said, "I know selling the business isn't easy for him. The negotiations are difficult, too. His lawyer has been on the phone with him often the past few days. Sometimes I'm not so sure he does want to sell. Retirement can be difficult for some men."

"He has his hobbies."

"Golf and skiing, and you know I hate skiing."

Louise disliked cold weather because it could often stir up that arrhythmia. So she never went skiing with her husband.

"Soon spring will be here and you can play golf together."

"Or maybe, better yet, we can be staying in a villa in Tuscany. Now that's some place I'd like to go."

"And Chet?"

"I think he'd prefer London or Paris, but I'm hoping with all the time in the world in front of us, we can compromise."

The bottom line was, that's how folks stayed married for thirty years. Lots of compromise.

As Caprice climbed out of her yellow restored Camaro that she parked in the Downings' driveway on Friday, she saw the greenhouse door was open and raised voices were spewing from inside.

"I do not want to have that kind of mortgage on the

next property," Chet announced, in a louder than usual voice, as if this argument had been going on for a while.

"We don't have to have *any* mortgage," Louise countered. "Let's just buy it outright."

"It's not an investment that way." He sounded as if he were talking to a child and trying to explain the basics.

This was the day before the open house and Caprice didn't know whether to walk into the middle of this argument or head in another direction. She remembered what Chet had said about Rachel when Louise was in the hospital. *Maybe we shouldn't take Rachel with us.* Was he trying to cut expenses, as well as downsize so they could travel more? Or was he cutting expenses for another reason?

Suddenly Caprice didn't have to make the decision whether to step into the greenhouse or stroll up the walk to the house because Chet said, "There's just no talking to you sometimes," and left the greenhouse with purposeful strides.

When he saw Caprice, he did a one-eighty and smiled. "Good to see you, Caprice. I hope you draw in a lot of buyers. I'm ready to sell."

Then he used his vehicle remote, climbed into his SUV, and started the engine.

Her sixties-style fringed purse on her arm with its large dangling peace sign charm, her boots brushing against her ankles, she went to the greenhouse and stood in the doorway. The glass enclosure was humid, warm, and bright with artificial light as well as sunlight. Louise was sitting on a stool at her potting bench, looking dejected, rearranging seed packets on the back shelf. She simply appeared to be going through the motions.

She didn't hear Caprice until Caprice said, "Hi, there."

When Louise turned around, she looked teary-eyed. Then she straightened her shoulders and said in an almost cheery voice, "Hi, Caprice."

"Is everything all right?" Caprice asked gently.

"I suppose it is." She motioned to the seedlings in the peat pots that had just started peeking up out of the ground. "They require so much care. You give them light and water, and even some dedication, but it's still survival of the fittest."

That was an odd way of putting it, Caprice thought. "You mean the hardiest ones grow," Caprice noted.

"Exactly. That's true in life, too, don't you think? For example, if you were still doing home-decorating instead of home-staging, your business would probably be down the tubes."

Louise was probably right about that. Caprice had changed her course when her home-decorating business had fallen off so much she couldn't pay her bills. It had been a risk to start making contacts to promote her unique staging techniques with a refurbished Web site, ads in the surrounding papers and professional magazines. The bottom line was, she was doing a good job, a different job, of promoting houses to sell, and it had paid off. She thought about the two murder cases she'd solved and the danger she'd been involved in while doing a job. Yes, indeed, she was a survivor.

"I see your point."

Louise pushed her stool away from the potting

bench and made her way to a jasmine plant that was blooming in the middle of winter. The greenhouse provided the right conditions. The vine's sweet scent, along with that of a nearby gardenia, wafted through the greenhouse.

"It's the same way in marriage, you know," Louise mused. "You have to survive it before you can enjoy it."

Caprice wasn't sure what to say to that.

"Sometimes men are so black and white, so cut-and-dried," Louise went on. "It doesn't mean they don't care. It just means they think differently. You know, the whole Venus versus Mars thing."

Caprice smiled. "That's true. Especially with my brother and my brother-in-law. They might have even come from Jupiter."

Louise laughed, and Caprice was glad when it sounded genuine.

"You're feeling recovered?" Caprice asked.

"I am. The medication for my heart is working as long as I stay away from the usual culprits."

"Are you worrying about the open house? You know Nikki and I will do our best."

"I'm not worrying about the open house, per se. I'm just worrying about life in general. Somehow it's gotten more complicated as I've gotten older. Maybe I'm just feeling too old today. Valentine's Day will make me young again. Chet and I always have a special celebration. This year, we're flying to the Bahamas over the holiday weekend. A little R&R away from here will help us both. By the way, he has to go out of town tomorrow during the open house. He couldn't postpone the meeting because negotiations to sell The Pretzel Party are at a critical stage. I'm just going to putter here in the greenhouse in the morning, and then I'll clear out before Nikki sets up. A friend, Gail Schwartz, has invited me to her house for the afternoon. Since Rachel will be off for the day, Nikki has the key and the security code to get in. Of course, if you need anything, you can reach me on my cell. Garden Glory delivered the plants early this morning. Is there anything we haven't covered?"

"I'm just going to go inside, take a last look around, arrange the plants to their best advantage, and make sure everything's exactly the way we want it. I'll give you a shout when I leave."

"Perfect."

If only everything had *stayed* perfect.

Caprice arrived at the Downing house the next day, glad the temperature had risen into the forties. The sun was even shining. She was eager to see Nikki. Excitement always swirled around an open house, right before all the guests started arriving. It could be quite a heady experience, with the food simmering in warmers, a party atmosphere abounding. That's why their open houses were such a success.

Caprice passed Nikki's van, knowing the waitstaff would be arriving soon. Pocketing the keys to her Camaro, she was surprised to see the garage door up, and Louise's luxury sedan still parked inside. Louise had said she'd be leaving.

Nikki emerged from the kitchen door and motioned to the back of her van. "I'm ready for the food warmers. My assistants should be here any minute to help."

Caprice went inside with her. "Louise's car is still here. Have you seen her?"

"No."

Puzzled, Caprice quickly searched through the first floor, then called up the wide stairway. "Louise?"

She received no answer.

Louise had said she was going to putter in her greenhouse this morning. Caprice gardened and her mom gardened even more. She knew how easy it was to become distracted by watering, examining, sorting. Maybe Louise was still in the greenhouse and was unmindful of the time.

"I'll check the greenhouse," she told Nikki as she passed her in the kitchen, her head deep in the refrigerator.

Caprice hurried to the greenhouse and saw the door was almost closed, but not completely. She pushed it open, calling, "Louise?"

There was no answer.

When she stepped inside—

She spotted Louise crumpled on the floor. She let out a loud "No," ran toward the older woman, and stopped at her prone form, aghast at what she saw.

There was blood everywhere on the earth floor . . . and what looked like three bullet holes in Louise's chest.

She was *dead*.

Chapter Four

Fortunately, or unfortunately—it all depended on one's point of view—Caprice was now familiar with crime scene procedure. With a lump in her throat and a knot in her stomach, with a wave of depressive sadness washing over her, she stood by a patrol car while official personnel entered information onto the crime scene log, while both the detectives and the forensics unit efficiently gathered evidence. She knew better than to move around, talk to anyone . . . or drive away. Oh, yes, she was familiar with this kind of scene.

Detective Carstead, who had questioned her with regards to another murder last summer, approached her now.

He said wryly, "At least you know better than to contaminate the crime scene. You didn't touch anything in the greenhouse, did you?"

"Not today," she said solemnly.

"What do you mean—not today?"

Caprice explained how she knew Louise, how she'd been in the greenhouse many times, how she'd come to find the body. It was hard to think of Louise Downing that way. After all, she'd been like a favorite aunt.

Detective Carstead jotted down notes in his small spiral notebook. Distracting herself, she wondered if detectives would ever use e-tablets. But as she watched Carstead's broad hand, his long fingers, the pad of his thumb, she figured he'd make lots of typos trying to input information on a tablet computer and writing was probably faster.

She glanced often at Nikki who was standing by the forensics van with Detective Jones. The tech had taken her fingerprints. They did that for everyone who'd been on the scene, for elimination purposes if for nothing else. Caprice's were already on file with AFIS—the Automated Fingerprint Identification System—because she'd been involved in other crime scenes. Detective Jones was the one who had grilled Bella and Joe so relentlessly last summer. He didn't even look her way. She guessed he didn't like her very much. Detective Jones thought she was an interfering woman who should keep her nose out of police business. The problem was, when it came to protecting her friend, or her sister or brother-in-law, murder had become *her* business, too.

Detective Carstead was watching Caprice carefully. "Would you like to sit down or something? You look a little pale."

"Of course I look a little pale. I found a body!"

"It isn't the first time," he commented.

She could have punched him, really she could have. Was he being totally insensitive or did he just want to get a rise out of her? Was he giving her grief because she'd solved two other cases before they had?

"Louise Downing was a good friend of my mother's." She heard her voice crack, and that annoyed her as much as his attitude. "She was . . . she was . . . she babysat me, for goodness' sakes. She liked my dog, and she loved hearts and flowers—" She stopped because Carstead was looking exceedingly uncomfortable now. Well, *he'd* started it.

He said in a softer voice, "Would you rather do this down at the station?" His dark brown eyes were almost kind as he tried to get the conversation back on track.

"No," she said firmly. "I'm fine."

After another penetratingly thorough study of her, he nodded. "Run through it all again for me from the moment you arrived."

Caprice did—how she'd arrived and gone inside the house with Nikki, how she'd called up the stairs for Louise, how she'd suspected Louise had lost track of time in her greenhouse, how she'd gone in there and seen—

She remembered now what else she'd seen, besides Louise's body on the ground. She'd seen a few seedlings that had been knocked over, maybe by Louise's collapse to the floor. Blood had been everywhere, and Caprice had been careful not to step in it. It had been more than obvious Louise was dead—from her unseeing eyes to her lack of a pulse. Caprice had carefully checked before she'd dialed 9-1-1.

Carstead wanted every detail, and she gladly gave it to him, hoping that would wipe it from her mind.

"Let me ask you this," he finally said. "When you

drove up the street to come here, did you see any cars driving away from the Downings' house?"

She thought about it. "No. I didn't see any other vehicles."

"And you said you did have to use the security code to get inside the house?"

"I didn't. Nikki might have."

"Or was the house still open when she arrived?"

"Possibly. That would make sense if Louise was still here."

"And while you and your sister were inside the house, you didn't hear anything unusual?"

Caprice felt at a loss. "Like what?"

"Like raised voices coming from the greenhouse, gunshots, anything that would have gotten your attention."

"No, nothing like that. I mean, Nikki's main focus was setting up the kitchen for the food, and I was concerned everything else was in place as I walked through looking for Louise."

He noted that. "Was anything out of place?"

Caprice concentrated on the rooms she'd quickly canvassed. "I don't think anything was out of place. I was focused on the arrangement of the furniture, the greenery that had been delivered, the heart pillows I'd added, and a vase of flowers for table adornment. Nothing was on the floor or disheveled, if that's what you mean."

He nodded as if that was what he'd meant. He made another notation in his book. "You said the deceased and your mother were good friends. Do you have any information on Louise Downing's closest relatives?"

"Her husband had a business meeting today. I have his cell number on my phone."

"Would you mind giving that to me?"

She was sure Carstead could get the information a million other ways, but if she gave it to him, he could notify Chet more quickly that his wife—

That his wife was dead.

Pulling her phone from a pocket in her fifties-style full skirt, Caprice scrolled through her contacts and read off Chet's number.

After Carstead noted it, he asked, "Any children?"

"No. But they have a housekeeper. Rachel had the day off. I'm sure Chet knows how to contact her."

"Was she a day worker?"

"No, she has a little apartment off the kitchen."

"You could be an asset to our investigation since you knew the deceased so well. Are you willing to come in if we have questions or we want to verify something?"

"If I can help you, I will."

"But you won't go looking for the killer yourself."

That wasn't a question, it was more of a statement, and it seemed to carry an inherent warning.

She said with some heat, "Right now I'm just concerned with notifying my mother. Her friend is dead."

She had no idea how she was going to do that.

Then something suddenly hit her. She glanced at her watch. "Oh my gosh. Security for the afternoon, as well as guests, are going to be arriving soon."

"That could be a madhouse scene," he muttered. "Who is the security company?"

"Bradford and Associates, out of York."

He nodded as if he was familiar with the security firm. "Do you have any idea who these guests are?"

"No. This is open to the public, though most will be high-end clients with luxury real estate brokers. I can contact agents and they can see if they can contact their clients. Some of these prospective buyers are coming from a distance."

"Do that. I'll call in more manpower to block off the street and barricade the driveway. Crime scene tape won't be good enough if we get a crowd. How long is this open house supposed to last?"

"From two to five."

"Are you sure you don't want to sit in one of the patrol cars? It's cold out here."

She did *not* want to do that. Those back doors on the patrol car automatically locked and even if the door remained open, she'd feel claustrophobic. It wasn't too cold for him, so it wasn't too cold for her.

"I'm fine," she assured him and started scrolling through her phone again as he moved away to speak with an officer ensuring the integrity of the crime scene.

Ten minutes later, she'd done what she could with the real estate agents. Now she turned to the phone call she didn't want to make. Her mother.

Her mom picked up on the second ring. "Aren't you in the middle of Louise's home-staging?" she wanted to know.

"We've had to cancel the open house."

There was a beat of silence before her mom asked, "Is Louise sick again?"

Maybe she should have done this in person. Maybe she should have driven over there. But she wasn't sure if Detective Carstead was really through with her yet. "Is Dad there?"

"You want to talk to him instead of me?"

"No, I just want to know if he's there."

"He's in the living room watching TV. Why?"

"Go in there with him and sit down."

"I won't be able to hear you with the TV blaring."

"Mom, go in there and sit down. Please. Ask him to mute it for a few minutes."

"If you're playing some kind of game—"

"No game. Just do as I ask, okay?"

A few seconds of silence passed, then Caprice heard the sound of the TV and heard her mom asking her dad to turn it down.

When all was quiet, Caprice said softly, "Mom, Louise is dead."

There was stark silence.

"Mom, give the phone to Dad."

"I will not," her mom protested vehemently. "Tell me what happened. Did she have a heart attack?"

"No. She was murdered."

Caprice heard the small gasp. She heard her mother turning to her dad and repeating what Caprice had said.

"Tell me what you know," her mother ordered.

"I don't know much. Nikki and I came for the open house, and I went to the greenhouse and found her."

"How was she killed?"

"I'm sure the detective doesn't want me talking about this."

"Caprice, I'm your mother. I'll keep my mouth shut if I have to. How was she killed?"

"She was shot. Three times."

"Oh my goodness. In her greenhouse?"

"Yes."

"Was anything taken?"

"I don't think so. Nikki and I were in the house looking for Louise and nothing was disturbed."

"There's a safe in Chet's office, and Louise has one of those boxes that look like a book where she keeps jewelry that isn't in her safe deposit box. That's in her bedroom on the bookshelf. You might want to tell the detective that."

"I'll do that. He might want to question you since you were a good friend, especially since you know where her safe was and that kind of thing."

"Just so it isn't that Detective Jones. I'll give him a piece of my mind if he tries to bully me."

Her mother knew what Roz as well as Bella and Joe had gone through with Detective Jones, and Caprice had no doubt her mom *would* give him a piece of her mind.

Detective Carstead was coming her way.

"Mom, are you going to be okay?"

"Of course I will, dear. Your dad's here, and I . . . I'll go tell Nana. She's going to be so shocked. I just can't believe Louise is—" Her voice broke.

"Mom, I'm so sorry. I know Louise was your best friend."

"Can you stop over . . . later?" her mom asked, with a catch in her voice.

"Sure, I can. Nikki will, too."

Detective Carstead watched Caprice end her call and pocket her phone.

"The real estate agents are going to do what they can?" he asked.

She nodded, and then said, "I called my mother, too."

"But you didn't give her every detail, right?"

"She wanted to know how Louise was killed and I told her, but she won't tell anyone else."

He rolled his eyes toward the sky. "This is one of the reasons Jones doesn't want you involved. You're a big family. And . . . you all know Captain Powalski."

Captain Powalski, who was chief of police, was also a good friend of her dad's, and he kept his distance when Caprice was involved in an investigation. Except . . . he had helped her out on the first murder she'd solved.

"What about Captain Powalski?"

"He doesn't want us to have to haul you in for obstruction of justice."

"I never obstruct justice."

Detective Carstead gave her a look that told her she'd better just keep quiet. Still . . . keeping quiet wasn't her strong suit. "My mother told me something you might want to consider." She related the information about the safe and Louise's jewelry.

"I made a note of it," he said.

Caprice spotted Nikki wandering toward her, looking a little dazed herself.

"Do you need us, or can we go?" she asked the detective.

"You're going to have to come to the station to sign statements. Tomorrow is okay for that. And you can't take your vehicles. You know the drill."

She sighed. Vehicles had to be searched since they

were on the property. She and Nikki would need a ride home.

When Nikki was beside her, she reminded her, "We can't take our cars. Who do you want to call?"

Nikki seemed to shake off her daze. "You could call Grant."

Yes, she could, but she didn't want to. Relying on him just wasn't in her nature, maybe because she had a trust issue where most men were concerned. Her last serious relationship had been with a divorced man with a child. He'd ended up going back to his ex, and Caprice had been left out in the cold. Whenever she was with Grant, she couldn't help remembering that he was divorced, too. Not only that, but there was a painful story in his background.

When Nikki saw Caprice's look, she decided, "I'll call Vince."

Icy slush crunched under Vince's sedan's tires as he pulled into Caprice's driveway. Just like visiting her childhood home where Mom and Dad and Nana lived, Caprice found the same welcoming sense of homecoming when she landed here at her own house after a busy day. The 1950s-style Cape Cod had unique features that set it apart—such as the stone around the arched door and the copper roof above the porch. Winter was the only season when bright color didn't dot the gardens. In spring, azaleas under the bay window bloomed. In summer, zinnias and geraniums danced in the wind in the sunny gardens while clumps of impatiens spotted the shaded ones.

They all climbed out of Vince's car without a word and went up the curved walk to the small front porch. Lady began barking from inside.

"I have to break her of that habit," Caprice mused.

"She's a dog," Vince muttered. "Dogs bark."

"She's a pup who still has some manners to learn. When I undo the gate and let her out of the kitchen, do not let her jump up. Turn away if she does. I've almost broken her of that." Caprice inserted the key in the lock in the door.

"You and Grant with these pups. You treat them like kids. I don't know how it's going to go when he starts bringing Patches to the office. But clients don't seem to mind having a dog around when Grant meets them in his town house. I've asked them."

"I'm glad it's working out for him. My neighbor was going to check on Lady at three and take her out for a walk. The Kong toy filled with doggie goodies and her kibble release ball would have kept her busy until then. I'll have to call Dulcina and tell her she won't have to come over."

"I suppose you taught your neighbor how to give her commands and treats?" Vince said with wry disdain.

"Now you're sounding like Bella," Nikki warned him.

Once inside, Caprice had Lady sit and then lie down before giving her a treat and releasing her. Lady wove in and out of their legs, wagged her tail against them, yipped with delight that she had company again, but didn't jump up on any of them.

"Good dog," Caprice said, over and over, because praise and rewards definitely worked with this pup.

Caprice's first floor had a circular walk pattern. The

powder room and Caprice's home office were down the hall to the left. The hall stretched past the stairway into the living room and small foyer. To the right, she could see through the dining room into the living room. Lady took advantage of the circular floor plan when she needed exercise. Sometimes, Sophia joined in. But right now, her long-haired, strikingly colored calico cat was sprawled on the seat of the oversized dark fuchsia chair. She was eyeing her floor-to-ceiling, turquoise-carpeted cat tree as if that might be a good place to perch with the invasion of humans that had disrupted her afternoon.

Caprice went over and scratched the ruff around her neck that was pristinely white and fluffy. "I can see you've been good. I'll put some crunchies in your dish in case I'm late getting back for supper."

Sophia's large golden eyes seemed to accuse her of abandonment again, so Caprice answered, "I'll give you an extralarge dollop of cream tonight. I promise. You won't have Lady to contend with because we're taking her with us."

At that, Sophia stood up on all fours, arched her back, jumped down, and headed for her cat tree, which she climbed in two seconds flat.

Vince said, "I'll take Lady out back while you change."

Nikki added, "I'll put the crunchies in Sophia's dish."

Fifteen minutes later, Caprice had called her neighbor, telling her she didn't have to stop in. She knew Bella would never approve of her outfit, but then Bella wasn't going to be present at her mom and dad's. She'd changed into a pair of wide-legged jeans, and added a sweatshirt from a Pennsylvania wolf sanctuary, opting for practical clothes. After all, her nod to retro could go beyond the Beatles and her collection of John, Paul, George, and Ringo T-shirts. Vintage styles had become a pastime for her, and she enjoyed mixing and matching eras, falling back into styles that could still be classic or funky. Bella often criticized her sense of style because it was unique. Tonight she didn't care about "unique."

By the time she ran downstairs, she could smell coffee brewing and Vince was calling Lady inside.

She went toward the kitchen, still feeling numb. She knew the feeling from before. She'd known the victims in the other two murders she'd solved, too, but not the way she'd known Louise. Louise had practically been family, hadn't she? As an adult, Caprice hadn't seen her around as much, hadn't visited her as much, hadn't talked to her as much. But like all good memories from childhood, when you saw someone who'd been in your life that many years, a warm feeling bumped around your heart. Now, thinking of Louise lying there on the earthy floor of the greenhouse, Caprice felt sudden tears burn in her eyes again.

Stopping in the living room by the cat tree, she petted Sophia. Sophia seemed to understand something was wrong because she bobbed her head into Caprice's hand and then licked her thumb. Caprice stroked her feline's silky fur for a couple of seconds until Lady bounded in, wet paws and all, and stood at her feet.

Animals understood. They really did.

But her sister and brother did, too, so she joined them in the kitchen.

Usually the buttercup vintage-style appliances made her feel as cheery as the kitchen looked. But not now.

Nikki took one glance at her and nodded to the

coffeepot. "I thought we should talk a little bit before we go see Mom. We have to absorb what happened before we can comfort her."

Vince pulled lime green, yellow, and turquoise mugs from the mug tree and set them on the table. "You two haven't told me much, and I think you ought to go over it for me again, just in case the police call you in for questioning."

"Detective Carstead said he might want to talk to me again because I knew Louise," Caprice said, heading to the refrigerator for the cream. Situations like this definitely called for sugar and cream, even though Nikki had probably used one of her chocolate-flavored coffees. Comfort came in many packages, and chocolate-flavored coffee, cream, and sugar were one of them.

Vince spied the round, brightly colored, tightly lidded canister that sat on the counter and peeked inside, finding more of the cranberry and white chocolate cookies that she had baked for Bella's family. A little stale? Vince would probably dip them in his coffee.

"Help yourself," she said.

Vince did and looked thoughtful. "You told me Louise was shot three times. All in the chest?"

Caprice sank into the chair at the table. The yellow braided seat covering slid a little as she made herself comfortable and crossed her legs.

"Three times in the chest. It was awful."

"You said there was a lot of blood, but was she like totally torn apart?"

"Vince," Nikki reprimanded. "We're supposed to be absorbing it, not reliving the gory details."

Caprice shook her head. "I think there was lots of

blood because of where the bullets hit, so I don't think it was a shotgun or anything like that, if that's what you're getting at. But I have no idea what caliber the gun might have been."

"You didn't see a weapon lying around?"

"I only got a quick look but no, I don't remember a gun lying on the floor."

"That brings us to the next question," Nikki said. "Who would do it?"

Vince took his coffee black. Once Nikki had poured coffee into all three mugs, he lifted his, blew on it, then took a sip. He made a face.

"The only person I know anymore who drinks straight coffee without some exotic flavor is Dad."

Nikki and Caprice just stared at him.

"Maybe this would be better with a shot of bourbon," he decided, possibly having trouble with the idea of Louise Downing's murder, too. "Do you have any? It wouldn't hurt the two of you to have a swig either."

Her brother, who was mostly a wine connoisseur, seemed to be shaken up. He was the oldest sibling. He'd known Louise longer.

"I have the rum I use in my rum cake. How about a dash of that?" Caprice asked.

"Sounds good."

After their coffee was topped with the liquor, they thought again about the question Vince had asked.

"Who might want to murder Louise?" Caprice repeated. "I just don't get it. Louise has collectibles sitting around—Waterford crystal, Limoges china, sterling silver even. So I think the bigger question is, not only who killed Louise, but did the killer *know* her? Did a stranger shoot her or was there motivation for murder that went deeper for a family member or an employee? Maybe an enemy of Chet's because of business dealings. He has the reputation for being a shrewd businessman."

Nikki chimed in, "He's in the process of selling The Pretzel Party. What if those meetings aren't going so well? What if someone's angry about that?"

"But would they take it out on his wife, rather than him?" Vince asked.

"Maybe that's the easier thing to do," Caprice decided. "Unfortunately I don't know much about Louise's life the past few years. Mom might."

"Do you think she'll be up for questions?" Nikki asked.

"I think she's going to want some answers."

Vince eyed Caprice. "I think she's going to want *you* to find some answers, and I think this time, you should stay far away from it."

Weren't they famous last words? Caprice wondered. She'd been warned before. But this time would she heed Vince's warning?

Chapter Five

Caprice saw the evidence of her mother's tears when she, Nikki, and Vince arrived at their childhood home. Seeing her mother hurting made her feel helpless. Usually it was her mom fluttering around with something to eat or drink, but tonight her dad did that with Nana's help.

From the moment they'd walked in the side porch to the foyer that led to the living room, dining room, and upstairs, Lady had made a beeline into the dining room and Caprice's mom.

In Caprice's experience animals just seemed to sense when someone was hurting and they wanted to give comfort.

The cuckoo clock in the dining room struck six. That clock had been there ever since Caprice could remember. This house had seemed like an albatross to most market-goers at the time when her parents were ready to buy one. They had known it would be a fixer-upper for most of their lives.

In Pennsylvania, the pale yellow stucco exterior was

an anomaly, along with the red barrel-tiled roof. Its Spanish style with black wrought-iron railings, a first-floor Juliet balcony off the library, and a second-floor balcony protruding over the downstairs sunroom were unusual in this area. However, they'd needed a house with some room for three children and bargained for a good price. Since Caprice's dad was a brick mason, he was skilled in a lot of the work that had to be done or had friends who were skilled in ways he wasn't. The tall casement windows in the dining room and living room certainly hadn't been energy efficient then and weren't now, but they had a European charm that her parents loved. A few years ago, they'd built on a side apartment for Nana Celia so she could move in with them, not worry about stairs and be independent yet close enough for them to discreetly watch over her.

The long mahogany dining room table had seen so many family dinners when Caprice and her brother and sisters were still living here. Her mother believed in family dinners as the best method of communication, and that's why her parents and Nana hosted a family dinner once a month and expected all of them to be there. It was just something that the De Luca family did to stay close. They bonded over food and wine and conversation, and Caprice believed that's what kept them strong as a family. Sure, they had their squabbles and rivalry, but the bottom line was they'd do anything for each other.

After they'd piled their coats on a chair in the foyer, Caprice sat beside her mom at the dining room table while their father poured them all a glass of wine. She supposed he thought they needed a bracer for whatever they were going to talk about. Nana Celia sat across from Fran, Caprice's dad on her mom's other side, while Nikki and Vince took seats at the table, too. Lady sat halfway under Caprice's chair and halfway under her mom's.

Her mom stooped down to pet the cocker and Lady licked her hand.

That little gesture of doggie kindness almost made her mom's face crumple. Her dark brown hair was laced with a bit of gray and fell softly in waves around her face, helped by a body perm every now and then. She was still attractive at age fifty-seven, and didn't dye her hair. She was fashion conscious, though, and usually wore classic styles. Tonight she'd wrapped herself in a comfortable old tan sweater of Caprice's dad's that she said was out of style for him, and just right for her. It was one of those go-to garments on a chilly night . . . or on a night when she needed comfort.

Nick De Luca wrapped his arm around his wife's shoulders. "She has a lot of questions," he told Caprice.

"We all do," Caprice responded. "I still can hardly believe what I saw. Why would anyone want to shoot Louise?"

Her mom just shook her head, but Nana said sagely, "Everyone has enemies, even if they don't know they do."

Was that true? Caprice wondered. Did *she* have enemies? Did Nikki? Sure, Vince might because of his law practice. Sometimes it was adversarial in nature. But she tried to please her clients with home-stagings. Nikki tried to make food everybody would enjoy. Nana Celia certainly didn't have any enemies. Did she?

Yet something in Nana's eyes told Caprice that what she'd said was all too true.

"Louise was a little bossy sometimes," Nikki said softly, as if she was afraid she'd offend her mom. "But that's just part of who she was, wasn't it?"

"No one at the Garden Club would want to kill her for that," Vince said. "There are a lot of bossy women there."

Nana gave him a scolding look and he shrugged. "You know it's true. Get a group of women together and you have 'bossy.'"

This time Caprice's father cleared his throat as if to warn Vince to be quiet.

"Louise was confident," Fran said, as if that explained it all. "That confidence came off sometimes as arrogance, I guess."

"You knew her a long time, Mom. Was she always like that?" Caprice asked.

Her mother seemed to consider the question carefully. "When I first met Louise, we were both so young. We'd volunteered to decorate the church for Advent. That's how we met. Thinking about it now"—she stopped—"Louise wasn't at all confident. In fact, the opposite, really. She was a little shy and stayed to herself. I even had to coax her to come to dinner. But when she did, I think she enjoyed being part of our family."

"What about *her* family?" Vince asked. "Didn't she have any?"

Their mom's brow crinkled. "No, she didn't. In fact, she never wanted to talk about herself. Now that I think about it, I don't even know where she moved here from. After she met Chet, she talked about *him* most of the time, and her work for The Pretzel Party. Come to think of it, her confidence grew as her relationship with him grew. Over the years, our lives here and now were important, not what had happened in our past."

Fran looked pensive. "But you know, I don't know *anything* about Louise before she started her life in Kismet. I remember thinking when I met her that she had a slight accent. Maybe a touch of a Texas drawl." She shrugged. "But I could be wrong. Sometimes I can't tell a North Carolina accent from a Texas one."

"What was her maiden name?" Caprice asked.

"Her maiden name was Benton." Suddenly her mother reached for her hand. "Are you going to investigate her murder?"

Vince said, "Mom, you know she shouldn't. You know what happened last time."

"This is different," Caprice said. "Louise is a family friend."

"You'll go too far, you always do," he protested. "Besides the fact that you almost got yourself killed, I have a feeling if you step on Jones's toes this time, he'll toss you in jail."

Caprice's father studied her with worry in his eyes. "Honey, you are apparently good at finding answers. But we don't want you putting yourself in danger to do this. Do we, Fran?"

"Of course not. I don't want you in any danger. But you know how the police work so slowly, and this just seems to be very complicated."

"Most murders are," Vince maintained. "If it was simple, it would be a crime of passion and the killer would be obvious. But that's not the way of it."

Her mother's shoulders straightened. "I know that house inside out. I'd know if anything was taken. Maybe I should go through it."

"As I told you, Detective Carstead might want to talk to you about Louise, her house, everything. But I don't think you should offer," Caprice advised her.

"I have so many questions, honey," Fran said. "I want to know what she was doing in her greenhouse. She should have been ready to leave. I want to know why Chet couldn't have pushed that meeting to next week. She'd just spent time in the hospital. He should have stayed with her and made sure she was okay. If he'd been there, this wouldn't have happened."

Maybe, Caprice thought. *Or would he have been shot, too?* "If I would start investigating," Caprice responded, "I'd want some of that past history that you don't have. I don't want to stir up more grief with Chet right now, but he could possibly tell me where she came from. If I find out anything, it has to be through the people who knew her the best and the longest."

"I don't know when will be a good time to talk to Chet," her mother said. "He's probably so grief-stricken, he can't think straight."

"I know that," Caprice agreed. "In the meantime, maybe Rachel could give me some information. She's been with the Downings for years."

"I really don't think you should poke around," Vince warned her and exchanged a look with his father.

But Caprice's dad just shook his head and said to his son, "You know if you tell her not to, she'll be even more determined to do it."

Her father's gaze met Caprice's and she saw knowing and love there.

"I'll be careful," she assured him.

"Stay under the radar," her father warned her. "If you just act like a concerned friend, you should be okay."

Yes, she should be. But Caprice knew one thing her father didn't. If one clue led to another, and then another, she'd have to follow each one.

Suddenly she realized that maybe he did know that. He was just playing this low-key because he didn't want the rest of her family to worry.

Hopefully she wouldn't give them anything to worry about.

Caprice sat in her home office around eleven P.M. with her two housemates. She knew she wasn't being very good company to either of them. She'd had caffeine and would be awake for a while. They, of course, hadn't. Lady was curled at her feet, her head across Caprice's toes. Since she had the habit of going barefoot in the house, even in the winter, the feel of Lady's warm head on her skin was comforting. Sophia, on the other hand, had settled on top of her printer, which was a favorite spot of hers.

Caprice was trying to take her mind off of her mother's sadness . . . and the murder. At least for a little while. At least until tomorrow when they gathered at her mom and dad's for dinner and would go over it all again. She turned her attention to her computer and her Web site.

Time was getting short before Valentine's Day, only

a week away, and Caprice had to give the okay for changes to her Web site. Her webmaster had redesigned it for Valentine's Day, creating a special badge that led to a separate page for Give-from-the-Heart Day. Anyone going to the Web site could make donations from there. Every penny was welcome.

"You two can help me think up my daily posts and tweets for the campaign. We're going to bring in lots of money for food and clothes."

At the word *food,* Lady lifted her head.

"Uh oh. I said a code word."

Caprice's cell phone lay by her keyboard. It began vibrating as well as playing "Good Day Sunshine." Bella's picture appeared on the screen.

Caprice swiped across it and answered the call. She had a sixth sense some of the time, but she didn't need it tonight to know what Bella was calling about. She probably felt left out, even though Caprice had called her while she was at her parents' house and filled her in.

"How's Mom?" Bella asked.

"She's taking it pretty hard. Vince dropped me off at home, but Nikki is going to stay the night."

"I should have been there, too, but with Benny just getting over his cold, and bringing over the whole brood, and having to talk about—I don't know what we would have been talking about, but it wouldn't have been happy. It just didn't seem like a good idea. Yet it didn't seem right not to be there either. Even Joe said so."

After a few moments of silence, Bella asked, "Do you know when the viewing and funeral will be? I'm going to have to get sitters."

"Since this is a murder investigation, I don't know when they'll release Louise's body. My guess is a few days at least. It depends on what the detectives find, and how much Chet pushes."

"Does pushing really help?"

"No one's going to answer that one, but I do know Chet has some powerful friends—state representatives and state senators. I really don't know how much politics is involved in running the police department. Dad says Mack never talks about that."

"Knowing Mack when we were kids, and knowing him now, are definitely two different things," Bella agreed.

Caprice sank back in time as she thought about Louise and how much *she'd* been around when they were young. "Do you remember those dresses Louise gave us to play in when we were kids?"

"When we went to her house and played dress-up?"

"Yeah. They were all taffeta, voile, and frothy."

"She hadn't worn them very much. They were like new," Bella remembered.

"She always said Chet didn't like to see her in the same dress more than once when they went to a party."

"Do you remember that white dress she had that hung in the back of her closet, and she wouldn't let us dress up in it?" Bella asked.

Caprice took a journey back, thinking about Louise's bedroom, the huge walk-in closet, the way it was organized and divided. That white dress had been separated from all the others. It had looked like . . . Caprice thought about it. It had looked like a First Communion dress for a sixteen-year-old.

"She would never answer us when we asked her what it was for. What do you think it was for, Bee?"

"You know more about old fashions than I do."

"Not old, vintage."

"Yeah, well, vintage. It sort of looked like a dress that a girl might wear to a prom back then."

"Maybe it could have been a low-key wedding dress."

"It was lacy, and almost went to the ankles."

"Do you remember it well enough to sketch it? You're good at that. If you could draw a sketch, then maybe I could look up some old patterns or old fashion designs and get an idea of the year it was in style, and what it might have been used for."

"And you think this is going to help how?" Bella asked, puzzlement in her tone.

"I don't know. But Mom wants me to help figure this out. If not who killed her, maybe why. We only know Louise from when she and Mom became friends. Mom doesn't know anything about her background before she moved here, and that seems odd."

"Maybe she was running away from something painful and didn't want to talk about it. She started a new life here and that was all that mattered."

That was a story that could be woven into murder motivation, Caprice supposed. "Her life in Kismet isn't all that matters now. I don't know, but if you can sketch the dress, Bee, sketch it, okay?"

"In my spare time, when I'm not too sleepy to hold a pencil."

"Speaking of your spare time: How would you like to have some with just Joe and Benny? After I stop at the police station to take care of my statement tomorrow,

I can take the kids ice skating before dinner at Mom and Dad's."

"You'd do that?"

"I know this isn't an easy time for you. Sure, I'd do that."

"What do you want in return?"

"I don't need anything in return, except of course, sometime when I'm in a pinch, it would be great if you could stop in and walk Lady."

"I knew it. With you, there's always something to do with animals. Okay, it's a deal. Lady's a cute pup."

"I can't believe you're admitting it."

"Let's just say, I like her better than I like Sophia. Cats are so—"

"Don't mention 'independent.' Sophia sleeps beside me every night. She nuzzles my arm. She purrs. She puts her paw on my stomach."

"Oh, please," Bella said. "Don't give me details. Someone should be in that bed with you other than the cat."

No, they weren't going to talk about that.

Changing the subject abruptly, Caprice asked, "Did you call Mom to tell her you were thinking about her?"

"Not yet."

"It's not too late. You could call her now. I'm sure she's going to have trouble getting to sleep tonight."

"Aren't we all?" Bella asked in that hollow tone that spoke of murder and the people who committed it.

On Sunday morning, Caprice drove her work van to early Mass at Saint Francis of Assisi Catholic Church.

Usually she would go home and make something to take along for the family's monthly dinner. But today, she'd created a recipe she could just make at her mom's when she arrived. The bread she planned to bake was best warm from the oven. She'd take Lady along to her mom's, but right now, she had two other stops to make before ice skating with Bella's kids and dinner at her parents'.

After taking care of her statement at the police station, she headed for the Downings'. She didn't know if forensics was finished with the crime scene, but she'd soon find out. At almost noon, it was possible that they would be.

She certainly wasn't going to question Chet the day after his wife was murdered. The police had probably done it and maybe would do it again. She didn't want to add to Chet's sorrow or his discomfort.

She thought again about whether or not she'd be able to enter the house. Maybe officers were still stationed there, though the York County Forensics team would try to release the crime scene as soon as they'd collected every bit of evidence. Paying manpower to secure a crime scene would get expensive.

Would Chet still want to sell the house where memories of Louise were potent? With a murder happening there, would the value of the property tank? Caprice had seen that happen before.

After driving down Middlebrook Drive, Caprice headed to the back of the house and found the greenhouse area was still sectioned off with crime scene tape. At least one officer would be on-site to make sure nothing was disturbed.

Since her car and Nikki's van had been parked in the driveway when the murder was committed, they'd been impounded. Caprice missed her Camaro and hoped she could pick it up soon. Nikki needed her van to work, so she was in worse straits than Caprice.

Circling the house again, she parked at the curb at the front, and she noticed no crime scene tape stretched there. Had the police found anything as they'd gone through the house? She imagined they'd been searching for the murder weapon. Still, the place had looked so pristine, she couldn't imagine them finding it there. Unless, of course, they spent extra time searching for someplace Chet might have hidden it . . . or Rachel.

Neither seemed likely. But who knew? She supposed everyone had to be treated like a suspect.

Parked at the curb, Caprice studied the front of the house, the architecture, the beautiful windows, the pillars. She thought about the chintz and gilt-edged mirrors inside, the hearts and flowers that Louise had loved so much. What had brought this down upon the Downings?

Murder could be a crime of passion. It could be premeditated and well thought out. It could be revenge. It could be the goal of someone gaining an advantage, the means of winning something valuable.

Probably one of the first questions the detectives were asking was, Who gained from Louise's death?

Maybe Rachel could help her with that one.

Two minutes later, Caprice stood at the front door ringing the melodious bell. After a few minutes of waiting for someone to open the door, she was ready to turn away. But then the door did open.

Rachel stood there in her black slacks and white blouse, looking a bit flustered. "Caprice. I wasn't expecting anybody. I'm not used to having guests come to the front door. Mr. Downing's not here if you came to see him."

Caprice wasn't exactly sure how to proceed so she just prodded a little. "He's not here?"

"Oh, no. He stayed in a hotel in York last night and I stayed with my sister. The police and that whole team of investigators were here until a little bit ago. An officer is still at the greenhouse. Mr. Downing called me about an hour ago and told me Detective Carstead had notified him that the police were finished with the house but not the greenhouse. He asked me to come on over and put everything back the way it should be in the house. Come on in. Would you like some coffee?"

Caprice hadn't yet had her morning fix. "Sure, if you have time. I don't want to interrupt. When will Mr. Downing be home?"

"Oh, he said something about this evening. I don't think he can stand being here, you know, without Mrs. Downing, without Louise. She always wanted me to call her Louise, but when she had visitors or I talked about her, I always spoke of her as Mrs. Downing. It just seemed right."

Caprice followed Rachel through the living room, down a hall, past Chet's den, into the kitchen. Through all that, she hadn't seen anything amiss.

"What do you have to clean up?"

"The walk-in closet in the master suite is a bit of a mess and drawers have been emptied or shuffled through.

I'll have to remake the beds. I guess the police were looking in between the mattresses and under the pillows. I'm not sure. They even questioned and fingerprinted me yesterday."

Standard operating procedure. Caprice was sure they'd been looking anywhere a gun could have been hidden. And as part of the household, they'd be looking at Rachel as a suspect.

"Tell me something, Rachel. Do you know of anyone who would want to hurt Louise?"

"The police asked me the same thing."

"Do you know of anyone?"

"There were women who didn't like her. Some of those Garden Club friends. When Louise would leave the room, they could be so catty. They acted like I wasn't even there. But I don't think they'd have a reason to murder her."

"How long have you been working here now?"

"Seven years."

"And in those seven years, did Louise ever tell you she was afraid of anyone?"

Rachel moved to the coffeepot and poured. "Louise wasn't the type of woman to be afraid of anyone. I don't think I ever saw her afraid, though sometimes she seemed sad."

"When were those times?"

"She'd hear a song play on the oldies station, or she'd be sitting on a bench in the rose garden. Once, I caught her crying there."

"Did she tell you what was upsetting her?"

"No. She just said the roses were so pretty they made her cry."

Caprice would have to ask her mom about that. Where had Louise gotten her love of roses, or was it just a hobby that had popped up as she'd gotten older?

"So you don't know of anyone who might have been a threat?"

An unusual look crossed Rachel's face.

"What?" Caprice asked.

"Since you put it that way . . ."

"Who do you think might have been a threat?"

"The housekeeper who was here before I came." She said it with a lift of her chin.

"I was just getting started in the decorating business around that time. When I was little, Louise had a really nice housekeeper who baked cookies whenever I came over. But when I was a teenager, she left. I never knew her replacement very well. Her name was Pearl, wasn't it?"

"You have a good memory. Yes, it was Pearl. From what I heard, she made lots of threats before she left. Louise had more help back then. Pearl was the housekeeper, but she also had a cleaning lady, and someone who came in for the laundry. They used to tell stories."

"And why did Louise let Pearl go?"

"I'm not exactly sure, but the official reason was that she'd become too cocky. She thought *she* ran the house rather than Louise, and Louise didn't like that one little bit."

If there was one thing Caprice had known about Louise, it was that she liked to be in control. "So what happened?"

"When Louise fired her, Pearl made threats."

"Life-threatening threats?"

"That depends on how you look at it. She said she'd give details of Chet and Louise's life to the gossip chain in Kismet. So Mr. Downing gave her a settlement and she went away."

"Was it a meaningful settlement?"

"It was enough to make her be quiet and to move to York and set up a cleaning business. She hasn't come back since. Only Mr. Downing or his lawyer would know if she was in contact with him again."

"I see. Pearl was a large woman, wasn't she?"

"She was. She was quite intimidating. She left in a harrumph the day I came for an interview. I wouldn't want to meet her in a back alley."

Apparently Caprice had just found her first suspect. The question was, Would Pearl be her last?

Chapter Six

Gracefulness on the ice didn't come easily for Caprice. She envied Megan and Timmy who were skimming around the rink Sunday afternoon, looking as if they actually knew what they were doing. Although Caprice had had access to this rink since she was young, that hadn't seemed to help her skills. Maybe it was because when her sisters and brother enjoyed coming here and meeting friends, she'd preferred staying home watching over whatever pet had followed her home recently. Or when she was older, volunteering at the SPCA and giving some lonely pets much-needed affection.

Her thoughts wandering helter-skelter, like the individuals on the ice striving to keep their balance, she found herself zooming much too fast toward a raven-haired woman in green slacks and a green jacket, her tweed scarf flying out behind her. The woman stopped abruptly and it took Caprice every detail of instruction she'd ever learned about ice skating to stop before she ran smack-dab into her. The woman must have felt Caprice's breath on her neck because she turned abruptly.

Instead of the watch-what-you're-doing warning Caprice expected, she heard, "Caprice De Luca! Imagine seeing you here."

Caprice knew that high-pitched voice anywhere. Millicent Corsi ran with the Kismet country club crowd. She could be scathing with gossip when she found someone to listen to her. She was older than Caprice's thirty-two, but probably wouldn't admit she was a few years over the hill. She was the type of woman who would use every scientific advance in plastic surgery to assure she looked at least ten years younger. From the scuttlebutt, not only from the Country Squire Golf and Recreation Club but at the Garden Club, too, Millicent had had breast augmentation and a tummy tuck, possibly liposuction. No one was sure about that. Caprice hadn't seen Millicent since she'd spoken to the Garden Club about simple decorating rules to help flower arrangements spiff up any room.

Automatically Caprice looked toward Timmy and Megan to make sure they weren't in any trouble. Megan was skating around the rink, trying to keep up with her brother, and doing a fair job of it.

Before Caprice could even say, "It's good to see you, Millicent," or some congenial opener, Millicent leaned close to Caprice and asked, "Did you hear about Louise Downing?"

As she was thinking about how to respond, Millicent went on. "Well, of course you have. Your family was sort of close to her and Chet."

Caprice wasn't exactly sure what that "sort of"

meant, so she stuck with "Yes, we were. It's awful. Mom's really broken up about it."

"I guess she would be, but on the other hand— Could anyone really be surprised? Louise rubbed lots of people the wrong way."

The remark was so catty, Caprice responded defensively, "She was *shot,* Millicent. Who would have ever expected that? She was a respected member of this community, as is her husband. I don't quite understand why you weren't surprised." Caprice wasn't letting any information out she shouldn't. The shooting was the lead story on local news outlets.

"Oh, my dear. I *was* shocked. But Louise wasn't the paragon everyone thought she was. You know that, don't you?"

Paragon. Who wanted to be a paragon? Louise had been wealthy and admired by many. Caprice supposed she'd been envied, too. Had Millicent envied her? Was that where this was coming from?

"Louise was never anything but kind to me and my family."

Millicent's eyes narrowed and she studied Caprice with a shrewd smile. "Maybe you just didn't look under the surface. For one thing, she was a perfectionist, and critical of anyone else who wasn't."

Yes, Louise had been particular. Yes, she'd wanted Rachel to do things a certain way . . . and Chet, too. But was that so unusual? She demanded much of others, but she demanded much of herself.

"She *was* a perfectionist," Caprice agreed, wanting Millicent to go on because listening in this situation would be wiser than talking.

"She wanted things her way, and she didn't trust easily either."

That remark puzzled Caprice. "How do you know that?"

"Their grand love story. Everyone in Kismet knows how she fell in love with Chet. But what they don't know is that it took Louise a long time until she trusted him. Months. He wanted to get married long before she did."

Caprice didn't know if Millicent was spinning a tale or had real knowledge to back it up. "A lack of trust shouldn't lead to murder."

"Maybe not, but I believe if she'd been able to trust more, she would have been less critical and would have made fewer enemies."

"Who do you think were her enemies?"

Millicent lowered her voice. "There were women at Country Squire and in the Garden Club whom she pushed around when she wanted her own way. But I think you could even look closer to home than that. Certainly you know about the housekeeper she let go after ten years."

Caprice hadn't paid attention to any gossip around Pearl's departure, but now she wondered about it more since her history with the Downings had come up again.

Because Millicent seemed to know the whole story, Caprice asked, "Why did she let Pearl go?" She wanted to see if the story Rachel told and the one Millicent had heard matched up.

"I heard the woman had become too cocky, that she started changing the menu without Louise's permission, that she was taking liberties and inviting friends over, and using Louise's own living room when she did. So Louise let her go, with severance, of course. But Pearl wasn't happy. I think she thought she'd be there the rest of her life. She made threats. To prevent anything detrimental from happening, Chet gave Pearl a settlement, and Pearl slunk away. If you really want to know the scoop, you should talk to Louise's manicurist about Pearl at the Nail Yard, and to Louise's best friend, too."

An odd expression must have crossed Caprice's face because she was definitely taken aback by the idea that somebody else, besides her mom, was Louise's best friend.

Keeping her tone even, she asked, "Who do you think her best friend is?"

"Oh, that's easy. Her best friend was Gail Schwartz, the manager of that headhunter agency."

Caprice knew Gail slightly. They'd worked together on a few church projects. Gail was also a member of the Chamber of Commerce and the Organization of Women for a Better Kismet that Caprice also belonged to. She was an entrepreneur herself. In her early fifties, she'd been running her headhunter agency for about fifteen years.

"Tell me why you think Gail is Louise's best friend." Caprice tried not to sound defensive.

Millicent could see right away why Caprice was surprised at the idea of Gail being Louise's best friend. Close to her shoulder now, Millicent said, "I understand that you think your mom and Louise were best friends. But the fact is, Gail and Louise ran and played in the same circles. They knew what money was and how to use it. Your mom, on the other hand—"

Millicent didn't have to elaborate. Francesca De Luca was simply a high school teacher who'd known Louise before she married Chet. She'd connected with Louise on a personal level and they had a history. But it was true that other than that, they didn't have much in life in common.

Caprice realized how hurt her mom would be by that idea.

"Can we build a snowman?" Timmy asked the adults in general as the De Lucas gathered in the living room where logs crackled and blazed in the fireplace.

Lady had run to Caprice to welcome her. Caprice had dropped off Lady here before going to pick up Timmy and Megan, thinking her mom could use the comfort of a furry friend.

"Aren't you tired after ice skating?" Caprice's dad asked them as he rocked Bella's baby back and forth in his arms.

"No!" Megan and Timmy answered at once.

"It will soon be time for dinner," their grandfather told them.

"Not for another hour," Nana said, brushing her thumb across the infant's forehead.

Sitting beside Nana, Nikki asked Caprice, "Aren't you going to mix up pepperoni bread?"

"That will take about five minutes," Caprice explained. All she had to do was collect all the ingredients, mix, turn the dough into a bread pan, and shove it into the oven.

Just then, the front door opened again, and Vince, Grant, and Patches burst inside.

"I brought someone along who needs a good meal," Vince teased. "And his dog. I figured Lady would be here."

Grant shook his head. "For some reason, he thinks I'm like him and I don't cook. But I've got to admit, a meal here is a great bribe so I don't beat him too badly at one-on-one in basketball the next time. He assured me Patches was welcome, too—" As soon as he released Patches from his leash, the pup scampered to Lady.

Timmy ran over to Vince. "Do you want to build a snowman with me, Uncle Vince?"

Megan crossed to Grant. "Can you build one with me?"

Caprice's dad got into the act. "That sounds like a fine idea, and I'll judge which one's the best."

"What does the winner get?" Timmy asked, already competitive.

This time her father answered, "How about a ride around the yard on your uncle Vince's old sled?"

That seemed to please both Megan and Timmy, and they went to grab their coats.

"I'll watch Benny so you and Joe can join the fun," Caprice's dad told Bella.

"Building a snowman could be fun," Bella admitted and turned to Joe.

He said, "I'll get our coats."

"I'll watch the pups," Nana offered. "You won't want to leash them while you're building a snowman or take the chance they'll run into the street unleashed." She putted her hip as Caprice and Grant did, said, "Come," and the dogs bounded after her into the library.

"I'll go pull out the bread pan," Caprice's mom offered, heading to the kitchen.

Before Caprice could also escape to the kitchen to mix up the pepperoni cheddar bread, Grant caught her elbow and leaned close. "How's your mom holding up?"

She glanced toward the kitchen. "I'm not sure. I'm hoping a meal and some company will help. She's trying to act like nothing's wrong, but we all know something is. Losing Louise was like losing a little piece of her heart."

Grant was silent for a moment, then asked, "Are you going to join in the snowman making?"

She cocked her head and looked him straight in the eye. "I think you ought to make a snow*woman*."

He raised his hands in a stop gesture while shaking his head. "Oh, no. I'm not going there. We'll just see what Megan wants to do with it. If she wants to put a fancy hat on its head, that's fine."

"I'll see if I can find an old one in Mom's closet before I come out."

"Don't you have to watch the bread?"

"It will be fine with a timer. Mom or Nana can tell when it's done. I have a feeling Nikki will be in the thick of it with you and Vince."

Suddenly Megan popped back inside and asked, "Grant, are you coming?"

"I sure am. Let's show your brother and his uncle what we can do."

When the snowman brigade left the house, Caprice went into the kitchen.

After another glance at her mom who was standing at the window looking out, Caprice gathered ingredients from the refrigerator—shredded cheddar cheese, a pack of turkey pepperoni, milk, and five eggs—and lined them all up on the counter near the mixer. Next, she reached for the bread pan. This really was an easy recipe. In no time at all, she'd popped the batter-filled pan into the oven.

As she closed the oven door, her mom moved to the counter and poked the pot roast that was cooking in a large Crock-Pot. "An hour will do it," she said. More softly she added, "We often had pot roast when Chet and Louise came to dinner."

Caprice went to her mom and stood beside her, then wrapped her arm around her waist. She didn't know whether to go into this now or not, but it might be a good time.

"I saw Millicent Corsi at the ice skating rink."

Her mom turned to her. "Millicent is a gossip."

In a town the size of Kismet, there were a lot of gossips, and a lot of gossip centers, like the Koffee Klatch, the Cupcake House, even the local drugstore. Where anyone gathered regularly, people talked. But her mother was right about Millicent Corsi. She liked to be in the know and spread the news. After all, the Garden Club and the country club were two more of those gossip centers.

The subject Caprice wanted to broach was delicate, and she wasn't exactly sure how to go about it. "Did you consider Louise your best friend?"

Her mother thought about that. "She was a good

friend, and an old friend. Other women in my life have come and gone, but she was a constant. Why?"

"I just wondered."

Her mom narrowed her eyes. "Did Millicent say something about my friendship with Louise?"

She wanted to be truthful with her mother, but she didn't want to be hurtful. "Did Louise ever talk to you about Gail Schwartz?"

Her mother considered her question. "Louise and Gail were on the boards of several fund-raisers together. They also played golf and lunched at the Country Squire. Now and then they asked me to join them for lunch, but I rarely could. Sometimes in the summer it worked out. Why do you ask?"

"Millicent made a comment about them being best friends. I thought *you* were Louise's best friend."

"I thought I was, too," her mom said, looking a little hurt. "But over the past five years or so"—she shrugged—"Louise and Gail did seem to do a lot more together than Louise and I did. But she and Chet seemed to keep to themselves more, too, and didn't come over to dinner as often when I invited them. Everyone's so busy nowadays. Too busy for long dinners and old friendships. There was a time when we talked on the phone a few times a week. That was replaced with e-mails, and over the past year, texting. Now I'm wondering if we both just didn't drop the ball on our friendship."

Caprice capped her mom's shoulder with her hand. "You could only be the kind of friend to Louise that Louise would let you be. You can't force friendship, just like you can't force love. I don't think a text will really tell you what's in somebody's heart."

How could you really know what was in a person's heart unless he or she told you?

Automatically Grant came to mind. Because he'd saved her life? Possibly. That night last summer, he'd really seemed to care. Yet he wouldn't tell her what he felt. He wouldn't make a stand. Heck, he wouldn't even ask her to go with him to the Valentine's Day dance.

Maybe she should push a little if she wanted to know Grant better. Yet if she had to push, would anything about their friendship be right?

Caprice's mom sighed. "I need to make a salad, then check on your father. Handling a newborn isn't as easy as it seems. He might have forgotten that. And if you want to be part of this snowman building, you'd better get outside or they'll be finished. If Grant and Vince are competing, they'll be men on a mission."

"I think I'll find a hat in the closet upstairs. The last time I looked, you had an old straw one you use for gardening. Do you mind if I use that?"

"I don't mind. It's getting a little dilapidated. Whose team is it for?"

"Team Grant," Caprice said with a wink.

"Of course," her mother responded with a knowing look.

Ten minutes later, hat in hand, Caprice stepped out the door onto the side porch. She'd no sooner reached one of the brown rope-style pillars that supported the porch when she heard Bella and Joe arguing. That wasn't an unusual occurrence, but since last summer, they'd argued less.

Joe was saying, "It's too soon for you to go back to work."

Bella kicked the clump of snow at her foot. "I'm in the house all day with the baby. You're at work. Of course you can handle it all better at night. Maybe if I was at work all day, I could handle it all better at night."

"And who's going to take care of Benny? If we have to pay through the nose for daycare, you might as well not work."

"I found someone who's reasonable through a network at church. Her kids are teenagers now and she loves babies."

"Has anyone done a background check?"

Suspecting this argument wasn't going to go anywhere soon, Caprice quietly stepped away from the pillar and went down the porch steps, hoping to reach Vince and Timmy before Bella and Joe had even known she'd passed by. But her boots must have clicked on a patch of bare pavement, and Joe swung around her way.

She gave him an I-didn't-hear-anything expression and was going to keep walking when he beckoned to her.

"Caprice, come here, would you?"

Uh oh. She really didn't want to get into the middle of this. "I have to warn Vince that Grant's team is going to use a hat."

Joe stared blankly at the two partially assembled snowpersons. "I want your opinion on this," he said firmly.

She had no choice but to cross to the couple and enter the conversation. Maybe the cold wind would convince them this discussion was better if held inside . . . or later.

"Are you sure you want my opinion? I know nothing about marriage, remember?"

"Maybe not," he conceded, "but I've seen the way you look at Benny. I've seen how you hold him, and how you walk him, and how you burp him. So just answer one question for me. If he were yours, could you leave him this soon?"

Caprice shook her head vigorously. "Joe, that's not fair. Bella isn't thinking about herself, or Benny. She's thinking about all of you. She's thinking about the extra money, especially if you're considering buying a house. Right, Bee?"

"Of course, that's what I'm thinking about. I've already told him that. This babysitter would be reasonable, and I'd still have money that we can sock away, or use toward a mortgage."

Joe's expression was set. He still wasn't buying it. Caprice looked at Bella and knew she had to support her sister. That's what sisters were for. So she considered a tactful way to do it. Tact was all important with these two.

She studied Bella again. "You want to go to work."

She changed her focus to Joe. "You want her to stay home. I understand both of you. But working isn't like making a marriage succeed. I mean, it's not all or nothing. Why can't Bella talk to Roz about working part-time for now? Maybe she can increase her hours as Benny gets older. Maybe she could work a good part of a Saturday and you can watch the kids, instead of taking Benny to a babysitter. I don't know. That's for the two of you to work out. But isn't this like everything else? Wouldn't compromise be best?"

They were both quiet. She took that opportunity to say, "You two mull that over while I take a look at these snowpersons."

After telling Vince that he and Timmy would have to do something spectacular to compete with her straw hat, she let her boots sink into the snow as she clomped through it to Grant and Megan. Their snowperson was smaller than Vince's, but it seemed to have a little more character. It actually had arms on the sides. With this hat, they could win this challenge.

Megan showed Caprice a handful of stones she'd picked up somewhere in the yard. "These are for the eyes and mouth."

"You'll have to ask Gram for a carrot for her nose."

"I'll go in right now," Megan said, and ran up the walk to the porch steps.

Caprice called, "Wipe your feet before you go in." Turning to Grant, she asked, "Are you having fun out here?"

"Playing with kids is always a life-altering experience." From the look in Grant's eyes, he was serious.

"I suppose so. You look at life differently when you're with kids."

He never talked about the child he'd lost, and she'd never pushed that button. Standing out here in the snow with the wind kicking up wasn't the right time to do it, either.

He stared at the house—Caprice's childhood home. "I want to start looking at houses soon. It could take a while to find something I'll like."

A house that didn't remind him of a house he'd once shared with a wife and child?

"That *could* take a while," she agreed.

"You have a fireplace. Your mom and dad have two. Do I want a fireplace or don't I?"

His question surprised her. He was thinking about details already.

"I like my fireplace. Dad keeps telling me I should put a wood-burning unit in it to make it more efficient. But that's not the same thing at all. And he hasn't done that, either. When I light a fire, even the animals feel mellow. So, yes, if I bought a house, I'd want a fireplace. Not a gas fireplace, but a *real* fireplace."

Grant cocked his head, and the breeze tousled his black hair. "I had a feeling you'd say that. I've been looking at photos online, just sort of deciding how big a house I want and neighborhoods where I might want to look."

"Wouldn't you miss Donna if you moved from your town house?"

Uh oh. What imp made her ask *that* question? A jealous one maybe. No, she shouldn't be jealous of Grant's divorced neighbor. He'd said they were just friends, hadn't he?

Grant's lips quirked up in almost a smile. "Friends stay in touch no matter where they live."

Caprice thought about Seth's last rushed e-mail. Had their romance changed into simple friendship? Did he think about her as much as she thought about him? Or tried not to think about him?

And why was she trying to distract herself with thoughts of Seth when Grant was right here?

"Would you go along and give your opinion if I find something I like?" he asked. "February isn't the best month for house hunting, but I thought I'd start actually touring some."

"I always have an opinion no matter what month it is."

Grant laughed. And when he did, she felt the two of them were making progress toward . . . something. Something more than friendship?

Caprice hoped dinner, as well as family around the long table, helped ease her mom's sense of loss. After cleanup, she was about to join the men and dogs in the living room when Bella swooped in beside her and grabbed her arm.

"I want to show you something," her sister said, pulling Caprice toward the library. Lady wandered after them at Caprice's side now.

The fireplace in the library shared a chimney with the one in the living room. Built-in bookshelves lined the wall around it. Caprice could remember her dad working on those bookshelves when she was little. He was somewhat of a perfectionist in his work and the project had lasted months as he'd found the time to do it. After they were finished, they all had shelved favorite books there. Two of hers were *Anne of Green Gables* and *The Black Stallion*. They were still there.

Bella led her to the two comfy club chairs that were covered with a nubby deep claret upholstery fabric. As Caprice sat in one chair, Lady rested on the floor at her feet. Bella perched on the ottoman.

Pulling a folded sheet of paper from her pocket, she

opened it, pressing the folds. "I couldn't sleep last night. So instead of staring at the ceiling thinking about Louise being shot, I did this."

Caprice took the piece of paper Bella handed her. She recognized the sketch right away—the dress in Louise's closet. "This is terrific, Bee. You've captured it perfectly!"

"You forget I used to want to be an artist before I decided to go to fashion school."

Yes, sometimes she did. She had the habit of seeing her sister in one dimension—as a woman who'd wanted a home, family, and children more than anything else. But Bella *was* talented and expressed that talent in ways other than a career.

"I would have never remembered all this detail." She pointed to a design on the lace.

"That detail is what led me to something else." She turned the sketch over and Caprice saw notes on the other side.

Bella seemed pleased with herself.

"Did you do some research, too?"

"I did. I have access to a few design databases. I thought this style looked very seventies. So I pored over some of the designers from that decade. I found Boyce Johnson. He had a brief period of fame designing one-of-a-kind wedding dresses. But in addition to those, he designed 'coming-out' dresses."

"Like debutante gowns?"

"Exactly. And I found one almost identical to this— the sleeve detail, the neckline, the skirt, the lace. Same design on the lace."

"Do you think we could get hold of this Boyce Johnson?"

"He died in a car accident about eight years ago. From what I found, after a few years of success, he went downhill. Died penniless."

Caprice tapped the sketch. "Where did he design from? New York?"

When Bella shook her head, the curls around her face bobbed. "Nope. He sold his first gown to an oilman's daughter in Houston."

Considering that, Caprice murmured, "Mom said she thought Louise had a Texas drawl when she first met her."

"Maybe she was right."

And maybe Caprice had just gained her first clue to Louise Benton Downing and her background before she came to Kismet.

Chapter Seven

After an evening with the family, Caprice had no sooner stepped inside her house with Lady when her dog ran over to the sofa and barked.

Caprice kept a light on a timer in the foyer. The small Tiffany lamp glowed its warmth into the living room. She could barely see Sophia at the far side of the area, stretched out on the afghan Nana had made that was folded over the back of the sofa. But she didn't seem to be concerned about Lady's greeting.

Since that was true, Lady barked again.

This time, Sophia rose slowly, stretched her front legs before her, and lifted her tail high in the air. Then she jumped down to the sofa, right above Lady.

Lady barked a third time as Sophia jumped to the coffee table, then landed on the rug. With Lady chasing her, she dashed to the kitchen. Apparently they were going to participate in before-bedtime gymnastics this evening.

Caprice took off her coat and hung it on the high mirrored, oak clothes-tree bench in her foyer while

Lady and Sophia ran around the circle she called home.
A few times around, and they'd both be ready for their
bedtime snack. This was their way of communing after
an absence.

She was making her way through the dining room to
the kitchen, turning lights on as she went, when her cell
phone played. She pulled it from her pocket and saw
Nikki's picture.

Swiping her finger across the screen, she put the
phone to her ear and asked, "Didn't I just see you?"

"You saw me, but we really didn't get a chance to
talk, not with Mom feeling so sad, and snowperson
building, and Bella corralling you. It's no surprise Grant
and Megan won the snowman contest, you know. Grant
has a much more artistic eye than Vince does."

"And you know this how?"

"Because Grant has actual artwork in his law office,
and Vince doesn't."

Caprice smiled. That was true. Grant's office had a
masculine Southwestern flavor to it while Vince's was . . .
executive boring.

"So you called to talk to me about the snowman competition?"

"No." Nikki paused, and Caprice wondered why her
sister was hesitating. The two of them were usually
pretty free with each other. She waited.

"I want to run something by you. What do you think
about me taking on a partner?"

Nikki had grown her catering business from simple
hors d'oeuvres and desserts to much more elaborate
fare. But she was often busier than she could handle and
had to turn down work.

"I'm certainly not complaining that I have clients who want me to cater for them," she went on. "But I'd like to have a life, too. As it is, I'm working sixty hours a week."

"I understand."

Sometimes Caprice's weeks were like that. "You want to know if I approve?"

"Sort of. How would you feel about working with me and someone else? I mean, I'd still cater all of your open houses, but a partner could help and could give me some time off."

"Do you have anybody in mind?"

"No, not specifically. I'm going to be interviewing three possibilities this week."

"So you've already decided to do this."

"Not if you're totally opposed. I don't know how this will affect us working together. I'd like to do all of your open houses, and I'll still help you plan them. But it would all depend on what kind of schedule a partner and I would come up with."

Caprice thought about it. She tried to roll with the punches in her life. That seemed to be the least stressful way to handle her family and her job. But this was one very big roll with the punches. Nikki understood her, and she understood Nikki. They had discussions about their menus, but their ideas always gelled and meshed. What would happen if she had to work with Nikki's partner?

Still, she couldn't just think about her own stake in this. Nikki did need a life. She also needed time off, or she'd burn out.

"Nikki, you do what you have to do. We'll adjust."

"You're saying you'd just rather work with me."

"Well, of course I would. But we never know what's going to happen tomorrow, do we? Louise's murder proves that. So interview your candidates for partner, then we'll talk."

"Are you going to investigate who murdered Louise?"

"I'm going to do some snooping, starting with Isaac's antique shop tomorrow morning. I need pretty touches for the model homes I'm decorating. Valentine's Day might be a big weekend for them. While I'm looking around for some interesting glassware, I'll see what Isaac knows about the Downings. You know Isaac. He has his ear to the ground, and gossip is almost as rampant at Older and Better as it is at the Koffee Klatch."

"At least I don't have to worry about you at Isaac's shop."

"No, you don't, or at anyplace else. When do you interview your first candidate?"

"Tuesday morning."

"Let me know how it goes."

"I will."

After Caprice said good-bye and ended the call, she set her phone on the counter and plugged it in to charge. She had a charger down here and one upstairs to make life a little more convenient.

Convenient. She had a feeling Nikki having a partner wasn't going to be convenient at all.

When Caprice stepped into Isaac Hobb's antique shop, Older and Better, she stepped back in time. Some of the furniture, such as the apothecary cabinet and a vintage icebox, were more than a hundred years old. She'd purchased 1940s glassware here for her mom's birthday and her mom had added it to the glassware Nana Celia had bestowed on her.

Caprice waved to Isaac who was sitting in his captain's chair behind the cashier's desk. As she wended her way through the musky scent of old wood, a dash of potpourri, and the vestiges from the past, she called to Isaac, who was tall, husky, and in his early sixties. His life was this shop, and the trips he took to find more unique pieces for it.

Lady snuffled along the wood plank flooring as if she'd caught scent of the past and was following its trail. The first time Lady had accompanied Caprice to the shop, Caprice had worried that she might be too rambunctious and break something. But ever since that first trip, after a few sniffs, she made her way around the cashier's desk to Isaac. Today was no different. Caprice firmly believed animals were a good judge of character. Lady confirmed that on a day-by-day basis.

Now, Isaac chuckled as he spotted Lady. "I know what you want," he said. "You know I keep a pack of dog treats back here just for you."

"We had a walk this morning, and she and Sophia had a grand chase through the house. So she's probably ready to sit on your foot and nap."

"She's welcome to do that after I sell you something. What are you here for today?"

"Maybe I just came to visit," Caprice teased.

"I know that look. You have something in mind. I went to an estate sale this weekend and found a cute turquoise-colored glass Fenton cat. It's signed and hand painted."

"That's the problem, Isaac. I come in here for my business and I end up buying something personal."

He laughed out loud this time. "If you buy enough other stuff, I might give you the cat at a discount."

She shook her head, and eyed the many tabletops and cubbyholes that held glassware. "I staged the model homes in Keystone Village. We're hoping for a good turnout of looky-loos over Valentine's Day weekend. Garden Glory will be delivering potted plants, but I need those extraspecial touches that a woman would look at. As silly as it seems, a piece like a hobnail vase can sell a house. A prospective buyer could look at a piece of glassware in the hutch and think, 'My dishes will look good here, too.' I'm thinking of maybe a lead crystal nappy that can hold rose petals, possibly a Capodimonte vase, maybe pink Depression glass."

"I have all three. Let me see what I can scrounge up."

For the next half hour, Lady followed them around the shop as Isaac produced possibilities, and Caprice made choices and bargained. She and Isaac always bargained like thieves, but that was part of the fun of coming here.

After Caprice had made her selections, and Isaac wrapped the little turquoise glass cat, too, he asked. "Do you have time for coffee?"

This was another reason Caprice came to Isaac's shop. He liked to talk when other customers weren't standing around waiting, although his coffee often tasted stale and grainy. Caprice ignored that for the conversation.

This time of the day, the coffee should be fresh.

"If I brought you a pound of caramel-cinnamon coffee, would you use it?"

"Caramel-cinnamon? That sounds like coffee for the petticoat set."

"How about blackberry rum?"

Isaac hiked one gray brow. "Now you're talking."

Caprice laughed and went around the back of the desk to one of the captain's chairs with its red plaid cushion. She sank onto it as Lady plopped right by her boot. She shrugged out of her coat, letting it cushion the back of the wood chair. Then she straightened the Peter Pan collar of her blue plaid blouse that looked as if it had come straight from the *Happy Days* wardrobe. Her wool slacks had a pleat from calf to ankle that flared when she walked. How she loved retro fashion that was definitely making a comeback.

Isaac took milk from a refrigerator under the counter, then handed her a mug that he'd doused with a teaspoon of sugar. "I hear your open house was canceled over the weekend," he said casually.

"It certainly was."

He gave her a sideways glance. "The *Kismet Crier* reported the murder. I happened to have my scanner on when the police were called in. Were you involved?"

Isaac's records had been a huge help when she'd solved her first murder case. It seemed everyone in Kismet had passed through his doors at one time or another and he could be an encyclopedia of information.

"I found Louise Downing."

Isaac sighed heavily. "Does this mean you're going to be involved in figuring out who did it?"

"Louise was a good friend of my mom's."

"Uh oh. It looks as if you didn't learn your lesson when you almost got dead yourself last summer."

Caprice was quiet because Isaac was right. If it hadn't been for Grant—

She shoved thoughts away of what had happened last summer. "Did you know Louise or Chet Downing?"

"I don't know if I know anybody who walks through that door," Isaac said honestly. "But if they come in more than once, I usually learn something personal about them. Chet Downing never came in here. I think I was too low-brow for him. But Louise came in now and then. She particularly liked hand-crocheted doilies. She would stop by every so often to see if I'd found any more. She was also on the lookout for dresser scarves with lace trim, and anything with hearts and gold trim, from perfume bottles to candy dishes."

"Her house was full of all that. Her theme for the open house was hearts and flowers."

"Is Downing still going to sell?"

"I'm not sure. His real estate agent is giving him time and space to absorb everything that happened."

"Hard enough with a death, let alone with a murder."

Caprice took a sip of coffee. Not too bad. "My mom wants me to help figure this out, and I can't let her down."

"Where are you starting?"

"Louise's background, I think. My mom doesn't know much about her before Louise moved here. Louise was pretty quiet about it. When someone's quiet about their past, that usually means there's a secret hidden there."

"There are lots of secrets hidden in the past," Isaac mused, glancing around his shop.

Lady stood, shook herself off, and wandered over to Isaac's chair, where she promptly sat on his foot. He smiled down at her and patted her back.

"When Louise came in here," Isaac started, "she mostly talked about the Garden Club and her greenhouse. Once in a while, a trip she and Chet were taking. I do remember one time, though—"

"What?" Caprice asked, knowing Isaac remembered details better than almost anyone she knew.

"She liked antique jewelry, too. She always stopped and looked at the case. One day when she came in, she saw a diamond necklace. I took it out and she thought about buying it. But then she said, 'I had one almost like this that was stolen.' She didn't say any more."

"What kind of necklace was it . . . besides the diamonds, I mean?"

"It was delicate. From the seventies."

Caprice thought about that.

The seventies again. A diamond necklace that was stolen. Another clue.

When Caprice returned home, she decided to take Lady for a walk before she went inside. She'd feed both Sophia and Lady an early lunch before she went shopping for a dress for the Valentine's Day dance. Then her pets could settle down for the afternoon. Of course, she'd leave Lady's play ball with kibble to keep her busy if she wasn't napping.

As she and Lady walked down her driveway, she saw that her neighbor across the street, Dulcina Mendez, was at home. She was outside on her front walk, shoveling away some of the slush that had accumulated. As soon as they crossed the road, Lady was in a hurry to get to Dulcina. Caprice jogged a little until they reached her neighbor, who was smiling already.

Dulcina was in her late forties, and usually wore her pretty black hair tied back in a ponytail. Strands of gray laced through it, but she seemed unmindful of it. She worked at home doing medical transcription for a local pediatrician's practice. She and Caprice both liked to garden, and they'd easily talked about that once Caprice had moved in across the street. Since then, they'd had coffee now and then, and always chatted when they ran into each other. They'd actually gotten friendlier since Lady had joined Caprice's family. Dulcina often looked in on Lady for her, or took her on a walk when Caprice was going to be late. Caprice didn't know a lot about her neighbor, just that she'd grown up in York and had lost her husband unexpectedly to a car accident when she was in her thirties.

Now she bent to Lady immediately, and played with her ears. "You're such a pretty girl."

"Walking in this slush and snow, she's soon going to need a bath. I'm going to have to take her to the groomer."

"Are they going to put pretty bows at your ears?" Dulcina teased.

"I don't know," Caprice returned. "A jeweled collar could be next. According to my family, I pamper her too much."

"One can never be pampered too much," Dulcina said with a laugh. "Are you staging a house today?"

"Actually, I have a video consultation late this afternoon. But after Lady and I take a walk, I'm going to go shopping," she said wryly.

"You don't sound too happy about it."

"It's more of a case of not knowing exactly what to buy. I need a dress for the Valentine Day's dance."

"I'm going, too," Dulcina responded with a smile.

"Did you get something really dressy?" Caprice wasn't sure *what* kind of outfit she wanted.

"Cocktail dress-style. It's a little more sparkly than what I usually would wear, but that's because I have a date."

"You do? That's great."

Caprice had to admit, she felt a little burn of jealousy. Her curiosity took over and she asked, "Is this someone new, or have you been dating him for a while?"

"This will be our third date. I met him New Year's Day. I was alone so I decided to go to the movies."

"The old theater downtown or the new one at the shopping center?"

"The old one downtown. I love that place. They were having a silent film day that I thought would make me laugh, and I guess he wanted to laugh, too. We started talking between the films, and we seemed to get along well. We went to dinner together afterward. I thought that might be the end of it, but then a couple of weeks ago he called and we had supper at the Blue Moon Grille."

Talk of the Blue Moon Grille brought back memories for Caprice. She and Seth had eaten there. In fact, that had been the night he'd told her he might be getting the fellowship at Johns Hopkins. They'd had a great time together on the outside deck, under the stars, a guitar player playing close by. It had been romantic, and she thought with an inward sigh about how much she missed him.

"I like the Blue Moon Grille, especially in the spring

and summer when you can eat outside," she responded softly.

"They put in a gas fireplace so it's cozy inside now, too. Those pretzels with the crab and cheese topping are to die for," Dulcina said.

"And how about the man you're seeing?" Caprice asked, focusing once again on her neighbor. "Is he to die for?"

Dulcina laughed. "He is tall, and he is handsome in his way. He has custody of his daughters and they keep him pretty busy. But for Valentine's Day, he said he wants to do something special. That's why I bought a sparkly dress."

Since the women were in conversation, Lady went up to the porch of the two-story Colonial and sat in front of the door.

"She wants to come in." And Dulcina sounded as if she'd let her.

"She can't always do what she wants." Caprice had to be a good mom.

"Think about this," Dulcina suggested. "If you're going to be gone, she could stay with me for a while."

"I don't want to impose."

"You're not imposing. I'm caught up with work, and I'd like the company. Seeing you with your animals, I'm thinking of getting a dog or a cat. I just haven't decided."

"If you want exercise and an animal to get you outside, a dog would be great," Caprice advised. "But if you'd rather stick close to your home and inside, then a cat would be better."

"It's a commitment, and I just don't know if I want that. Even dating . . . It's been so long since I've done it that it seems strange. Sometimes I don't know what to say or do."

"You're not the only one with that problem," Caprice pointed out, remembering how she'd felt with Seth.

"Do you have a date for the dance?" Dulcina asked.

"No, actually, I don't. Somebody I know is going, and I was hoping he'd ask me to go with him, but that didn't happen."

"Then you know what you have to do."

"What's that?" Caprice asked warily.

"You have to absolutely wow him. You'll have to find a dress that he can't possibly ignore."

Hmmm. Maybe finding that kind of dress would take longer than she expected. "Are you sure you don't mind watching Lady?"

"Not a bit. I even have food left from the last time she stayed with me. Will Sophia be lonely without her?"

"I'll give Sophia some time before I leave. She'll probably sleep all afternoon, especially if she has peace and quiet. Thanks, Dulcina. I really appreciate this."

"Anytime," she said. "And when you get back, I want to see what you found."

Caprice hoped she could find that wow dress that would be everything Dulcina expected . . . and everything Grant *wouldn't* expect!

Chapter Eight

The primary store for Caprice's clothes shopping efforts had always been Secrets of the Past. Suzanne Dumas' shop was known for its actual vintage fashion as well as for up-and-coming designers delving into the past for new looks. Caprice found most of her professional and casual clothes there. But today, her drive downtown, and her delving into the racks in her favorite shop had left her clueless and disappointed.

What exactly was she looking for?

Suzanne had even checked in her storeroom but couldn't find anything suitable. Caprice suspected that other residents of Kismet, shopping for dressy clothes for Valentine's Day weekend, had wiped out the small store's cocktail dress inventory.

But she wasn't out of ideas. Roz's fashion boutique, All About You, had opened this past October in time for the Christmas holidays. Bella, with her associate degree in apparel design, had worked with Roz and made the opening a success. Toward the end of her pregnancy, Bella had acted more like an office manager than a sales representative. For the most part, Roz's fashions were pricey. She purchased with current trends in mind, and Caprice's taste didn't always fit into current trends.

Roz's inventory could be picked over, too, but not every woman in Kismet went to the Valentine's Day dance, did they?

Roz's shop was worth a try.

All About You was located in what Kismet residents called Restoration Row. It was a street of row houses in an old section of town. The street had been a scab on Kismet's pretty face until a developer from Harrisburg had bought the whole section of town. He'd named the street Bristol Row, refurbished the houses, sand blasting brick, refacing the fronts, putting siding over clapboard, adding black shutters, and making the street respectable once again. Roz had decided to rent one of the houses for All About You.

The store had an unusual layout, with two stories and separate rooms for specific types of fashions. But that was the point. Roz had wanted her boutique to be unique. The back entrance had an inside stairway with a chairlift for anyone disabled who wanted to shop there. There was a ramp out back, too, for the first floor, and limited parking. Roz had gone to a lot of trouble to make this boutique exactly the way she wanted it. She'd inherited tons of money from her deceased husband, and she was using it the best way she knew how.

On a Monday in the middle of winter, Caprice was pretty sure Roz could give her one-on-one time.

When she opened the door to All About You, a bell rang. She heard a little yip-yip to accompany it and realized Roz had brought her dog, Dylan, here as she did most days to keep her company. Dylan had been one of the strays Caprice had taken in last year. But Roz had fallen in love with the little dog and the dog had fallen in love with her. They made the perfect match.

Caprice hadn't walked three feet into the store when Dylan came running to her, yipping, winding in and out of her legs, greeting her in an I-missed-you kind of way. She stooped down and picked up the mixed breed—part Pomeranian, part shih tzu.

"Hi there, fluffball. How are you today?"

Roz laid her clipboard on top of one of the clothes racks. "He was playing tug-of-war with an old scarf I brought in. But he takes every opportunity to get attention from the people he likes."

Caprice laughed. "Don't we all."

As she rubbed Dylan's back, he settled in her arms. He'd always been a cuddler.

"What brings you here today?" Roz asked. "Nana Celia has given me a list of everything she wants me to do for the Give-from-the-Heart Day on Saturday, so I'm sure she's tied you up, too."

"I haven't started on a list yet," Caprice admitted, "other than making calls for donations and posting on social media. I'm going to stop at Grocery Fresh and talk to the manager on the way home. I'm hoping they'll have a ton of food to donate. My Web site's bringing in monetary donations. That should please Nana and the coordinators."

"I'm sure anything will. Donations are down on all the charities I work with. It's the state of the economy. I'm donating clothes I was able to buy wholesale."

"People need food and clothes as much as ever. It makes me feel guilty for why I came here today."

"Guilty?"

"I want a pretty dress for the Valentine's Day dance. Something special. But I decided whatever I buy, I'll match it in a donation to Give-from-the-Heart Day."

"You usually buy your clothes at Secrets of the Past." Roz said it without any defensiveness or rancor. She'd often shopped there with Caprice and advised her on what to buy.

"Suzanne's party dress section was almost nonexistent. How about yours?"

"My clientele is a little different. I had a lot of special orders, but I also had a new shipment come in that I ordered specifically for my cruise-taking clients. This is a big time of year for cruises, and I get a lot of inquiries about formal wear. So . . . Come with me upstairs and we'll take a look. In fact, I have something I think you'll like a lot."

"In my size? Not a size four?"

"You know I believe every woman should be able to look pretty no matter what her size. So I always order a wide range. Your waist is your best feature, and curves right now are in."

"Uh oh. What does *that* mean? Because I won't wear something too clingy."

Roz laughed and shook her head. "Come on, follow me. Trust my fashion sense."

And Caprice did.

Caprice carried Dylan up the stairs, but let him down at the second floor. He followed them through the shoes and handbag room into the formal fashion area.

Roz went straight to a rack built into the wall, pushed a few dresses aside, and found the one she was looking for. She held it up in front of Caprice and said, "What do you think?"

The color was fabulous. It was dark fuchsia, one of her favorite colors. Roz knew that, of course, and the style was—

"Forties glamour fashions are coming back. Don't you think this looks like something Susan Hayward would wear?" Roz asked.

The dress had long sleeves and a lovely scooped neck. It was a satiny material that formed a fitted bodice. The waist was form fitting, too. There was a slight flair to the hips of the dress that arrowed down into a pencil-thin knee-length skirt.

"Do you really think I'm going to fit into that?"

"This material is forgiving. It might be a vintage style, but it's a current fabric. It's your size, and this designer's sizes aren't skimpy. Try it on, then decide."

Caprice liked the dress so much, she was afraid to hope it would fit.

In the spacious dressing room, she quickly disrobed, then reverently handled the dress, unzipping the zipper, then slipping the garment over her head.

Roz rapped on the door and then came in. "Need help?"

"Can you zip me?"

"Of course, I can." Roz carefully pulled the zipper up its track, and Caprice couldn't believe the way she looked. She looked . . . glamorous. It fit her like no dress she'd ever worn before. She was almost speechless.

"Didn't I tell you?" Roz asked.

Caprice couldn't help the grin that spread from one corner of her mouth to the other. "You did, and I'll never doubt you again. The pearls Mom and Dad gave me when I graduated from high school will look perfect with this."

"Just the right touch. How about wearing your hair up for a change? I'm sure my hairdresser could find a forties style to do you proud. You never treat yourself like that. Why not go all out?"

Caprice's hairdresser trimmed her hair about every six weeks, fringed her bangs, and made sure the side layers fell just right. But specialty hairdos weren't her thing.

"Could he fit me in?"

"I'll text him and see." Roz took out her phone and did just that. "If he has an appointment, it might be a little bit before he gets back to me."

"A texting hairdresser," Caprice mused. "The world sure is changing."

"But one thing doesn't change," Roz said. "Friendship. Don't you agree?"

Their friendship had grown stronger through Roz's crisis last spring. They were almost like sisters now, and that's why Caprice could ask, "Do you mind that I shop at Secrets of the Past?"

"Of course, I don't mind. A woman's fashion sense is her fashion sense. You like vintage. I don't always have that."

Caprice's conversation with her mother made her go beyond the dress shopping subject. "About friendship . . . Do you mind when I talk to Bella and Nikki several times a week? Do you feel left out?"

Roz looked puzzled. "No, I don't feel left out. You and I talk when we can. We're both busy. Where's this coming from?"

Caprice had called Roz to talk about Louise's murder,

finding the body, all the feelings associated with that. Roz understood because of what had happened with her husband back in May.

Because Roz could understand, Caprice explained, "Mom thought she and Louise were really good friends, maybe even best friends. But I ran into Millicent Corsi and she told me Louise and Gail Schwartz were best friends. My mom seemed hurt by the idea and wondered if her friendship with Louise had been as solid as she'd thought. Women can be jealous of other women's closeness to friends. I've seen it before. In fact, Bella sometimes gets jealous of everything I tell Nikki, and what Nikki tells me. So I was just wondering."

"After what we went through, our friendship is solid no matter who else is in our lives, don't you think?" Roz asked.

Caprice was glad Roz felt the same way she did.

"Well, since we're such good friends, just what do you expect out of going to the dance with Vince on Saturday? I mean, are you two dating?" This was the first time she'd brought up that subject because she hadn't been sure what she wanted to say.

"This will be our first date, and the truth is, I don't know if I'm ready for dating. But I'm comfortable with your brother, and when he asked me, *yes* just popped out of my mouth."

Caprice was glad Roz's response had been instinctive. "I think you and Vince can have fun together, but Vince's romantic track record isn't the best."

"I know that. My eyes are wide open. One date won't hurt."

Caprice was about to say she hoped that was true

when her phone played from her purse. She'd settled her fringed bag that seemed to gain weight daily on a shelf in the dressing room.

Roz's phone beeped at about the same time. "I'll check mine. You get yours," she said as she exited the dressing room.

Caprice took one look at caller ID and saw Grant's number. She didn't have a picture of him on her phone. She'd have to take one, though she didn't know how he'd feel about that.

She answered with "Hi. Are you going to puppy class tonight?"

"I didn't call about puppy class," he said seriously. "But yes, I'm going. I'm calling about Louise Downing. Her body's been released. From what I heard, the viewing is Wednesday evening, and the funeral is Thursday morning. I thought you'd want to know."

She did want to know. "I'll tell Mom," she said.

"Are you planning on going?" Grant asked.

"Of course, I am."

Grant paused and then went on. "If you're going to the viewing to support your mom because you feel Louise is part of your family, I understand that. But if you're going to try to pick up clues, after what happened to Louise, I think you should shut down your intentions. This time, leave it to the professionals."

Caprice always bristled at this type of Grant's protective advice. "And if I don't?"

"If you don't, this time you could end up just like Louise Downing."

Chapter Nine

Caprice didn't like viewings, not one little bit. She liked funeral homes even less. But when someone you loved passed on, this is what families did to help heal. The support of family and friends and shared memories just seemed to help. Being Catholic, there was a certain amount of ritual involved. Not so much tonight at the viewing, but tomorrow with the Mass and the funeral and the burial, there would be.

Caprice had left Lady in her puppy apartment in the kitchen tonight, unsure of how long she'd be gone. She was hoping to soon give Lady the run of the house, at least for short periods, when she left. But with plenty of pup still in her, keeping her in her puppy safe-area seemed the wise thing to do, the practical thing to do. However, sometimes Caprice just didn't like to be practical.

She thought she'd been practical tonight. She'd toned down her usually bright dressing style and gone with a Katharine Hepburn style of high-waisted flared pants in a pretty violet wool, a pale lilac silky blouse, and a blazer in the same wool with a fitted jacket. She might wear something like this to a particularly conservative business meeting. But there was so much black when she walked into the sea of men and women lined up to give their best regards to Chet that she wondered if she'd made a mistake.

Caprice stood at the guest book stand and thought, *Louise can't see the color we're wearing anyway, what does it matter? She knows I love color and want to share it with her. She loved color. She raised brilliantly colored flowers. Just why would she want everybody around her to be in black? It doesn't make sense.*

Vince magically appeared at Caprice's elbow from somewhere. "You look different tonight."

Caprice wasn't sure whether she should be insulted or not. "Different how?"

"Grown-up. Mom will be proud."

Had she dressed tonight partly for her mother? Maybe so. Even though her mother would never try to tell her what to wear, she would consider the tone-down a benefit, and more appropriate. Funeral homes always had that over-the-top cold temperature. Coats, jackets, and sweaters were welcome.

Mr. Shultz, the funeral home director, motioned to the front of the room where the flower arrangements stood on height-adjusted stands. Sometimes, at a Catholic viewing these days, there weren't so many flowers because friends opted to give Mass cards instead. A Mass would be said in honor of their friend, maybe to get them a better place in Heaven? Caprice wasn't sure about that, and when she started asking questions, everyone just got uncomfortable. But saying prayers to help a person's soul or energy or whatever it was reach its highest good wasn't out of her belief realm.

Rows of chairs were arranged sort of like at a wedding. There were about ten rows with about eight seats in each row on either side of the center aisle. Of course, at the center of it all was an open casket. Red and white roses decorated the open lid. There was one red rose, long-stemmed, tucked into baby's breath lying close to Louise, and Caprice guessed that was specifically from Chet.

She didn't want to go up there, she really didn't, but her mom and dad and Nana had come in the door and so had Nikki.

"Did you see Bella?" she asked Vince before they reached her.

"She came early to pay her respects and left not long before you got here. She said she'll come to the funeral tomorrow."

The De Lucas gazed at each other and didn't have to say a word. They hugged, then walked together to the receiving line and waited for friends and colleagues of Chet to offer condolences.

Caprice leaned close to her mom. "How are you doing?" They had both been called to the police station yesterday, along with Nikki, to talk to Detective Carstead.

Her mom, dressed in black, sent her a weak smile. "I'm fine."

That was an out-and-out lie. Her mom looked pale. Caprice squeezed her hand.

The line moved slowly. When the family reached

Chet, her mom gave him a hug first, then spoke to him in low tones.

Caprice took the opportunity to study him. He looked like a broken man. After so many years of marriage, what was he feeling, what was he thinking, and what was he going to do?

There were plenty of people behind them in line, so they didn't tie him up long, but moved over to the casket, and took turns on the kneeler there beside the flickering candle. No one but Caprice and law enforcement knew exactly what damage had been done to Louise's body. Caprice hated kneeling there because this wasn't Louise anymore. Louise's soul or energy or whatever left a person when they died simply wasn't there. That body was now an empty shell, no matter how perfect the funeral technician made it look.

Caprice, Nikki, her mom, and Nana each knelt a respectful amount of time with Vince standing behind them, their dad standing there, too. After they rose to their feet, they all made their way around the outside of the chairs to a row that was vacant. Her mother would want to stay a little while and talk to some of Louise's friends, maybe other parishioners of St. Francis. Either the rosary would be said or there would be a short prayer service. Caprice was sure her mom would stay for that, too. She wasn't sure if she would.

Sitting there, she heard snippets of conversations.

"I remember when Louise—"

"Louise looked so great in those Easter hats. Remember the one that was yellow straw with the big pink roses?"

"Louise loved lace, and anything pretty, really. I'm

surprised Chet didn't kick up a fuss about the chintz and lace."

Not for the first time Caprice wondered if Chet would sell the house where he and Louise had lived for so many years. She glanced toward him . . . and then took a second look. He wasn't standing near the casket anymore, but rather ten feet away with a very attractive woman. She looked about fifteen years younger and she was touching his arm in a familiar way.

Just who was the attractive ash-blonde? Had there been discord in the Downings' hearts-and-flowers marriage?

The woman must have said something about the people who had come to pay their respects because he looked over the friends and family in the chairs. His gaze caught Caprice's and a flush stained his cheeks. He looked . . . guilty?

Hmmm. There was only one way to find out what was going on and who that woman was. She knew her mother was upset enough just by being here, so she wasn't going to pull her into *that* discussion.

Caprice tapped her mother's arm. "I'll be right back." She stood and easily made her way to Chet, as if it was the most natural thing in the world to do. When she approached him, he stopped talking to the blonde and gave his attention to her.

He said smoothly, "Thanks so much for coming, Caprice. I know Louise meant a lot to you and your mom, and your brother and sisters. It's so hard to be here, isn't it?" His voice held sorrow that seemed sincere.

Seemed sincere.

Caprice didn't answer, hoping the silence would create room for introductions. It did.

Chet said, "I don't know if you know Malina Lamont? She's my CFO."

Chief Financial Officer. That meant they worked together.

"It's good to meet you," she said politely. "Even under circumstances like this. I just wanted to ask you, Chet, if there's anything I can do. We rearranged some things for the staging, and I didn't know if you might want to put everything back the way it was, especially your den. I can have Juan replace the second leather recliner and the side tables that used to be in there."

Chet gave her a weak smile and shook his head. "No, I'm fine. I told Ms. Langford I still want to sell the house, though I don't think an open house is suitable right now. The work you did will still help sell the place. My den is about the only place I'm comfortable right now. Louise never came in there very much, so I don't have those memories to wrestle with. The rest of the house is a little difficult."

He stepped closer to Caprice and lowered his voice. "Your mother said she asked you to look into Louise's death. Are you going to do that?"

"How would you feel about it if I did?" Caprice asked, watching Malina's expression, too. She just looked slightly uncomfortable.

Chet shrugged, the expensive tweed of his suit catching the overhead light. "The police think this was a robbery gone wrong, or possibly an attempted kidnapping. When folks are well-to-do, law enforcement always believes money is involved."

Caprice glanced at the pretty CFO again. If Louise and Chet's marriage wasn't what it seemed, there would be money involved there, too, along with a divorce. Chet had scheduled meetings so he'd be away the day of the open house. Could he have hired someone to kill his wife?

Caprice felt terrible for even thinking it.

"I am going to look into it, Chet, just to satisfy my mom. Rachel told me that the housekeeper before her was fired. Would you mind if I spoke with her?"

"I don't mind at all. But Pearl Mellencamp might still hold a grudge. She moved to York and started a cleaning service with the settlement I gave her."

"Was the settlement a large one?"

"Essentially it was a severance package, much more than she deserved. But it kept her quiet and out of our hair and that's what was important."

Caprice asked Chet, "Can you tell me where Louise was from originally before she came to Kismet?"

Chet gave her a blank look, then admitted, "Louise wouldn't say. I know that seems a little odd, but she told me she was escaping her past and just wanted to live in the present."

He took Caprice's arm and pulled her away from everyone, including Malina.

"Louise never talked about her past and didn't want me to know anything about it. She simply said she had no family and she'd had a disastrous marriage when she was younger. The man died. But she wouldn't say more. And the truth is, I loved her so much, I didn't care. Let's face it. I had secrets, too, and I didn't want to spill those.

Past romances just weigh down what two people have now. Full disclosure isn't always best."

That might be true. But what about the practical aspect? "When you apply for a marriage license, past paperwork has to be disclosed—divorce, death."

"I dealt with that. I set up a private appointment for Louise with the marriage license clerk." Chet was thoughtful for a moment. "Do you think her past had something to do with her murder?"

A shadowy past could definitely have something to do with murder. "It might. Do you have your marriage record?" She remembered her mother had often said something about keeping hers in a safe deposit box.

"I have it in my safe," Chet revealed. "But it doesn't say much. Just that Louise was a widow and her husband's date of death."

The date wouldn't do Caprice much good unless she discovered *where* Louise had been widowed.

Suddenly their attention was taken up by a woman at the kneeler in front of the casket who had started crying. Caprice recognized her in her smart navy dress with the lace collar and cuffs.

Chet said, "Gail's taking it hard. She and Louise were close, too."

Gail Schwartz left the kneeler and ducked behind the flower arrangements. "I'll see if I can help," Caprice offered and went to Gail.

When Caprice reached her, Gail shook her head. "Sorry, I didn't mean for that to happen."

"This is hard," Caprice empathized. "No one expected anything like this to happen."

"No," Gail agreed. "If anything happened to Louise, I expected it to be her heart, not something so . . . violent." Although she took a handkerchief from her navy purse and wiped her nose, she kept glancing at Chet standing with Malina.

Caprice said, "I'd never met Chet's CFO. Do you know her?"

Gail shook her head. "No. Louise always said they were just colleagues."

So apparently Louise had talked about Malina and Chet.

"Louise and Chet always seemed so happy," Gail said, as if she might be doubting it now.

"They honeymooned in Hawaii, didn't they?" Caprice asked, remembering Louise's stories and what her mother had told her.

"They always took such romantic trips. Louise was looking forward to going to the Bahamas over Valentine's Day." Gail sighed. "Thirty years is a long time to be married. Even if they did have a rocky start."

"A rocky start?" Caprice prodded, remembering what Millicent Corsi had told her.

"Louise was quite anxious about starting a relationship when she met Chet. She and I had been friends for a few months and she talked to me about getting involved with a high-powered man like Chet and what that entailed. When Chet asked her to marry him, she wasn't sure she should. And he did propose pretty quickly. She backed off, almost broke it off."

"Why didn't she?" Caprice prompted.

"Because he was head over heels in love with her. He was so in love, he even showed her his bank account, and had her talk to his financial advisor. After that, Louise agreed to marry him."

Now wasn't that interesting? Exactly what did finances have to do with trust? Exactly why had Louise been so hesitant?

Caprice studied Gail who had tears in her eyes, as she thought about her past friendship with Louise. It seemed odd that her mom, who thought she was Louise's best friend, hadn't known Louise and Gail were that close. Or even this early story about Louise and Chet's romance.

Caprice considered this new information that Louise hadn't trusted Chet. She'd been in her early twenties when she'd met him. What had happened to make her not trust easily?

Glancing over at Chet and Malina once more, Caprice decided a visit to Pearl Mellencamp was in order. She'd have to fit that into her schedule tomorrow.

York was a city with tons of neighborhoods, from rich to poor, and everything in between. There were shopping centers and malls in the east end, the west end, and the north end. There were two hospitals and urban sprawl that crawled into what once had been beautiful farmland. Whatever residents of Kismet couldn't find in their town, they could find in York. Caprice had staged houses here, but not in the section of town where she and Nikki and Lady were headed now.

"I can't believe you were going to drive over here by yourself and question this woman you've never met who might hold a grudge," Nikki berated her from the passenger seat.

"I was going to bring Lady along," Caprice joked.

Lady heard her name and barked from her crate in the back.

But Nikki wasn't laughing. "You've got to be careful this time, Caprice. You know you do. Mom would never forgive herself if you put yourself in a situation where you got hurt."

This morning they'd sat beside their mom in the pew at St. Francis during the funeral Mass. At the cemetery, their dad had escorted their mom to one of the chairs Chet had designated for their use. As the cold wind blew, they'd all stood behind their mother, each of them with a hand on her shoulder as the priest had said his final words, as everyone who had thought highly of Louise or loved her had taken a rose from the huge spray on top of the casket to keep as a remembrance.

"Mom and Louise were friends like you and I are," Nikki said.

"I'm not sure about that," Caprice responded, wishing she didn't have to.

"What do you mean? You saw how heartbroken Mom was. Dad was, too."

"Yes, they were. But how broken up would Louise have been if something happened to Mom?"

"What an awful thing to say!"

"It's an awful thing to think. But I've been thinking it ever since Millicent Corsi told me that Gail and Louise were best friends. Mom never knew that. What else didn't she know?"

But Nikki was still thinking about best friends. "Maybe best friends can change."

"Do they? Really?"

They thought about the concept of best friends for a few moments until Caprice reminded Nikki, "My best friend never changed. You've always been my best friend."

"That's different, Caprice. We lived together. We loved each other. We were pals."

"We were still two years apart, though, not in the same classes, not dating the same level of boys. Other girls could have snuck in there and put a wedge in our friendship. Bella certainly tried sometimes."

Nikki shrugged. "We lived with the De Luca history. We knew everything there was to know about the family. We heard our aunts and uncles complain and get a little tipsy and tell things they shouldn't. All of that bonded us in a way and made us feel even closer. So close, we could talk about anything, even with Bella. You know that's true."

Nikki continued. "The whole situation with Mom and Louise could have boiled down to Louise not wanting to hurt Mom, not wanting her to know she and Gail were close."

Caprice made a left turn. "I suppose. Sometimes when we share something, we try to protect Bella."

"It never works out, though, because she can see it on our faces. She keeps poking and prodding until she figures out what we're holding back."

Caprice thought about the differences between her generation and her mother's. "Mom never would have poked and prodded with Louise. They were both women who knew what 'classy' meant. There just isn't so much class around anymore. Haughtiness, maybe, but not class. Does Chet have any brothers or sisters?" Caprice asked.

"You'd have to ask Dad for sure, but I don't think so. And I didn't see any relatives of his there. He's nine years older than Dad."

"I never really delved into his business success," Caprice mused. "I heard Dad say once that whatever Chet Downing did always turned out right . . . that he had a mind for business."

As the GPS voice told them they had arrived at their destination on the right, Caprice pulled up to the curb and examined the houses along the street. Most were row houses, two stories, freshly painted. This time of year, many had some kind of Valentine's Day decoration on the door in the form of a wreath, a bouquet, or a plastic heart.

She left her van running so it would stay heated, but she cracked her window and told Nikki to do the same.

"You should let me go to the door with you," she advised Caprice, not for the first time.

"No. I'll have my phone with me. You'll be able to hear every word. Talk to Lady until I get inside so she doesn't start barking."

Caprice dialed Nikki's number, then exited the van before Nikki could give her any other advice or warning. Caprice had to admit she felt a little twinge in her stomach, not knowing what she was going to find here. But her stomach would get over it, and so would she.

On the small porch, she confidently knocked on the wooden screen door. When Pearl Mellencamp opened the door, Caprice recognized her immediately, although she was older . . . and looked it. Her brown hair was turning gray, and it was all frizzy around her head as if she'd tried to give herself her own perm. She wore no make-up, ragged jeans with holes, and a sweatshirt.

"Hi," Caprice said with a lot of energy and held out her hand.

"I'm not voting in the next election," Pearl mumbled and started to close the door.

"Oh, I'm not a politician."

"I'm not buying any cookies or Tupperware or wrapping paper or magazines either."

Caprice shook her head. "I'm not selling any of those." She reached into her purse for a business card and handed it to Pearl.

Louise's former housekeeper glanced at it and narrowed her eyes, then said, "You're a home stager. Do I know you?"

"It's been a long time, but I visited Louise Downing's house when you were her housekeeper. I have some questions."

At that, Pearl backed up a step and attempted to close the door again.

Caprice asked quickly, "Do you know she's dead?"

That stopped Pearl. She took a step forward, the door opening wide.

"Dead?"

"She was murdered."

Pearl looked . . . astonished, but Caprice supposed that could be an act. After all, Louise's murder had been all over the local news.

"That house had security," Pearl informed Caprice.

"Chet Downing had a gun. And Louise knew how to take care of herself, unless that heart condition of hers got the best of her if she got scared—" Pearl broke off as if she'd said too much.

"I'm trying to help find her murderer," Caprice told Pearl truthfully, watching the woman's eyes. "So I thought maybe we could have a cup of coffee or tea and talk."

Pearl avoided Caprice's gaze, but then said grudgingly, "Come on in. I'll get the kettle."

Five minutes later, the kettle had whistled and Pearl was pouring water into two mugs. She plopped in the tea bags. "I've been buried in paperwork from my cleaning business, trying to get everything together to do taxes. Not watching much TV. Maybe that's why I didn't hear about Louise. How was she . . . killed?"

"Someone shot her."

Pearl didn't react to that news.

The kitchen was shabby. There was a crooked blind at the window but no curtains. They sat at a small rectangular table for two, looking down at their tea mugs on plastic, well-used flowered and faded place mats. Caprice didn't even have a spoon to take the tea bag out, and she didn't want to just lay it on the table. So she left it in, watching the brew get darker and darker.

"Can you tell me a little about working at the Downings'?" Caprice asked.

"I worked there ten years," Pearl announced proudly. With a scowl, she added, "But then suddenly they decided they didn't want me there anymore."

"Who decided?"

"It wasn't one or the other. Mr. and Mrs. Downing came to me together and said they thought it was time for me to go. But every household has secrets, and housekeepers usually know what they are."

"What were the secrets in the Downing household?"

Pearl shook her head. "As part of my settlement I can't talk about the Downings."

"I see. The thing is Louise is dead."

A smile suddenly broke across Pearl's face. "Yeah, she is, isn't she? You know, she was shrewder than she looked."

"I don't know what you mean."

"Louise wasn't no shrinking violet, not like her husband thought she was. She was a schemer." As if she couldn't wait to reveal what she'd been hiding for years, Pearl gave Caprice a conspiratorial smile and continued. "Mr. Downing put a household allowance in her account every week."

"That makes sense," Caprice prompted, wondering where this was going.

"Oh, yes, it does, to buy groceries and supplies and whatever else she might need. But . . ." Pearl's voice lowered a notch as if someone might overhear. "Louise skimmed money off that account and transferred it into an account Mr. Downing *didn't* know about. That poor man must have thought expenses for food and bedsheets were rising faster than inflation."

"You said households have lots of secrets. Did Louise ever mention anything about her past before she married Mr. Downing?"

"Like what?" Pearl asked.

Caprice didn't want to get too specific because she wanted the information to come from Pearl. "Did she ever mention past relationships she'd had before her marriage?"

Pearl considered that, then shook her head.

Before Caprice could even think about what Pearl *had* given her, barking came from her phone. She'd forgotten to press mute.

"What's that?" Pearl asked, motioning to Caprice's pocket.

"It's just my phone."

"Yeah, but I heard something. It sounded like a dog. And if I heard something, that means you've got the phone open. That means somebody can hear me. Are you taping us?"

"No, I'm not taping."

Pearl got to her feet. "Get out, and get out now."

"Miss Mellencamp—"

"Don't you 'Miss Mellencamp' me. If you want information, you get it from the people involved. I got my settlement. No, I don't like the Downings. No, I try not to think about them. But they did give me a settlement, and I have my own business now. So you just leave, and you forget about me."

With that, she practically pushed Caprice out the door.

When Caprice returned to her van, she told Nikki, "I messed that up. I didn't mute my phone."

She thought about the conversation she'd had with Pearl. "I'll tell you, that woman has some push behind those arms. She might be older than I am, but she's stronger, and I think she could do harm to somebody if she wanted to. In fact, I believe she's capable of murder."

Chapter Ten

For the rest of the afternoon, as Caprice worked on upcoming projects, she couldn't help thinking about Pearl, her attitude, and her settlement with the Downings. On the other hand, she also remembered Chet's familiarity with Malina Lamont last evening, and everything Gail had told her. Sometimes people weren't what they seemed on the outside. Sometimes *couples* weren't who they seemed on the outside.

After she finished eating a slice of pepperoni bread she'd baked for herself along with a square of thawed lasagna, she placed an order for furniture from a rental company in Harrisburg. In eight days she had a Sherwood Forest-themed staging and needed a few unusual living room pieces.

She was studying the invoice when her phone played an airy signal that told her she had a text coming in. It was from Nana. Yes, some grandmothers did text.

Can you come over? Bella needs to see everyone.

After the funeral, Bella had decided to spend the afternoon and evening with their mom and Nana. Joe and the kids were supposed to join them for supper.

But now Bella wanted to see everyone?

Lady looked up at Caprice hopefully. After all, that excursion to see Pearl Mellencamp hadn't been much of a playtime. This afternoon, work had taken precedence. Her pet would enjoy the attention the rest of the De Lucas could give her.

It didn't take long to text Nana back, let Lady out for a quick bathroom run, give Sophia a little catnip and a few brushes through her thick undercoat and longer hair, and she was off to her mom's. It was probably good her mom and dad had company tonight. It would keep them from dwelling too much on the funeral, from end-of-life issues no one wanted to face.

At her mom's, Caprice left Lady with her dad, Joe and the kids, as well as Vince—who had been texted too—then joined Bella, her mom, Nana, and Nikki in Nana's apartment. The smell of coffee wafted through the rooms, and a tray of biscotti sat on the table. No matter what Caprice did, her biscotti never came out exactly like Nana's. Close, but not exact. The biscuit with its lemon icing wasn't anything like the twice-baked biscotti you could buy at the grocery store or at the Koffee Klatch. These were quite different—soft and smooth rather than hard and coarse.

Bella was wearing one of those swaddling slings, and Benny was asleep against her chest. Tonight, she was dressed in jeans and a pretty green sweater. Her curly black hair was loose around her face and looked just washed. Maybe switching Benny to the bottle had helped and she was getting more sleep.

With a smile, she pointed to a white box on the corner of the table. "Take a look at that, Caprice. It's Benny's christening outfit." She patted her baby and cooed against his head.

After a glance at Nikki and a shrug, Caprice opened the box and turned back the tissue.

"I made the suit," Bella explained. "Barbara from the Rosary Society at church knitted the sweater, cap, and booties. What do you think?"

First Caprice lifted out the sweater, cap, and booties made from the softest, fluffiest white yarn. "Barbara's knitting is impeccable. How pretty this is, Bella."

She handed that part of the outfit to Nikki who could pass it along to Nana and their mom. All of the women examined it and pronounced it perfect for the christening.

Next Caprice lifted out the little white suit, and she couldn't help but gasp. It was absolutely adorable. The white shirt was enhanced with a swirl design right in the fabric. There were small white pants that were perfectly tailored for a baby. Along with both of those pieces was a white vest with tiny little lapels that came to a V.

"Oh, Bee, you made this? It's wonderful. You could make these to sell as well as costumes."

All the women crowded around, examining every stitch and every seam, as well as the fabric.

Fran wrapped an arm around Bella's shoulders. "I always knew you were talented, but this little outfit, Bella . . . It's so beautiful because of all the love you packed into it. That makes the difference between ordinary and special."

"Bella never makes ordinary," Nana said, with a sweeping gesture of her hand. "She always goes beyond. This idea of children's costumes is going to catch on, you mark my words. She'll be famous someday. Maybe she should forget about going to work for Roz."

"Joe would like that," Bella admitted with a laugh. "But my business is going to take time to build. Now if I had a really famous client, with a child who needed a costume, that could help. But until that opportunity rolls around, I need to bring in money every week. Besides, I like being around the fashions in Roz's store. That's in my field, too."

Bella had a different confidence about her when she talked about fashion, making costumes, and what she might like to do with a business. Although her sister was a little worn-out from the first few weeks of motherhood, Caprice had never seen her more happy. Maybe that was because her life had so many more directions and new ways it could grow.

"Everybody have biscotti," Bella said. "I have to get Vince."

Vince, with all these women? Caprice supposed that wasn't a stretch. Vince was good with women since he'd had to deal with three sisters all his life. At least he was good with women until he dated them and then didn't date them anymore. She thought again about him and Roz, and certainly couldn't see them as a couple that would last. But what did she know? Roz needed some fun and he could provide it. Vince needed some grounding, and Roz could provide that. Weren't relationships all about having mutual needs filled?

Vince looked perplexed as he straggled in behind Bella into Nana's apartment. Caprice suspected he didn't spend too much time here, whereas she and Nikki and Bella often had tea with Nana. Vince didn't want to be grilled, not that Nana outwardly grilled. She just seemed to have a sixth sense that led her into certain questions and certain comments that were always right on the mark. Vince had always believed she was psychic, but Caprice . . . Caprice knew Nana had terrific intuition. Mostly she was observant. She missed nothing, and that's how she put two and two together to come up with four when everyone else might get five or six.

"I don't drink tea," Vince announced, as he stood at the table and picked up a biscotti.

"That's good because we brewed coffee," Nikki offered, giving him a wink. "Tea's just for afternoons with Nana, when we like to think we're refined."

"Oh, and coffee is for family when we're not?" he asked dryly.

They all laughed.

Bella held up her hand and waved it, signaling that she wanted them all to be quiet. Nothing new there. Bella liked to hold court. Tonight, however, they all soon realized she had good reason.

"Benny's christening is coming up quickly in just over three weeks. Joe and I have been discussing who we want to be his godparents."

Caprice's heart quickened a bit. After all, being a godparent was a great honor.

"We've had discussions about it ever since Benny

was born, and the reason for that was, we couldn't decide. We listed pros and cons for everybody." She shook her head. "But that didn't help. How could I choose between Nikki and Caprice to be Benny's godmother? So this is what we decided. We'd like both of you to be his godmothers and we'd like Vince to be his godfather. How about that?"

A cheer went up from Nana and they all laughed and then hugged. Nikki and Caprice worked well together on almost everything. Being Benny's godmothers together would just give them another bond. And having Vince as godfather would bring them all even closer. She was sure of it.

"Would you like to have a light dinner after the christening? I'd be glad to cater it for you," Nikki said. "It will be my gift to Benny."

"Oh, that would be lovely," Bella agreed. "We'll have to make sure to take lots of photos."

Caprice was already thinking that a wall collage of photos would be a great birthday present for Bella. She'd have to make sure both her phone and her camera were handy.

As they talked about the ceremony and the hope for good weather, they finished the biscotti and most of the coffee.

"I bet Megan and Timmy are asleep on the sofa. Joe, too, for that matter," Bella said with a grin.

"I really should be going, too," Caprice said. "Tomorrow I have those model homes to spruce up for the weekend. I found nice glassware pieces at Isaac's shop. Once I add chocolates and plants, I'll be ready for Valentine's Day weekend."

"At least with the model homes," Nana said wisely.

"At least with the model homes," Caprice agreed, thinking again what Valentine's Day would bring if Grant came to the dance on Saturday. Would he even want to sit with her? Would he dance with her?

That thought sent a little tingle up her spine, but she shifted her thoughts away from it to ask, "Does anyone want to doggie-sit tomorrow?"

After all, wasn't that what family was for?

"Tell me about your next staging project," Nana suggested the next morning.

"How do you know I have one?" Caprice teased. She wanted to let Lady romp around a little before she left so her cocker would settle down for Nana. Though she'd never tell her grandmother that. Nana would be outraged at the thought that she couldn't handle her granddaughter's pet.

Nana pulled a toy from the wicker basket by her sofa, sat on her couch, and wiggled it at Lady. Lady scampered to her, ready to play. So much for letting her romp so she was ready for Nana!

"You are a businesswoman. You always have your next project lined up."

Actually, she tried to schedule four to five jobs ahead. "My next theme is Sherwood Forest."

Lady gave a wiggle as she tried to pull the braided colorful rope from Nana.

"I like that. Brings to mind Robin Hood and Maid Marian."

"The serving staff will dress in period costumes.

Nikki and I haven't come up with the menu yet but it will be very Old English."

"How did you come up with the theme?"

"The house is in a forested area by the old mill. But the idea really came to me when I spotted the gigantic treehouse at the rear of the property. The boys who lived there even had a heavy rope to lower themselves to the ground."

"What are you decorating with?"

"I used lots of earth-tone fabrics, chair swings that are really comfortable, rustic shelves. The house is stone and cedar-sided, practically encased in oaks, sycamores, and silver maples."

"Copper pieces would make nice accents along with pewter."

Caprice considered that. "I'd found wooden crocks and vases but I do believe you're right. I think I have a primitive copper tray in my storage unit as well as pewter steins. I'll have to check my inventory list."

"And the family?" Nana inquired.

"They're moving to Hilton Head. They're tired of Pennsylvania winters."

"Oh, so now they can run from hurricanes," Nana said acerbically as Lady stopped pulling and just stood her ground.

Letting Lady have the toy, Nana caught Caprice's gaze and held it. "Do you think Bella and Joe are mending their marriage? She doesn't talk to me like she talks to you."

Nana was the family overseer in a quiet way. She kept tabs on them all.

"I think they're on the right track. Sessions with Father Gregory have really helped them communicate."

"Yes, I noticed that. But does Bella still keep things from Joe? Is he just trying hard for our benefit or for his?"

Those were questions Caprice had asked herself. "I don't know, Nana. But I do think they're both trying. And they both adore Benny." She really did have to get on the road. One thing more before she left. "How's Mom?"

"She's grieving. One of these days I'll suggest she pull out her old photo albums, and she'll have a really good cry. That will help. Maybe we can start a special fund at the Garden Club for a scholarship for a young person interested in flowers or plants. That will give her thoughts a positive place to fall."

Lady gave a little yip, rolled on her back, and gazed up at Nana.

"You want a treat?" Nana asked.

Caprice smiled. Spoiling was something grandmothers did best.

Hearts, flowers, chocolates, plants, and a touch of antique glassware would put the finishing Valentine's Day touches on the model homes that Derrick Gastenaux had built and was now attempting to sell. There had been a few hiccups with the ceramic tile experts and the landscapers that had put finishing the homes behind schedule. They'd gone on the market right before Christmas, definitely not a prime time to sell. However, through Caprice's staging efforts, she'd actually garnered business for future stagings.

During this weekend over Valentine's Day, the houses would have real estate agents present all day Saturday and Sunday. There had been an extensive ad campaign as well as social media coverage. Derrick had pulled out all the stops. Caprice had already been paid for her contracted staging effort but she felt invested in the homes. Sales contracts on these houses would almost guarantee her more work when Derrick developed the land more completely.

Hence she pulled up to the first model home, switched off her van's engine, and got ready to unload those extra niceties that could convince prospective home buyers that they could live here.

This development was part of a new neighborhood that would expand and grow. The problem with these newer neighborhoods, in Caprice's estimation, was that they didn't have tall trees already growing, or stately bushes out front. The landscaping with ornamental evergreens and unusual grasses was pretty but she much preferred mature oaks, ivy climbing up brick, hydrangeas that had survived many winters. Yep, she was old-fashioned in a lot of ways because she didn't think "newer" was necessarily better. Yet there was something to be said for a family starting a life in a house that had never been lived in, with brand-spanking new roofs and siding and a picturesque gas fireplace instead of a sootier wood-burning one.

The idea of a fireplace brought back her conversation with Grant: whether or not he should look for a house with a fireplace. Would he actually go to the Valentine's

Day dance? Would they spend any time together there other than in polite conversation? Would he tell her any more than he had before about what he was thinking and feeling, maybe even hoping? Hopes were as private as prayers. You had to really trust someone to tell them your hopes. She trusted *him*. Did he trust her?

Caprice carried two boxes and three bags into the first model home, thinking about Nana's smile when she'd left her with Lady. Her grandmother liked the cocker's company.

When Caprice checked her watch, she realized Jamie from Garden Glory should be arriving shortly. Greenery as well as knickknacks warmed up a house. It didn't have to be obvious. But even philodendron on a windowsill could add that homey touch.

Caprice arranged potpourri in the lead crystal nappies she'd found at Isaac's. It was a combination of rose and cinnamon that seemed odd but went together really well. The gentle smell sifted through the living room. Positioning a cupid-shaped pillow on the window seat, she thought it might capture prospective buyers' attention and encourage them to smile. When she arranged the heart-shaped milk chocolates in a glass-covered dish, it reminded her of one her mom used to have on her bureau. Isaac had claimed this one was from the 1950s.

Caprice was about to move on to the second model house when she heard a vehicle pull into the driveway. Crossing to the front window, she watched Jamie emerge from the Garden Glory delivery van. She went to the back, opened it, and hefted a carton into her arms.

As she carried it toward the house, Caprice opened the door to let her inside.

"What do we have?" she asked of the knowledgeable nursery clerk.

"I have plants for sun and shade."

Caprice understood that inside gardening was an art just as outside gardening was. You couldn't put a sun-loving plant into a dark corner. You couldn't put a shade plant in front of a sunny window. Just as with people, they had to be happy in their location.

"I have more in the car," Jamie said, as she set the box on the floor. "Let me go get the money tree. That one doesn't require much looking after. It's great with bright indirect light. You can let the soil dry out between waterings. The only thing you have to be careful about is not to overwater it because it will get root rot. Hold on and I'll get it."

Two minutes later she was back.

"Oh, how pretty," Caprice said. The thin trunks of this plant were braided and each leaf had five to seven more bright green leaflets.

"Sometimes the containers we put these in look a little too small, but they're not," Jamie explained. "You don't want a big container that will hold too much water. If the plant starts getting brown leaves, it doesn't have enough light. That's not going to happen over one weekend. I'll place it for you because we don't want it near a heat vent or a cold-air return. In fact, this would be great for an office, too, because it thrives under fluorescent light. Do you have any of that here?"

"There's fluorescent lighting in the kitchen in the next house. How about that?"

I have a second one in the van. We can take that one over there. Now let's look at what I have here. I've potted combinations of plants to give variety."

She brought forth the container that held a Boston fern and a ponytail palm. She'd mixed the schefflera with trailing ivy and a cascading fern. The pièce de résistance was a combination peace lily, which seemed to bring a sense of serenity to any space, combined with a broad-leafed dumb cane.

"Louise loved the peace lily," Jamie mused. "She said she could breathe easier knowing it does an excellent job of purifying indoor air."

"I wish it would have done a more peaceful job for her," Caprice murmured, still thinking about what she'd seen in Louise's greenhouse the day of the murder.

"I heard you found the body," Jamie said, in a little voice as if she almost didn't want to utter the words.

"It was awful."

"I suppose the police are still working on what happened."

"I haven't heard anything. A friend of mine has a contact in the D.A.'s office. Maybe I'll find out something this weekend."

Jamie looked around the living room, seeing the touches that Caprice had added. She seemed to put Louise's murder out of her mind. "Valentine's Day weekend. That's a special one for lots of people. How about you?"

"It's going to be a busy one. I don't know how special it will be. I'm helping with the Give-from-the-Heart Day food drive. I am going to the Valentine's Day dance, but I'll probably just spend time with friends. How about you?"

"I'm too old for Valentine's Day dances."

"You're never too old for a Valentine's Day dance. Who knows? You could meet someone there."

"Heaven forbid!" Jamie said with a negative shake of her head.

Caprice laughed.

"I'll arrange these plants, then move on to the other houses," Jamie assured her, already doing it. "We're pretty busy at work today, so I can't dawdle."

Fifteen minutes later, Jamie had left and Caprice was arranging more chocolates in a pretty dish when her cell phone rang. Slipping it from her pocket, she smiled. Ace Richland.

Ace was a former rock star now making a comeback. He'd bought a house that Caprice had staged last summer. She'd also redecorated some of the rooms for him, including his twelve-year-old daughter's. Trista had come to visit Shasta's pups after they were born and had fallen in love with them. When they were old enough, Ace had delivered one to her at her mom's place in Virginia and Trista had named her Brindle. Caprice hadn't seen much of Ace since then, but that wasn't unusual. Though she did try to keep in touch with former clients. Ace had even given her a recommendation for her Web site.

"How are you?" she asked, after his initial "It's Ace."

"I'm pretty good. I know this is short notice, but I'm calling to invite you to a party I'm throwing to debut my new single. It's Monday."

She loved music, and she even liked Ace's old stuff.

She'd had some of it on her playlist before she'd even known he was moving to Kismet.

"I'd love to come."

"Well, score one for my side," he said, sort of grumpily now.

"That doesn't sound good. Don't tell me you're having problems finding guests who want to listen to this new single?"

"No. Even though my label decided to roll this out early on short notice, the guest list is filling in." He sighed. "But I don't think my ex is going to let Trista attend the party."

"Why not?" She knew since summer he'd intended to try harder to connect with Trista as a dad should bond with his daughter.

"I don't know. Trista and I are good. She seems to have a swell time now when she visits. Especially when she brings Brindle. I assured Marsha that the party's going to be tame. But she won't budge, and I can't push too hard if I want to see my daughter, can I?"

She knew Ace was in a tough spot. He hadn't been an exemplary dad when he was married to Marsha and his ex-wife maintained full custody. He'd like to change that, but again, he didn't want to push too hard. And after all, he was a rock star. Just how would a judge look at that?

"Is there anything I can do?" Caprice asked.

"If there's anything you can do, I'll let you know. My family will be there. You met them at the pool party last summer."

"I did."

The pool party he'd thrown then had been the same

night that Lady was born. It had also been the same night she and Grant had become friendlier.

"I just hired your sister to cater before I phoned you," Ace informed her.

Nikki was probably over-the-top excited about that.

"This isn't a huge party, Caprice," he went on. "That will happen in L.A. next weekend. But I wanted you to be among the first to hear 'Second Chances.'"

"I'm honored you included me."

"I like you," Ace said and Caprice could hear the smile in his voice. "I'll see you Monday at seven P.M. My place."

After Caprice said good-bye, she thought about Ace and his ex and Trista. So many families were broken apart. So many kids had to shift from one parent to the other. That's what happened when a marriage disintegrated.

More than once, she'd wondered exactly what had happened with Grant's marriage. Who had wanted out? Who had blamed the other? Who had said, "I want a divorce"?

She knew divorce wasn't always the final ending. Her relationship with Travis had proven that. She'd fallen in love with his little girl as well as with him. When he and his ex had gotten back together, that had left Caprice bereft from losing both relationships.

Divorced men meant baggage and trouble. She'd have to keep that in mind whenever her interest in Grant became a little too keen. She'd have to keep that in mind if she saw him at the dance.

She would concentrate on solving Louise's murder and not on what she and Grant had in common. Because at the end of the day, it really wasn't that much.

Chapter Eleven

Caprice was getting a manicure.

On her way home from the model homes, she'd made the decision to stop at the Nail Yard where Louise had had her nails done. Going over the murder scene in her mind, everything her family had said, everything Pearl had said, everything Rachel had said, Caprice wanted to push forward.

A manicurist was very much like a hairdresser. These professionals could be sounding boards because they knew how to listen. They were neutral, usually accepting any information without judgment. Therefore, they could become confidantes. Now, it was quite true that Louise might not have confided anything in *her* manicurist. On the other hand . . .

Of course, it wasn't so easy to go to a stranger and inveigle information. But Caprice had an "in." Nikki went to Judy Clapsaddle—also Louise's manicurist—at the Nail Yard. She wasn't above cashing in on that sisterly bond today.

As she entered town, she glanced at the Arts And

Crafts Mall that was topped by the Blue Moon Grille, remembering again the evening she'd spent there with Seth. Pushing those thoughts aside, she drove through the oldest part of town.

Downtown Kismet reeked of tourist charm, rooted in its early 1900s heritage. Stark white trimmed the windows and eaves of the redbrick buildings. Many businesses had agreed to showcase oval wrought-iron signs that were less garish than larger placards to advertise their service or goods.

She glanced at Secrets of the Past. A few more storefronts down the street, she gave her attention to the old movie theater that ran marathon film fests. Nearby, the ice cream parlor—Cherry on the Top—was another of those date places where she'd spent time with Seth. Sighing, she quickly focused on a deli where Vince bought take-out, and the old school transformed into condos where he lived.

The Nail Yard wasn't part of one of those glitzy chains set up in malls. Nope. It was tucked into what used to be a bicycle shop. It was a narrow little space, with plate glass windows on either side of the entrance. Judy Clapsaddle, the manager, had decorated the storefront in a frothy way for Valentine's Day with a large hand-drawn sign surrounded by red paper hearts. It proclaimed the Valentine's Day Special—ANY COLOR, FREE ADORNMENT, $12.99. GIFT PACKAGES TO $100. GIVE A LITTLE MANICURE LOVE TO A SPECIAL SOME-ONE TODAY.

Clever, really. What woman didn't like to be pampered and have her nails looking like a model's in a fashion spread? In fact, she hadn't found anything in the

hospital gift shop, so this could be the perfect gift for
her mother. This was going to be a multipurpose stop.
Her mother's spirits needed to be lifted. A few sparkles
on her nails could at least make her smile.

Caprice parked along the curb in front of the store.
She didn't frequent the Nail Yard, for a multitude of
reasons. The smell was the main one. Even though an
exhaust fan labored to rid the shop of the odors, even
though new polishes weren't as noxious as the old ones
used to be, paint was paint. It carried fumes. Still, as she
walked into the Nail Yard, she realized business must
not be booming. There were no other clients waiting,
and there was only a faint smell.

Pleasantly surprised, Caprice smiled at Judy who sat
at a narrow table reading a magazine. She was flipping
the pages of a national tell-all, not something Caprice
read on a regular basis, though she really was intrigued
by the alien stories sometimes.

Judy looked up, immediately asking, "How can I
help you?" She was a short redhead with a pixie-cut
hairdo and freckles. Her small frame and turned-up
nose, her skinny jeans and sequined T-shirt, made her
look about sixteen. But she knew, from what Nikki had
told her, that Judy was closer to twenty-five. Twenty-
five seemed like ages ago.

Goodness. When had she started thinking about approaching middle age? She had a lot to accomplish and
experience before she even hit thirty-five. No, she was
still on the first step of a young adult life. She had a
ways to go before approaching any hills.

"Do you have time for a manicure? My sister Nikki

comes in here all the time, and she told me you do a beautiful job."

Judy checked her watch. "I have a client in half an hour. We can accomplish a lot in that amount of time."

Caprice laughed. "I imagine we can."

Two displays of nail polish stood on either side of Judy, with multicolored bottles of polish that were for sale and color palettes to choose from. In addition, placards beside the bottles showcased charts with adornment possibilities. Caprice studied them now, wanting to choose something that would complement her new dress, that would look a little vintage yet glamorous. No small feat.

As she perused the displays, Judy said, "I saw the articles about you in the *Kismet Crier*. I think it's wonderful you take in stray dogs and cats and give them homes. Do you have a network for that?"

So Judy was one of the residents of Kismet who actually read the paper. She'd had others recognize her from the articles Marianne Brisbane had written about her—both human interest and murder-solving. "Mostly friends, neighbors, and family are my network. A veterinarian, Marcus Reed from Furry Friends, is a big help, too. Do you have any pets?" Caprice asked.

"No. I live at home with my parents, and I'm not there very much. I don't want to give them extra work."

Because of the economy, young adults were living longer at childhood homes before they went out on their own. "I certainly understand that. When I was a kid and brought home a stray, my mom would roll her eyes, then say, 'You're going to take care of him or her.'"

Judy laughed. "Nikki has told me stories about growing up with two sisters and a brother."

"I'll bet she has."

As Caprice was deciding on the color of nail polish, Judy pointed to the brass clothes tree. "Take off your coat and get comfortable."

Caprice was unbuttoning her coat as Judy arranged everything she'd need on her table. "The last two articles I read were about the murders you helped solve."

Caprice had given Marianne Brisbane an exclusive both times. Marianne could be a big help when she was digging around for clues. At first, Caprice had been afraid to trust her, but the reporter had proven to be a competent research source, as well as a journalist who was just looking for the truth.

"I don't know how I got involved in both of them," Caprice admitted, deciding to go with a silver-toned polish instead of trying to match a color to her dress.

She held it up for Judy to see. "I'm wearing a fuchsia dress for the Valentine's Day dance. It mimics a forties design. What appliqués might go well with this?"

"I guess you don't want little red cupids."

"Not hardly."

Judy glanced at the placards. "What about a layer of mother-of-pearl stars to top off the silver?"

Stars, a glamorous dress, and Valentine's Day? They seemed to go together. "Sounds good."

Caprice checked out the massage chair sitting in the corner that seemed to take up half the shop.

"Shiatsu massaging," Judy explained. "After you get up from ten minutes on that, you feel as if a masseuse has worked magic."

"Is that included in one of your gift packages?"

"Absolutely."

As Caprice settled on the white stool, Judy said, "Let me see your left hand, and we'll get started." Judy examined Caprice's hand. "A little dry. You must wash your hands a lot."

"With pets, I have to. I do a lot of cooking, too."

"Like Nikki." Judy picked up a sanding block. "Are you involved in Kismet's latest murder?"

Caprice supposed that was an obvious question since they'd been talking about the articles. "I knew Louise well. She was a family friend. I understand you were her manicurist?"

"Yes, I was," Judy said somberly. "She was very particular, sometimes made me do her nails over. But she tipped well because we often went overtime."

"You had a lot of get-to-know-you time."

"Once a week, ever since the shop opened three years ago. She didn't want anything to do with those acrylic nails that last longer."

Caprice nodded. "I don't want anything to do with them either."

"I can understand that," Judy said neutrally.

Caprice had heard horror stories about those nails, but even besides that, with her hands in water as much as they were, they just didn't seem practical. If and when she polished her nails, it was for an evening out and that was it.

"So what was your overall impression of Louise?" she asked the redhead.

Judy shrugged. "She was a woman who knew what she wanted. Yet she seemed so insecure sometimes."

Instead of jumping on that comment as she wanted to, she let it sit for a few moments, then asked, "Insecure? How so?"

Judy studied Caprice as if thinking about what she wanted to say. Then realizing they'd both known Louise, she revealed, "Oh, she let little things slip."

"What kind of little things?"

As Judy hesitated again, Caprice waited. She knew this was where her relationship to Nikki paid off. If Judy liked Nikki, it meant she was more likely to trust Caprice.

She buffed Caprice's nail with the sanding block. "I don't usually talk about my clients with other clients."

"I understand that, but I *am* investigating, trying to get at the reason for the murder. She was my mom's best friend, and my mom is really torn up about this. I'd like to help her put it to rest."

Judy thoughtfully brushed Caprice's nails with a buffer, then nodded. "Maybe it was just because Louise was older, but I think she felt her husband didn't notice her anymore. She changed her hairstyle last year, waited for him to say something about it, and he never did."

"Sometimes men don't notice things like that."

Judy screwed up her face. "Well, husbands should, and he didn't, and she felt bad about her hair. She even talked about dyeing it, but she didn't. She also told me she joined town organizations, not because she wanted to, but to help her husband in his business visibility."

Had Louise's life been all about Chet's? Caprice thought she'd joined boards and charities and bridge clubs because she'd enjoyed being with other people.

"Gardening was her hobby. I'm sure she liked being part of the Garden Club," Caprice prompted.

"When the women weren't being snotty." Judy gave her a knowing look. "She told me stories about some of the disagreements there."

Maybe Caprice's mom would know about that because she didn't.

"She did tell me once that she loved roses because her mother grew them," Judy said.

That was something Caprice hadn't heard before— something about Louise's life before she came to Kismet. "Did she mention anything else about her parents?"

Judy shook her head.

"Anything about a first marriage?"

Judy responded, "Nope. Nothing about that. She mostly talked about her husband and places they went together." As the manicurist started on Caprice's other hand, she added, "She was a worrier, though."

Caprice knew Louise had been worried about downsizing and what her life and Chet's would be after he retired. But what else had she worried about?

"Can you explain her worries?"

"Something about prices on her husband's pretzel snacks going up. He was concerned about that because there was such a competitive market right here in Pennsylvania. She said a family name wasn't enough anymore to succeed in business."

That was certainly true. Was Chet selling the company because he didn't want to deal with the whole mess anymore? Maybe he wanted to turn it over to someone younger with more energy, who could make a

real niche in the business. Of course, why would he care
if he was getting out of it?

"And then, there was Louise's house," Judy went on.
"That and the heart condition she had. She constantly
worried about that. When she had coffee in here, she'd
ask me three times if I was sure it was decaffeinated. I
always have a pot of each, and I never mix them up. But
every time, she'd ask more than once."

Caprice didn't remember the worrying side of Louise.
Had that come to the forefront as she'd gotten older?
Were her worries about Chet's opinion of her something
every married woman thought about?

Caprice went over all the questions again in her head,
and then she asked herself the really big one. Had Chet
Downing been having an affair? Could he have been
involved in his wife's murder?

When Caprice picked up Lady at Nana's that afternoon, she assured Nana they'd have a long tea after the
Valentine's Day weekend was over. She still had a stop
to make before heading home—Nikki's condo. She
rarely took Lady to Nikki's in case Nikki was cooking
for a catering job. Confining Lady outside of the kitchen
and outside of her reach wasn't something Caprice liked
to do. But she and Nikki had to go over logistics for
decorating the social hall tomorrow. She also wanted to
run down the list of everything she'd found out about
Louise and Chet. Nikki was good at seeing the bigger
picture, or coming up with alternative theories.

Nikki's neighborhood was an older one that had been
somewhat renovated. There were clapboard as well as

brick houses in differing styles and character along the tree-lined streets. However, at the end of one of those streets, a developer had bought up a warehouse as well as a whole block of older homes and demolished them to build the Stonegate Corner Campus.

The sprawling enterprise was comprised of several sections. There had been much dissention about condos going up, mainly because one of the buildings was five stories high. Residents felt this just didn't fit into a quiet neighborhood. But that main condo building had every amenity, including the finest line of appliances, ceramic tiled floor, and solid wood cupboards. Besides the main building where Nikki lived, there was a lower-slung building three stories high. That building was for seniors and had extra-wide doorways for wheelchairs, step-in showers, and roll-out shelves in the kitchen cupboards.

Besides that complex, small cottages dotted postage-stamp-sized lots. The campus was well-maintained with spring, summer, and fall gardens overflowing with knock-out roses, pansies, and marigolds. In the winter, twinkle lights blinked around Stonegate Corner's massive stone entrance. It was a pleasant place to live with no outside upkeep or inside repairs. Of course, residents of the community paid a fee for that, but Nikki said it was well worth it.

Oh, yes, and it was a pet-friendly environment, though there were limits on the number of pets a resident could have.

Caprice leashed Lady and then walked her into the entrance of Nikki's building through double glass doors into a foyer that opened to the elevator. To the left was a

The door that led to a staircase. Briefly Caprice thought about running up the staircase to the second floor where Nikki's condo was located. But . . .

She didn't feel like exercise right now. She'd make time to go for a swim on Sunday. She really would. She'd joined Shape Up because swimming was the one exercise she minded least. But winter, wet hair, and swimming didn't always go together. Still she knew she needed the exercise. Maybe after church on Sunday. *Yes, Sunday,* she promised herself.

Stepping into the elevator with Lady, she moved to the back. The doors swished shut and Lady gave a small yip. The first few times they'd done this, she'd barked constantly until they'd arrived at Nikki's floor. But Caprice's "eh-eh's," a shake of her head, and her frown, along with no treat, had soon convinced Lady that keeping barks to a minimum was a better way to go.

A treat handy in her pocket now, Caprice gave it to Lady and patted her on the head. "Good girl. Very good girl. No barking in the elevator."

Lady's big brown eyes and the cock of her head said she got it now. If she kept quiet, there'd be another treat when those doors opened again.

Another treat and a short walk to the door of Nikki's condo and they were there. Caprice knew she should have called or texted Nikki, but sometimes unexpected drop-ins between sisters were the best visits.

Caprice rethought the drop-in idea when she rang the bell and the door flew open. A handsome man stood there with raised brows. His hair was mussed in that new run-your-hands-through-it-but-gelled way. He was

wearing a football jersey, jeans, and a white chef's apron
that had a few spatters. Just what had she interrupted?

Obviously nothing that required supreme privacy because Nikki called from her kitchen, "Who is it?"

The man called back, "I don't know, but she's got
a dog."

Her sister called, "Is it a golden cocker spaniel?"

"Looks like it," he called back.

Enough of this. Caprice stepped inside around him
and said, "It's me, Nik. What's up?"

"Cooking," her sister responded with a smile. "Drew
and I are experimenting. Come on in. This food isn't
going to clients so Lady can be in here. And I do have
news for you. I'm catering a party at Ace Richland's
estate."

The aroma of sautéeing onion and peppers, along
with simmering meat, had Lady's nose up in the air as
she sniffed her way to the kitchen. Caprice followed, no-
ticing the food spread out on the counters. The mixer
head was standing up and ready as if Nikki had been
about to stir up baked goods in there.

"You said you're not cooking for clients?"

Drew glanced at Lady as if wondering if she was
friendly or not and crossed to Caprice. "She's interviewing me."

Caprice waved to the counters. "Some interview. Not
name, rank, and serial number."

Nikki laughed. "No, more like past food preparation
history and can-you-pass-me-the-salt when I need it."

Drew grimaced. "Coordinating work in a kitchen
sometimes is a little tough, but I think Nikki and I are

getting it down." His green eyes twinkled with something other than food preparation.

"Do you mind if we mix up this batter before we talk?" Nikki asked her. "I'd like to get it into the oven."

"Go right ahead. I'll watch you work."

Drew groaned. "Oh, no. Two De Luca sisters interviewing me."

"Sorry I didn't introduce you," Nikki said. "Drew Pierson, my sister Caprice, though it seems you recognize her from my description."

So apparently Nikki and Drew had talked about her family. Maybe this wasn't their first "interview."

"Both of you come up whenever anybody talks about food and your open houses with a feast. Those open houses are always gossip among real estate agents, from what I hear. Finding a job as a chef or sous chef these days isn't easy, especially if I want to do more than flip burgers. So when I heard Nikki was looking for a partner, I decided to apply."

At least he was honest. Maybe. Men and honesty didn't always go together. For some reason, Caprice remembered Travis's declarations that he and his wife were finished. After all, they'd been divorced for two years. After all, there had been muddy water under their bridge. But their child had kept them glued together, and an old attraction had brought them back together. Had Travis been lying to her all along? Had he known those old feelings had still been there? It had seemed that way to Caprice.

So, no, she didn't always trust what men said.

As Nikki creamed butter and granulated sugar, Drew stood by, ready with a cup of brown sugar. Then he

handed her the two eggs as if he'd been doing it all his
life. Nikki used a spatula while he poured in a dry ingredients mixture, a quarter cup at a time. What looked like
melted chocolate went in next. After a minute of letting
the mixer do its work, Nikki was finished.

Drew had a loaf pan floured and ready, and slid it
over to Nikki while she lifted the bowl. He held the pan
while she poured in the batter. They worked as a unit,
and Caprice knew that's what Nikki was looking for.
Maybe this partnership would work out. That is, if
romance didn't get in the way.

Nikki had opened the oven door, and Drew was slipping the pan onto the rack when Caprice's cell phone
played. She didn't recognize the number. Then she
spotted the name—Pearl Mellencamp.

"Excuse me a minute?" she asked Nikki and Drew,
then said, "Come," and patted her hip so Lady would
follow her into the living room.

Nikki closed the oven door. "Go ahead. We're in the
middle of everything."

After Caprice's "hello," she heard an abrupt "Are you
sure you didn't tape our conversation?"

So Pearl must be worried that Caprice was going to
use her words against her. Should she end this call
quickly, or try to find out more?

Her curiosity always urged her to find out more.

Caprice thought about lying, but that simply wasn't
her style. "No, I didn't record it. I had my line open with
my sister and dog in the vehicle, just in case I might
need backup."

There was a pause as if Pearl was absorbing that.
After she cleared her throat, she said, "If you want to

know who shot Louise, you might want to talk with Don Rodriguez. He and Louise were friendly." Pearl made the word sound as if it were a major crime.

"And how do I find this Don Rodriguez?"

"You can look him up. I'm sure that fancy phone of yours can help you find his number." Then she heard Pearl sigh. "He owns a body shop in Kismet that's open from seven to eleven on Saturdays, eight to five rest of the week. It's not in the safest part of town. It's over near the community center. You might want to take along that dog."

"How will I recognize him?"

"Thick black mustache and heavy brows."

After that bit of information, Pearl ended the call.

Caprice had thought about thanking her.

She'd have time tomorrow morning to stop in at the body shop before she went to the social hall to help sort food donations and decorate for the dance. The question was, Did she want to go to Rodriguez's shop alone . . . or did she want to take Lady?

Chapter Twelve

It really was a no-brainer whether or not she should take Lady along to visit Don Rodriguez's Body And Auto Repair Shop. A dog usually helped and didn't hinder. A dog was an object of conversation. A dog could protect. And anyone on the outside of Caprice's circle didn't need to know that Lady *was* an absolute lady.

Caprice had arisen early because she had a full day. She found arriving at Rodriguez's shop at eight A.M. as a benefit because there wasn't much activity. She supposed most drivers didn't want to take their cars to a mom-and-pop shop, but rather wanted one of the bigger dealerships with the benefits of computer analysis. Rodriguez probably had a steady round of consistent customers who knew what he could do and liked what he could do. That's the way these shops stayed in business.

Lady seemed to understand that she should act like a more mature pup this morning. She walked side by side with Caprice and waited patiently while her mistress opened the heavy door that led into the small complex. Three chairs dotted the waiting area, if you could call it that. They looked like they'd been stolen from a hospital lounge. Orange vinyl, they could easily be cleaned. The counter was L-shaped with one half of it built against the wall. That half stored the computer. There was a corkboard behind the counter with hooks, and a few sets of keys dangled there with numbers attached to them. The place seemed clean enough but the two bays that were just beyond the outer area sent smells of grease and oil and lubricants and car motors and car parts into the reception area.

Caprice wrinkled her nose. Not really her kind of place.

Except today it might be.

The man sitting at the desk on a stool, studying what looked like a manual in front of him, matched Pearl's description. He had a thick black mustache, black hair that was gray at the temples, and dark bushy brows. To top it off, his red name tag with the white lettering read DON.

When he glanced at Caprice as she walked in, his gaze traveled down to Lady and he smiled. That was a good sign.

"Can I help you?" he asked, with what sounded like a Texas drawl.

Texas. Pay dirt? Of course, an accent didn't mean anything. Someone from Virginia could have a drawl.

She went right up to the desk and Lady sat as if she was waiting for the questioning to begin. Caprice almost smiled at that thought . . . but didn't. Instead she extended her hand. "I'm Caprice De Luca."

"Are you selling something?" Rodriguez asked with a raised brow.

Maybe she *should* sell something. Did investigators always get that question?

"No, I'm not. I thought about bringing my car in so I could strike up a conversation with you. It's a restored Camaro. But you might not have been able to take it today, or we might not have had time to talk, so I thought the direct approach might be better."

"Direct approach?" He looked perplexed. "If you're not selling anything, why do I need a direct approach?" He glanced down at Lady again. "Unless you think I need a watchdog."

Okay, so he had a sense of humor. That could be good. She'd see how he reacted to her next sentence. "I understand you knew Louise Downing."

A defensive rigidity came into his shoulders under his red plaid flannel shirt. His jaw tightened and his lips compressed. Even under the mustache, she could tell that. His dark brown eyes became more wary. At six-two and with those shoulders, he could easily throw her out of his shop. However, he didn't.

He returned politely, "And just why does it matter if I did or didn't know Louise Downing? Are you a cop?"

She attempted to lighten the mood. "Do I look like a cop?"

He didn't smile, and his posture remained rigid.

"No, I'm not a cop," she responded.

"A private investigator?"

"No, not one of those either, though I am investigating. Louise was a friend of the family. She and my mother were good friends. Francesca De Luca."

There was a glimmer in his eyes that told her he

might recognize the name. Just how friendly had he and Louise been?

"In addition to being around her as long as I can remember," Caprice added, "she was also my client. I was staging her house to sell. I'm the one who found her dead in her greenhouse."

Now an expression came into Rodriguez's eyes that could only be labeled as sad. "I'm sorry you found her like that. That had to have been difficult."

"It was. My mother needs some answers. My family needs some answers. I'm trying to figure out who might have killed her."

Rodriguez opened a drawer under his computer, and Caprice wondered if he was going for a gun.

But instead of a weapon, he pulled out a pair of glasses and settled the black-framed spectacles on his nose. "I thought you looked familiar. Your picture was in the paper. You solved that murder last summer."

"I did. But I had lots of help along the way. People answering questions and giving me clues. So that's why I'm here. I need leads."

He cocked his head and studied her speculatively. "Just who gave you my name?"

"I'd rather not say."

"Then maybe I'd rather not talk."

Lady whined a little and Caprice glanced down at her. She pointed to the rubber mat that lay in front of the desk.

"Down," she said firmly with a hand signal.

Lady obeyed and Caprice quickly took a treat from her pocket and gave it to her pup. "Good girl. You're smart!"

Then she returned her focus back to Rodriguez. "Someone told me you and Louise were friendly. If you were friends, then you'll want to help me. I intend to get to the bottom of this whether you do help or not. But if you don't want to help, then I have to wonder why."

He looked away for a moment and grimaced. "There are lots of reasons why I don't want to say anything, and none of them have anything to do with my guilt or innocence."

"Anybody can be a suspect. Give me a reason not to make you one."

He crossed his arms in front of him on the counter and glared at her. "What do you want to know?"

"Let's start with something easy. When did you meet Louise?"

Now he took off his glasses and fiddled with the side piece. "About twelve years ago."

"Did you meet her here?"

"Where else would I meet her? Do I look like I'm anywhere in her league?"

Caprice ignored that. "Did she come in to get her car fixed?"

"Not in the way you mean. She came in one winter day, something like this, all upset. She was so shaken up she was almost crying, all because she'd sideswiped a mailbox, scraped some paint off her fancy car, and didn't want to tell her husband. I honestly don't know what brought her here to this shop. I do believe serendipity plays a part in some of our lives."

He stared out the window of the door as if remembering that particular day. "She promised she'd pay cash. I needed cash, so I told her I could fix it right away. When

I was trying to give her an estimate, she kept me talking. I finally realized why. She asked where I was from. When I told her Austin, she was interested in the goings-ons there, like she missed it. She said she'd grown up around there. After that, when I listened to her talk, I could hear that little bit of Texas in her voice. So I fixed her car good as new."

"But you continued to see her after that? She stopped in again?" Caprice guessed.

"Now and then. She came to visit because we seemed to connect on some level. Or maybe she missed Texas. After a year of visiting every few months, I met her at a coffee place on the way to Harrisburg. She sometimes went there to meet with a financial advisor."

More and more questions were popping up about Louise's insecurity about money. What was that about? "These meetings with you. Were they ever overnight?" That was the most subtle way she knew to ask if they were sleeping together.

"No," he said loudly and firmly.

That resounding no told Caprice it had more than information behind it. It had Don Rodriguez's integrity behind it. She'd better step back from that one.

When Don gazed at Caprice, she saw a man who'd lost someone important to him. She saw a man who was grieving in his own way.

"How often would you see Louise?"

"She was always so busy. And we didn't like to be seen around town. That's why we went up to Harrisburg. She'd have a meeting and then we'd meet at the coffee place. Sometimes we were there two or three hours. It didn't matter much. Her husband worked long hours, never called her in between, which I didn't get. They'd been married a long time. He couldn't phone or text her and ask her how her day was going?"

"You would do that?"

"Sure, now and then. But not so much anyone would notice."

"There's one all-important question here. Did Chet Downing know about your friendship with Louise?"

Rodriguez thought about it. "Louise didn't tell him when she came in here. She certainly didn't tell him about our meetings near Harrisburg."

"But did Chet *know* about them, even if she didn't tell him?"

"That's possible," Rodriguez readily admitted. "If her husband checked her phone, he'd see my number during times when the body shop wasn't open. Louise and I called each other sometimes when she was lonely in the evenings. It was a simple friendship."

Simple or not, that friendship could have gotten Louise killed if Chet had known and been jealous enough.

She and Rodriguez were doing a defensive dance. He was trying not to tell her any more than he had to, and maybe there wasn't any more to tell. But on the other hand, all those years of friendship had to have resulted in something.

"It sounds as if you knew Louise pretty well. You said you talked about Texas. Did she confide anything to you about her life there before she moved to Kismet?"

He quickly shook his head. "Louise was funny about that. She talked about places she knew in Austin and even Houston, but she always skirted around personal

stuff. I didn't want to poke because that wasn't what
we were about. We kept everything easy . . . kind . . . and
just plain friendly."

Caprice didn't want to leave with Rodriguez regret-
ting anything he'd told her. After all, she might need him
again for further information. If he felt involved, he'd
want to solve the crime, too. She found the Texas aspect
intrigued her.

So she stopped the questions for now. "I might want
to talk to you again. Is it okay if I stop back?"

She thought he might say "no." But then he peered
over the counter at Lady. "If you bring her, you're welcome."

As she safely put Lady in her crate in the van and
gave her praise and a treat for being so cooperative,
Caprice could understand why Louise had liked Don
Rodriguez. There was a gentlemanly courtliness about
him. Before she climbed in her vehicle, she pulled her
phone from her pocket and scrolled down her contact
list for Rachel. She had some questions.

Once she was behind the wheel, she dialed. The
housekeeper answered quickly.

"Hi, it's Caprice," she said. "Do you mind if I ask you
another question?

"No, go ahead."

"Did Louise have any friends who visited with Texas
accents?"

"Texas accents? I don't know if I'd really know a
Texas accent, me being from here and all. But I can't
remember anybody with any accents, except . . ."

"Except who?"

"Except there was this man who would call every

once in a while. The call always came in to Louise's cell phone, but now and then if she was busy or her hands were full of dirt, she'd ask me to pick up the cell and answer. So I did. That man did talk differently, and after Louise spoke with him for a while, this little thing would happen to her voice."

Voices mirroring each other, especially if it was natural for them to do so. "That's the only one?" Caprice asked.

"I can't remember anybody else."

The other thing that was really bothering Caprice was Louise's sudden visit to the hospital the week before she was killed. What had *really* sent her there?

"I'm looking at some other avenues, too," Caprice told Rachel. "I know this might seem a little odd, but what did Louise have to eat the day she got sick?"

Rachel easily gave her the rundown. "Louise had her usual breakfast of yogurt and granola. Then I went out shopping, and I didn't get home until midafternoon. But she'd had lunch with someone who brought organic chicken wraps, a favorite of Louise's. I know that because Louise had left half of one in the refrigerator. It was still in the deli wrap."

Just who had Louise had lunch with that day? Had something she'd eaten made her sick?

"Of course you threw that half of chicken wrap away, right?"

"Oh, yes, down the garbage disposal."

A dead end.

* * *

The social hall adjacent to the fire company was a bevy of activity on Saturday morning. Caprice had taken Lady home, settled her with her Kong toy, her kibble ball, and her favorite chewing ring in the kitchen, then texted Nikki she was on her way.

As she walked into the social hall and greeted people she knew, she saw Nikki on a stepladder, adding yet one more glittering heart mobile to a ceiling light. But then Caprice's attention focused elsewhere. At a long table, Grant was sorting canned goods and loading the food into boxes.

Descending the stepladder, Nikki said, "He's been at it since seven A.M. He knows how to work for a cause. Do you think he left Patches alone?"

"His divorced neighbor's probably watching him," Caprice muttered.

Nikki gave her an odd look. "You said you didn't care."

"Yes, I did, didn't I?" Caprice sighed, not knowing exactly what she felt for Grant or what he felt for her. She certainly wasn't going to hold him up in conversation, not when there was work to be done.

"You know, Mom wasn't sure she wanted to come to the dance tonight," Nikki informed Caprice.

"She didn't tell me that. Because of Louise?"

"They were such good friends, she doesn't feel like she should go out and have a good time so soon after her death, I guess."

"What did you tell her?"

"I told her to go sort clothes this morning with Nana at the church, and she'd feel a lot better when she knew those clothes were going to needy families. Then she should think about her and Dad and how much they love each other, and they should come together tonight. No guilt. But I don't know if she's going to listen to me. You could call her and reinforce the idea."

"I will. After lunch. I imagine she and Nana should be done by around two."

"That all depends on how many people donated clothing. But for right now—" Nikki nodded to one of the tables where their dad was standing with a laptop computer. He was motioning to Caprice.

"Uh oh, Dad and the computer aren't getting along again," Nikki guessed.

Caprice smiled. Now that her dad was in his masonry company's office rather than in the field, he had to deal with his own computer more than he intended to. However, he wasn't tech savvy. He knew the programs he had to use for his business and he didn't want to learn more than that. Today he was dealing with lists on one of the volunteer's computers, and apparently there was a problem.

"I'm going to work on table decorations next," Nikki said, "but then I've got to scoot. Drew and I have a lot to get ready for tonight."

"So Drew's helping?"

"We'll see how it goes. You'd better get to Dad before he crashes the whole computer."

Caprice tried not to smile as she crossed to her father and asked helpfully, "A problem?"

"Computers are the problem," he growled. "I would have been happier if all this stuff was on a legal pad. I can't find the right screen." He leaned a little closer to her. "But you're the only one I'll tell that to."

She laughed. "There's no shame in asking for help."

"If that isn't the pot calling the kettle black. If you weren't so independent, you'd be engaged by now."

Usually she got this kind of advice from her mother, not from her father. Maybe Valentine's Day had put him in a think-about-your-kids-and-their-happiness kind of mood.

"And what makes you think I want to be engaged?"

"You avoided Grant when you came in. That tells me something."

"Yes, I avoided him. He's busy."

Her dad guffawed. "Yeah, right. Busy. You two have been dancing around each other since Vince was in law school. Too bad Grant married and cut himself out of circulation. Too bad—"

Her father shook his head. Then he glanced up at the hearts that Nikki had just attached to the ceiling, and all the other mobiles hanging along with the red and silver sparkling decorations.

"Your mother and I have been coming here to the Valentine's Day dance for years. It was the one night of the year we would get a babysitter even if we couldn't afford it. Nana Celia and Gramps used to come, too."

"Valentine's Day always seemed special to you and Mom."

"It was. It is. It's the holiday for lovers. But since you're already blushing, I won't go there."

Thank goodness! Caprice thought, but didn't say it.

Her father chuckled. "Your mom and I always see

friends and relatives here. That's something that cements a relationship—other people seeing your marriage grow and change, witnessing that the vows you made are going to last. You get my drift?"

"Sort of like Big Brother watching?"

"Now, Caprice, when did you get so cynical?" her father asked with arched brows.

"I'm not cynical. I just don't think we always know what's inside a marriage, even if we know the people on the outside." Her father was one person she could talk to about this. "You know, I didn't want to ask Mom about Louise and Chet's marriage. Were there any problems there?"

When her father didn't speak right away, she saw he looked troubled. "Few couples have a marriage like me and your mom do," he reminded her. "And kids can really bind a couple together. Chet once told me Louise couldn't have children. He never said more than that."

Caprice wondered if Louise's heart condition had something to do with that.

"Besides that, though," her dad went on, "I know Louise didn't always come first for Chet. His company and his recreational life did. Spring, summer, and fall he played golf. In the winter he skied. Louise wasn't particularly fond of trekking over the golf courses more than once a week so he played with colleagues and friends."

"And her heart condition could be triggered by cold weather," Caprice added thoughtfully. "So she didn't go skiing either."

When Caprice envisioned Chet and Malina at the

funeral home, she had a good guess about just who he might have gone skiing with. "Are you insinuating that Chet had affairs?"

"No, I'm not. I know nothing about that, and that's the truth. Men aren't often as forthcoming with each other as women are."

Grant passed by them as he carried a carton filled with canned goods to the loading dock.

She asked her dad, "Has Grant ever been forthcoming with you? Has he ever told you details about his marriage, or exactly what happened with his daughter?"

Her father appeared surprised by her question. "Why would you think he would?"

"Because I don't know how close he is to his own parents, and they're living in Vermont. He comes to our family dinners with Vince, and I thought he might look on you as a second dad. You can get anybody to talk about anything."

"I'll take that as a compliment. But no, Grant's never talked to me about any of that. That doesn't mean he won't talk to *you*."

Caprice just pursed her lips.

"Do you remember the story about how your mom and I fell in love?" her dad asked.

"Of course, I do. She was home from college for the summer, picking flowers in her mom's garden. She looked up at the roof and there you were, fixing the flashing around the chimney. You were shirtless, your hair was blowing in the wind, and she said it was love at first sight."

This time her dad laughed. "Maybe attraction at first

sight," he admitted. "But the last part . . . Honey, we
were as different as night and day. She was college-
educated and becoming a teacher. I was just someone
who knew how to handle bricks. I'd grown up with two
brothers and a sister, and she'd been an only child. Our
interests were as different as football and arranging
flowers."

"But you fell in love."

"We did, in spite of all those other differences. We
found that we thought alike. Our values were the same.
We even had the same dreams. That's what mattered.
You and Grant . . . You might be in different places now.
A man needs time to put the past really behind him. But
I don't think you should count him out."

Should she count him out? Maybe that depended on
what happened when they attended the dance together
tonight . . . well, not really together. Would he even talk
to her? Or ignore her then, too?

She tapped her dad's computer. "Tell me what screen
you need to get back to."

"You're changing the subject."

"What screen, Dad?"

"The one with the list of delivery drop-off points."

Caprice checked out the program for a minute,
tapped a few keys, and found the screen her dad was
looking for.

Navigating a computer was much easier than navigating a man's mind.

Chapter Thirteen

At eight P.M. Caprice walked into the fire company's social hall and thought the whole town seemed to have turned out for the Valentine's Day dance. Maybe that was an exaggeration, but not by much.

She'd borrowed a black velvet cape from her mother with faux fur around the neck and the sleeves. It was elegant, and beautifully complemented her forties-style dress. All she was missing was a muff. She'd even done something different with her hair tonight. Well, the stylist at Roz's beauty salon had. He'd wound her hair into a one-sided bun that looked stylishly vintage, even with her fluffed and waved bangs. He'd let a few stray tendrils wisp out for a modern version of the hairstyle.

Nikki waved to her from the table where the buffet was set up.

Caprice discarded her cape, hanging it on a coat rack in the reception area. Then she took her faux pearl beaded purse that was barely big enough for her phone, and headed Nikki's way. Her sister's slow smile told her she'd made the right fashion choices tonight.

In fact, Nikki asked, "Who *is* this woman? I don't recognize her." She tilted her head. "Except I think I recognize those brown eyes, that wide mouth, that long neck. That must be my sister." Then she leaned in and gave her a hug. "You're looking absolutely fabulous."

"I can't tell how *you* look under the apron."

"The apron will go once Drew and I have everything set up for the servers."

Speaking of that particular man, he came in the back door, carrying another silver chafing dish, and set it on the table. He was wearing slim black slacks and a black shirt with a bolo tie.

"He looks good in that outfit," Caprice noted in a low voice.

Nikki gave a little sigh. "Yeah, he does look good, doesn't he?"

"Uh oh, chemistry as well as cooking expertise?"

Nikki gnawed on her lower lip. "I'm not sure. We'll see how this goes tonight. We're trying out a working arrangement. For now, I'll pay him a salary. He's willing to work for me until we both decide if we want to be partners."

Drew crossed to them and said hello to Caprice. With a hiked-up brow, he said, "I'm on trial tonight. But I don't think Nikki's sure she *wants* a partner. She's not sure she wants to give up control."

"I can give up control," Nikki protested. "I grew up with a domineering brother, and a younger sister who had all the answers."

Drew stared at Caprice.

"No, not her," Nikki was quick to explain. "My other

sister, Bella. Caprice and I . . ." She shrugged. "I guess the two of us were always like partners."

"So I have to fill *her* shoes."

He looked down at Caprice's shoes, which were fuchsia and high-heeled with an ankle strap, and she was suddenly glad she was wearing them. If they made Drew take a second look, would they make Grant take a second look?

"I simply need the *right* partner," Nikki insisted.

"You need a partner who can help you set your limits," Drew offered with confidence. "You cook wonderful food, Nikki, but you shouldn't have to add every sprig of parsley yourself, or taste every piece of sautéed onion. Know what I mean?"

Nikki nodded. "I'm beginning to. Just look at these scallops in cream sauce that you made, and the sweet and sour pork. It's perfect."

"We work together well," he murmured, gazing into her eyes.

There definitely might be more than chef and sous chef going on here, Caprice thought. She knew chemistry when she saw it. But then again, maybe the hearts dangling overhead and the Valentine's Day mood tonight had turned her into a matchmaker.

Knowing Nikki had food to set up with Drew, Caprice smiled. "I'll see the two of you later."

As she glanced around to find the table where Vince and Roz were sitting, Denise Langford, the luxury property real estate agent, approached her. Denise was all prettied up tonight, too. Her hair bounced in tighter waves. Her slim figure was accented by one of those little black dresses that Caprice could never seem to find.

Denise said, "I was going to call you tomorrow. Then . . ." She waved her hand over the way Caprice was dressed. "Who could miss that gorgeous color?"

Caprice wasn't sure if that was a subtle dig or not. Trying to stay on the optimistic side of life, she decided Denise's comment was a compliment. "Thank you. Why were you going to call?"

"Chet Downing is going to sell his house, but . . . He's postponing his own house-hunting because he's taking a prolonged trip to Europe in a few weeks."

"Europe? I know Louise wanted to travel to Italy after he was retired, but I didn't think they'd planned anything yet."

"I get the feeling he just wants to get away."

"Are the police going to let him do that?"

"I think that's why he's waiting a few weeks. Maybe he thinks they'll solve his wife's murder in that amount of time."

That was naïve thinking. "I don't believe Louise had planned to take a trip yet. She'd been looking forward to finding a smaller place and moving in. I don't suppose he mentioned whether he's traveling alone?"

Denise's eyes widened. "Caprice!"

"I'm not suggesting anything. I'm just wondering. Maybe this is part business. Maybe since he's selling The Pretzel Party, he's going to start another business. I just wonder if he'd confided any of that in you."

"No, he didn't. You're the one who was the friend of the Downings."

"I spent most of my time with Louise. Even when I was a kid, Chet would take business calls during dinner, sometimes skip dinner with us altogether because he had meetings. I don't think his life was all about The Pretzel Party. He had his hand in investments and wheeling and dealing. I just hope—"

"What do you hope?" Denise asked curiously.

Caprice had been about to say that she hoped Chet and Louise's marriage had been all about hearts and flowers and lace, but she wasn't sure it had been. Still, she shouldn't voice those thoughts to Denise.

"I just hope the police find the murderer sooner rather than later."

"You and me both. It's hard to believe there's a murderer running around free in Kismet. Well, I'd better get to my table. I wouldn't want anyone to give my seat away."

Caprice was lost in thought for a few moments, thinking about Chet and his trip, thinking about Chet and the argument she'd overheard between him and Louise. How important had that argument been? Had it been ongoing? Had there been others?

This time when Caprice scanned the room, she saw Roz standing up and waving at her. She spotted her mom and dad seated at the same table. And then she spied . . .

Grant was seated across the table from Roz and Vince. Was she supposed to sit next to him?

Caprice was suddenly very self-conscious with her new hairdo. She touched it now. For good luck, she'd worn Nana's tortoiseshell seed-pearl comb, as well as the pearls her dad had given her when she graduated from high school. Double pearls dangled on her earlobes. The dress itself fit as well now as it had the first time she'd tried it on. She thought she'd been mistaken.

She thought nothing could look that good on her. But it
did. It cinched her waist and accented her breasts, and
even made her hips look flattering. The satiny material
swished a little when she walked. Walking wasn't the
easiest thing in the world in the high-heeled shoes.
When she'd slipped her feet into them, she somehow felt
like Dorothy from *The Wizard of Oz*. All she had to do
was click her heels together and she'd be home. That
idea brought a smile to her lips. She shifted her purse
from one hand to the other.

Caprice suddenly felt shy as well as self-conscious as
she made her way toward Grant. As soon as she reached
the table, her mom and dad grinned at her. Earlier,
before her hair appointment, she'd given her mom the
manicure gift certificate in a Valentine's Day card. Her
mom had gotten teary-eyed and told her Vince had
stopped in with a box of chocolate truffles. She was
especially grateful for her children at a time like this.
Her mom was leaning close to her husband and appeared glad to be here.

Grant cleared his throat and stretched his arm across
the back of her chair. "Do you mind if I join you? I
wanted to sit with someone I was comfortable with."

Comfortable. The two of them? What made her perk
up a lot was the way Grant's eyes scanned her from head
to toe, as if he hadn't seen her looking quite that way
before. Good. He shouldn't have her pegged. She wanted
to be an enigma like he was. But she knew that probably wasn't possible.

"The buffet line's set up," Grant said, nodding to the
table. "Are you ready to get something to eat?"

So, maybe they were going to spend the evening together. She'd have to readjust all of her mental buttons.

The servers had taken over at the chafing dishes and the buffet was indeed ready. Nikki and Drew stood nearby, watching Caprice as she nodded to Grant. He rose from his chair and they walked over to the buffet line.

Spotting Nikki and Drew, Grant remarked, "I've never seen him with her before. Does she have new help?"

"Possibly a partnership. They're seeing how the working arrangement goes."

"That's a good idea. You never know how exactly you'll work with someone until you do it."

They were quiet as they selected food for their plates. Caprice chose one of the hors d'oeuvres that was heart-shaped. She added a Waldorf salad and passed by the fruit cups. Pausing before the hot buffet, Caprice considered the variety of dishes, from the scallops in cream sauce to chicken to a rigatoni casserole to sweet-and-sour pork. Everything smelled wonderful and Caprice knew she shouldn't even think about eating any of the luscious desserts, from chocolate swirled cheesecake to apple tarts drizzled with caramel to coconut cake . . . and, of course, heart-shaped cookies.

Grant must have read her mind because he asked, "Should we pick up desserts later?"

"Sounds like a good idea." After all, it *was* Valentine's Day.

When they returned to the table, Grant asked, "Are you keeping an eye on Roz and Vince tonight?"

The couple had just walked up to the buffet line with Caprice's mom and dad.

"Roz can take care of herself, and I know Vince

won't do anything stupid. He knows where she's coming from."

"They seem to have a lot to talk about," Grant noted.

"That's always good on a date," Caprice agreed with a little smile."

As if the word *date* turned Grant in a different direction, he asked, "So did you leave Lady alone tonight?"

"I did. I'll be home by eleven. But I did put Sophia in my office. Usually I have someone to watch Lady, but almost everyone is here tonight."

"You're lucky to have so many people interested in watching her."

"You don't?"

"Donna stops in once in a while, but she's busy with Tanya and the two cats. I can't ask her to take care of Patches, too. I do have a neighbor on the other side. He's in his fifties and semiretired. He was a teacher for thirty years, and now designs Web sites for businesses. Anyway, he says I can bring Patches over anytime I'd like. But I hate to impose."

"Impose? It would be good for Patches, and if he really likes dogs, good for you, too. You won't feel so tied down if you have someone who can help a little."

"I don't feel tied down. In fact, I like working from home with Patches there. Vince has been handing over most of the corporate agreements that come in, except for Roz's, of course. It's less face-to-face client work."

"But you do like seeing clients."

"I do, to a certain extent. But making wills and estate planning is more Vince's forte."

They chatted in that congenial way through dinner until suddenly the music began playing. A DJ had set up and had started with "My Funny Valentine." Caprice saw a look her mom and dad exchanged, and soon they stood, held hands, and went out onto the dance floor.

"They look happy," Grant said.

Caprice leaned closer to him so he could hear her. "They make a lifelong commitment seem possible."

Roz and Vince stood and headed for the dance floor, too.

Caprice waited, but Grant didn't ask her to dance. Instead he said, "Why don't I get us some dessert? I'll be right back."

He returned in a few minutes with a sample dish.

They listened to the music and watched the dancers for a while as they tried the desserts. Caprice wished Grant would ask her to dance, wished he'd talk to her about something personal. But he didn't. As they ate and sipped coffee, she began to wonder why she'd gotten dressed up at all. Especially when he said during a music break, "I heard you're asking questions concerning Louise's murder. The police are aware of it."

"What questions have you all heard I'm asking?"

"Jones knows you talked to Rachel Cosgrove. Knowing you, if you talked to Rachel, that would lead you to someone else. Am I right?"

"It led me to another of Louise's housekeepers, Pearl Mellencamp. She told me a few things about Louise that I hadn't known."

"Like what?" he asked, leaning close.

His woodsy cologne distracted her momentarily. She shook off the intimate feel of being close to him and told him about Louise skimming money off the house fund.

Grant looked as puzzled as she'd been about Louise's money concerns. "Who else did you talk to?"

"Don Rodriguez. He owns a body and auto repair shop. Pearl told me that he and Louise were friends."

"Hmmm. I wonder if the police have his name on their list. Jones won't be happy if you're finding leads he doesn't know about."

Defensively she answered, "I'm not getting in their way. If I find something concrete, I'll tell them about it. All I have so far are bits and pieces. I can always use help putting them together."

It was an invitation to Grant of sorts and she wasn't even sure what it was an invitation to.

Grant's response was quick and dry. "I already have a full-time job, and a pup who requires the rest of my attention. So do you."

She wasn't daunted by his tone. "You know, sometimes if you have nothing to do, or sometimes when our dogs are running in the dog park, maybe I can run everything by you."

A romantic ballad was playing over the speaker system once again. She gazed into Grant's eyes as the slow song engulfed the room. She so wished again he'd ask her to dance. Instead, he looked away and picked up another cookie.

More disappointed than she wanted to admit, she said, "I need to freshen up," stood, and walked faster than she should have in those high-heeled shoes to the ladies' room. On her way, she happened to see Dulcina and her date leaving in what seemed to be a hurry.

Ducking into the bathroom, Caprice thought over each conversation she'd had lately with Grant. That mental exercise took about ten minutes and got her nowhere. With a sigh, she refreshed her lipstick and thought about Louise's murder, as well as everything she and Grant had spoken about in *that* conversation. He didn't want her pursuing it, for her own good. She understood that. But her own good was sometimes different from what everybody else thought it should be, including Grant.

She was recalling her conversation with Don Rodriguez and the possible Texas connection to Louise Downing when she pushed open the door to exit the ladies' room and came face-to-face with—

Seth Randolph!

She must be having hallucinations. Valentine's Day hallucinations. Was that possible if you ate too many heart-shaped cookies?

But when he stepped toward her and took her into his arms for a great big, giant hug, she knew he was no hallucination. She remembered the scent of his aftershave all too well. She knew the feel of his arms around her, her body pressed close to his. Although she would have liked to stay in his embrace all night, she had some questions.

Leaning away, she looked him straight in the eyes. "What are you doing here?"

He was dressed in a suit and a white shirt and a tie, and his blue eyes said he'd really missed her. "Can we talk while we dance?"

He wanted to dance with her!

He looked her up and down. "You look fabulous, straight out of the forties. Even the hair," he noticed, touching a stray tendril.

One of the qualities she liked about Seth was that he was observant, and she had really missed him.

"This is a Valentine's Day dance," she joked. "We should dance."

To her surprise, he looked relieved that she'd agreed. Taking her by the hand, he led her onto the dance floor, and then swept her into his arms again.

Once they'd settled into an easy embrace, he said honestly, "I thought you might tell me to go back where I came from."

Because his career was more important than she was? She told herself that was no way to think.

"You're here now. That's what's important."

"You still know how to roll with the punches."

"Do I need to?"

"I don't know. We'll see. In your last e-mail you told me you were helping with the Give-from-the-Heart Day, and you were coming to the dance."

Maybe tonight was the night for some honesty instead of flitting around what she wanted to say. "I was just making chitchat."

He squeezed her hand. "I know that, but it got me thinking. I was hoping I could get away over Christmas for a longer period of time, but I barely had time to go down to Virginia to see my parents, and I hadn't seen them for months."

"You know I believe family is important, Seth."

"I'm not making an excuse. I'm just telling you my thought process. The work is demanding, and tough, and intensive, and more challenging than anything I've ever done. We start at five in the morning and go until ten or eleven at night, some nights longer. When you e-mail me and I don't e-mail back right away, that's why. Sometimes I don't feel as if I have time to eat or breathe or . . ."

"I get it." She seriously looked him over again. "Have you lost weight?"

"Running around the hospital keeps you in shape. And now that *that* subject's covered, I don't want to talk about work." He held her a little tighter.

Caprice found herself grinning, enjoying being held by Seth. She hummed along to the song. It was a favorite of Nana's. "My Foolish Heart." She scolded her heart and told it not to be foolish tonight.

"I got a late start today, and just arrived when everyone was eating dessert. I didn't see you anywhere. But I spotted Nikki and she told me where you'd gone," Seth explained as he gazed down at her. "When I couldn't find you, I thought maybe the Fates were trying to tell me something. Do you believe in fate?"

"I'm not sure."

"Lately, I feel as if I'm bucking it," he admitted. "But one thing is for certain, I knew I wanted to spend Valentine's Day with you. In fact—" He suddenly stopped dancing. "Come with me."

His arm was firm around her waist and she let him guide her toward the back door of the social hall. When he reached the door, he took off his suit coat and wrapped it around her shoulders.

"What are we doing?"

"We're stepping outside for a couple of minutes, okay?"

A minute later, they stood outside the back entrance.

Seth held her face in his hands and kissed her. The world as she knew it dropped away.

After the kiss, he said, "I just couldn't wait another minute for that. I know it's cold out here, but I want to give you something."

"Now?"

"Now. You never know what's going to happen in the next minute or so."

He took a box from his trousers pocket and handed it to her. "This is for you."

"Seth, what did you do?"

"Nothing earth-shattering. I saw it and I thought you'd like it. After all, it is Valentine's Day."

The little box had a silver foil lid, and she removed it now as she peeked inside under the glow of the parking lot lights. Several charms and glass beads decorated a bracelet. The beads were painted with colorful flowers. One of the charms was a peace sign, another a kitten shape. A small heart dangled from the center of the circle of charms.

"Oh, Seth, it's beautiful."

"It doesn't exactly go with the pearls you're wearing."

"That doesn't matter. Can you put it on for me?"

He clasped it around her wrist.

This time she reached for him and kissed him full on the lips. "Thank you."

"It's a selfish gift, really," he said. "I want you to look at it and think about me."

She wasn't sure what this meant, except that Seth didn't want her to forget him. "I thought you'd forgotten about me, that you were too busy to even think about us."

"That's not true. Yes, I'm busy, and I still don't know what's going to happen after the fellowship. But I do think about you—a lot. Now come on, I'd better get you inside before you freeze to death."

When they returned inside, the DJ was taking a break. She felt the little charms along her wrist move as they walked to where she had been seated before. When they reached the table, her mom and dad stared at them speculatively. Vince's brows arched, and Roz just smiled. Grant was nowhere in sight.

When Caprice's eyes went to his empty seat, Roz stood and came around to say hello to Seth. While Seth was greeting the other De Lucas, she leaned close to Caprice. "Grant left when he saw you two dancing together."

Even though Seth's bracelet was a welcome weight on her arm, Caprice's heart cracked a little when she thought of Grant going out into the cold, dark night.

Just why did love and life have to be so complicated?

Chapter Fourteen

After only a few hours of sleep, Caprice awakened in her bed, felt the furry warmth of Sophia on top of the covers beside her left hip, heard the snuffling snores of Lady on her mat on the floor beside the bed. Glancing across at her dresser painted with hummingbirds and flowers and the pastel braided rugs on the floor, she thought back to the real reason she'd awakened, other than to feed the animals, who didn't seem all that ready to get up themselves.

There was a really good reason for all of them to sleep late.

Seth hadn't left until almost three-thirty. No, they hadn't done anything they weren't supposed to do, according to Nana, her mom, and church law. They'd seemed to have so much to talk about. Everything had poured from her—her feelings about Joe and Bella, the new baby, what had happened before, during, and after Louise's murder.

She and Seth also had had to get something straight about their communication. If she had more time than he did for e-mails, he wanted to know about her life. He'd insisted she didn't have to feel as if she were rambling on or boring him, because she wasn't. He wanted to hear it, and when he got the chance, he'd do the same for her.

After they'd come home from the dance, she'd made him real hot chocolate from cocoa, an imported chocolate bar, milk, and sugar. The sweetened whipped cream on top was just the bonus. They'd tried to have a *real* talk. But his idea of kissing after every few words was a little different from the serious discussion she wanted to have. She liked it; oh, how she liked it. Somehow their kissing had become their discussion. Somehow just sitting there together and holding each other tight had been what they both needed. But after he'd left, she'd felt as if she was in limbo again. The thing was, before he'd left, he'd taken her face in his hands and he'd told her it wouldn't always be like this.

But exactly what *would* it be?

Yes, she'd always been that girl, and then that woman, who rolled with the punches. But now maybe she needed more stability in her life. Maybe now she needed to know just what came next.

"That's it, troops," she said, sitting up and awakening both Sophia and Lady. "Enough of this whining about what could be and what might be. We have a murder to solve."

Lady got to her feet, ran to the door, and wagged her tail. Sophia just looked at Caprice as if she were crazy. She yawned, blinked her golden eyes, swished her fluffy tail, stretched out on the bed, front feet toward Lady, back paws toward Caprice. Then she meowed.

Caprice ran her thumb over Sophia's nose. She had a toothbrush on her nightstand she sometimes used on Sophia's little face. Sophia loved to have her cheeks brushed with it. But right now, Caprice had to let Lady out, feed both animals, and then get herself to early Mass. Shape Up would be open by then and she'd go for a swim. And if a swim didn't straighten out everything in her head, or at least put it in some kind of order, she'd text Nana and see if she was going to be home. When all else failed, when she couldn't wrestle a problem to the ground by herself, she visited Nana.

To Caprice's relief, Mass calmed her down. There was something about ritual, familiarity, something to lean on, that gave her renewed hope in finding love. Although the frigid temperatures outside prohibited her from visiting the statue of St. Francis behind the church where she'd often sat to contemplate life, she stayed after the service until everyone left. Lighting a candle for Louise, she recognized the fact that grief was weighing her down, too. How could it not be? She had to recognize it and accept it to get through it. If she'd learned nothing else in her thirty-two years, she'd learned that. She couldn't figure anything out until she got a grip on her emotions. But a grip didn't mean ignoring them.

Although she sometimes figured out staging ideas and decorating plans when she was swimming, today she tied her hair back, slid on her goggles, stretched a little, then swam. She swam hard, just wanting to burn off everything. This wasn't a Zen experience today, it was an exercise in energy output. It was a way to forget she didn't know when she'd see Seth again. It was a way not to think about the way Grant had left the fire company's social hall. It was a way to put the sight of Louise's body on that greenhouse floor in the recesses of her mind, at least for a little while.

Afterward, when she pulled into her driveway once more, she knew she was going to take Lady to Nana's.

A half hour later, after she'd texted Nana and found her at home, she knocked on her door. She wanted some quiet time with Nana, so she went to the outside entrance that led into her apartment.

Nana opened the door and smiled. "It's about time you came for a good, long visit. Did you have lunch?"

"I haven't even thought about lunch." She asked Lady to sit, removed her leash, and the cocker went inside.

"But I bet you gave Lady and Sophia lunch," Nana guessed.

"Before I left."

"You should treat yourself as well. But not to worry. How about chicken soup and peanut butter sandwiches?"

Caprice followed Lady inside, and unbuttoned her pea coat. "You're not having dinner with Mom and Dad?"

"We're going to join up tonight around six. They wanted me to go with them to visit friends after church, but I wanted to come back home. Good thing, too, or I would have missed you. Are we having tea or coffee?" Nana asked.

Remembering her lecture from Louise, she answered, "I'll have tea."

"Then tea it is."

Pulling pretty cups from the china cupboard, Nana studied her closely. "I think you need a little brightening today. What's wrong?"

There was that sixth sense of Nana's, alive and well.

"I'm just a little sleep deprived," she said.

"I suspect I know why that is. Your mom and dad said Seth turned up at the dance."

"Yes, he did. I didn't know he was coming."

"The way I hear it, you danced with Seth, Grant left, and then you left with Seth."

"It wasn't exactly like that," Caprice said defensively, feeling a little judgment in Nana's tone.

"How do I have it wrong?"

"Not wrong—" Caprice sighed. "I'd only had a couple of quick e-mails from Seth since September. I e-mailed him more often than he e-mailed me, and I knew that's the way it would be. He was busy."

"*You* were busy."

"But I'm not saving lives, he is, and sometimes his shifts go past twelve hours."

"Point to Seth," Nana said, as if she were keeping some kind of score.

"So for all these months, I've tried to forget about him."

"But you didn't do a very good job . . . unless Grant was around."

"It wasn't like that, either."

"Go ahead and explain," Nana instructed her, but said it as if she already knew the story.

"Grant and I have this . . . friendship. After he saved my life last summer and adopted Patches, I thought we were getting closer."

"So you began to have expectations," Nana filled in.

Caprice thought about that. Yes, maybe she had. "When he called me before the murder, he mentioned he'd be going to the dance, so I thought maybe we'd actually be there together, maybe even go together. But he didn't invite me."

"Hmmm," Nana said, as if that meant something important.

"He hardly talked to me when I was helping Nikki decorate, when he was working on the food drive, but I figured that was just because he was busy."

"Uh huh," Nana said this time, and it sounded just as weighty.

"Roz suggested I knock his socks off with a beautiful dress, and I found one that I thought would do that. I even had my hair done by Roz's hairdresser."

"Your mother and dad said you looked beautiful."

Caprice shrugged. "I thought I looked pretty good, and when Grant saw me, I was certain I'd surprised him with my appearance in a wow kind of way. We talked when we went through the buffet line and while we ate, but then the music started to play. Mom and Dad danced, Roz and Vince danced, and Grant just sat there. He didn't ask me."

"So you got angry and went off in a huff."

"No, I didn't. I didn't get angry. I got sad, and I was disappointed. So I decided just to freshen up and try to get a better attitude. And maybe when I got back, we could talk more and maybe he'd tell me why he didn't want to dance."

Nana shook her head and clucked her tongue.

"What?"

"A man doesn't want to have a conversation like that, in a place like that."

"He doesn't want to have that conversation *any-where*."

Nana stirred the soup on the stove. "Expectations, Caprice. There they are again. The more you expect, the more he'll back off."

When Caprice was silent, Nana finally suggested, "Come on, tell me the rest."

"When I came out of the ladies' room, there was Seth."

"Looking like Prince Charming."

"Looking darn close to it. He took me in his arms, danced me away, stole me outside, and he gave me this." She showed her Nana the bracelet, pointing out each charm that was special because Seth knew she liked peace signs and hearts and kitty cats.

"We talked until three-thirty, and then he left, and I don't know if I'm going to see him until summer. I'm not sure what to do."

Nana switched off the stove burner with a click. "Pull the jar of peanut butter from the cupboard. You're the one who doesn't use jelly. We'll toast the bread, though, and the peanut butter can melt on it. You used to like it that way when you were little."

"I still do," Caprice confessed.

Five minutes later, they were sitting at the table with their soup, tea, and peanut butter toast. Nana spooned up noodles, chicken, and a little bit of corn, blew on it lightly, and then ate it.

After she did, she picked up her napkin, wiped her

mouth, and set her hands in her lap. "Do you want my advice?"

"That's why I came over today."

"There isn't an answer, you know. At least not a right one or wrong one. You know two men who seem to be honorable men, worth your time, and maybe even your commitment. The thing is, you aren't committed to either man and neither man is committed to you. So there's only one thing you have to do. You have to stop trying to protect your heart. You have to figure out what you want, and which man is worth the risk."

"And then?" Caprice asked, almost holding her breath.

"Then you jump into it with both feet and without a net."

Without a net. She did that when she solved a murder case. But could she do it when it came to love?

Nana patted Caprice's hand. "It will work out, you know. It always does. Time, patience, and listening to that little voice inside of you. Trust me."

Caprice did trust Nana. That was easy. Because the subject of Seth and Grant had nowhere else to go, and no answers today, she said, "I need your help with something else."

"What is it?"

Caprice took her e-tablet from her large, fringed bag and opened it. All of her notes were on the notepad app. She read them off to Nana, knowing Nana's eyes sometimes bothered her. She went from the murder scene, to Chet, to Don Rodriguez, to Pearl Mellencamp and Rachel, and everything in between that she had listed in her notes.

Then she looked up at Nana. "So what do you think?"

"You found Louise's body, but you didn't tell me anything about the crime scene. What do you remember? I know it's difficult to think about her lying on that floor, but think about everything around her. That might give you a clue where to go next."

Caprice closed her eyes, making herself relive walking into the greenhouse. "Peat pots were knocked over. Tiny seedlings were destroyed. The stool was on its side, too, like Louise had grasped onto it and fallen over with it."

"What about her potting bench? What about anything that could have seemed out of place?" Nana prompted.

Ever since the murder, Caprice had been trying *not* to visualize the crime scene. So doing it now was like a splash of cold water on her face. It was a shock all over again, and Nana must have seen that because she pushed Caprice's cup of tea toward her and suggested, "Take a sip."

Caprice did, bent over to pet Lady, then she took another sip and a few breaths. When she closed her eyes and breathed deeply, she suddenly remembered something else.

She blurted out, "There was an open box of chocolate candy, and two of the candies were on the floor."

"What kind of candy?" Nana asked. "Was there a brand on the box lid? Something like that?"

"The box lid was plain white. Nothing on the box, either. But the candy on the floor looked like those peanut butter creams Louise liked so much. Mom was going to send her some. I wonder if she did."

Reaching for her purse, Caprice took out her phone and called her mother.

"Hi, honey," her mom answered. "How did it go with Seth last night?"

That wasn't a conversation she wanted to have again now. "Can we talk about that when I see you?" Caprice asked, knowing her mom wanted to stay in the loop, and Caprice wanted to keep her in the loop.

"Does that mean you're up or down?"

"Neither right now," Caprice said lightly. "I promise, I'll tell you all about it. But I have a question."

"Hold on a minute. Your dad's going to turn down the heater in the car so I can hear you. Okay, there we go. What's your question?"

"Did you ever send Louise that box of peanut butter creams?"

"No, I didn't. After her trip to the hospital and stomach upset, I didn't think it would be a good idea. Why?"

"Maybe Chet sent her peanut butter creams," Caprice mused.

"Maybe," her mother said cautiously, "but he was planning that trip with her over Valentine's Day weekend. I wouldn't think he'd send her anything beforehand, not Chet. He's so practical that way."

If not Chet, maybe Don Rodriguez? Caprice wondered. She didn't want to go into what she'd seen at the crime scene with her mom.

"Did *you* have a good time at the dance last night?" Caprice asked.

"I always have a good time with your dad, you know that. That's what I wish for you someday."

Someday.

But right now, she had to get to the bottom of a murder.

Dead ends. That was all that Caprice was finding. But maybe a visit to The Pretzel Party would turn up more.

After her morning routine on Monday, Caprice had surfed the Internet trying to find anything she could about Louise Benton—Louise Downing—before she'd arrived in Kismet. But she'd found zip. She'd even gone to real estate sites. She'd searched Louise Benton in Texas, too.

Some people had luck on search engines. She didn't . . . except for the obvious definitions and descriptions. She could call Marianne Brisbane, but she'd decided to try another avenue first.

The Pretzel Party's Outlet Store, factory, and distribution center were located on the outskirts of Kismet, near Pennsylvania Pharmaceuticals, a company that had plenty of legal woes right now. She remembered when she and Grant had gone there searching for another kind of evidence. But she wasn't going to think about that now, or Grant, or Seth. Valentine's Day was over and she had a life.

She didn't intend to buy any pretzels, so she headed for the building attached to the store, entered the lobby that was utilitarianly decorated at best, and went straight to the desk of a person she wanted to talk to—Verna Mae Ludwig. Verna Mae and her mom volunteered at the soup kitchen that the church helped with once a month. She was friendly and talkative and full of gossip.

If Chet was in his office, she'd talk to him about that candy and see if he'd sent it. But if he wasn't, Verna Mae might give her a new lead.

Even though Verna Mae was around her mom's age, she had silver-white hair that was thinning on the top. She kept it short except for the bangs that fringed over her brows. Carefully made up for her position as receptionist, she wore red lipstick and nail polish and her smoky eye shadow complemented her gray skirt suit. She was busily typing at the computer when Caprice walked up to the desk.

However, when she glanced up and saw her, she swiveled her chair around and broke into a smile. "Caprice. I was just talking to your mom about you yesterday after church."

Uh oh, that couldn't be good. What had Verna Mae and her mom been talking about?

"You were?" she asked after a bit of a pause.

Verna Mae fluttered her hand. "Oh, nothing scandalous. I asked if you found any stray animals lately. Your mom said you had your hands full with the pup you'd kept."

"She's right about that. In fact, Lady's at home right now probably whining to Sophia that I'm not there."

The smile faded from Verna Mae's face, and the wrinkles under her eyes and around her mouth seemed to grow deeper. "Your mom and I talked about Louise, of course."

"I'm so sorry. You knew her well, too, didn't you?"

"We talked a lot when she came to see Chet, or when we bumped into each other at church. But that was only surface stuff. I just feel so bad for Mr. Downing."

"Is he here? I'd hoped to see him."

"No, he stopped in on Friday to pick up some work, and I know he keeps in touch with his managers by phone. But he said he'd be out this week, too. This has certainly got to be hard for him. I'm not sure how he's going to get over it."

"It's going to take time," Caprice said, meaning it. She did feel sorry for Chet, even if his marriage to Louise hadn't been perfect. He had certainly felt the loss. But she aimed to find out exactly how much of a loss it was.

"I know he likes to ski," Caprice said. "Maybe he'll be able to go skiing and get away. Just being in the outdoors with the wind on his face might help ease the loss."

"That's possible," Verna Mae said with a nod. "He was just skiing the week after Christmas. Maybe he can get away again."

Taking a guess, Caprice encouraged Verna Mae to fill her in on details. "He told me the resort was beautiful, but I can't remember the name. Do you remember?"

"I do because he left the information with me before he left. He stayed at White Top Mountain Resort near Killington from December twenty-sixth until December thirty-first."

Killington. Now Caprice had a place and a name and she could find out more.

She was no sooner in her car when she took her phone from her purse. It was freezing outside. Even though she wore her boots, her toes were cold and her fingers were stiff as she swiped her phone, went to a search engine, and plugged in the name and location of

White Top Mountain Resort. There it was. A phone number.

The wind buffeted her car as she thought about how she wanted to play this. Just how could she get the information she needed? Of course, she could always call the resort a second time if the first time didn't go so well. After she thought about the resort and skiing and Chet, she decided on a plan. She plugged in the number.

"White Top Mountain Resort. Ski with us, and you'll feel as if you're on the top of the world," a chirpy voice told her. "How can I help you?" the woman rushed on.

"Hi, I'm Malina Lamont. I stayed at your resort with a friend . . ." She paused a little. "It was the week after Christmas, and we had an exceptional experience. We particularly liked the amenities in our room. We're thinking about making reservations again, but I just couldn't remember the room number. Being sentimental, we'd like to ask for that room again. Do you think that's possible?"

"That depends on our vacancies, and how soon you'd like to come. We'd be glad to make your reservations, and even if we can't get you that room—"

Caprice didn't give her a chance to go on. "But we'd really like that room. It was an expensive one, but I wonder if you could look it up?"

"Can you tell me your name again, and spell it please?"

"Well, I guess the reservation was made under Chet Downing—D-O-W-N-I-N-G."

Caprice waited a few moments, and then the woman returned to her call. "You said the week after Christmas?"

"I think those dates were specifically December twenty-sixth to December thirty-first," Caprice filled in.

"Hold on again."

The woman checked, and then said, "I don't have the reservation for a Chet Downing. You're sure you stayed with us?"

"Oh, I'm positive. Maybe he put the reservation in my name. Malina Lamont—L-A-M-O-N-T."

Caprice fully expected to strike out. She fully expected the woman to come back and tell her there was no reservation under that name either. But why hadn't there been a reservation under the Downing name?

"Oh, yes, Mrs. Lamont. You and Mr. Lamont were in room 260. Can you tell me the dates you're deciding on for a new reservation?"

"No, I have to consult with Chet. Then I'll call again. At least I know the room number. You've been very helpful. Thank you."

Caprice ended the call, hardly aware of the cold now as she thought about the repercussions of what she'd learned. There was no Mr. Lamont. Malina wasn't married. Verna Mae was positive Chet had stayed at White Top Mountain Resort.

This wasn't proof positive that Chet and Malina were having an affair, but it was close to proving the two had gone away together for the trip. Was it possible Louise found out and confronted Chet? Could that have led to a terrible argument?

Supposedly he'd been on the road to his business meeting when she was killed. But in reality, what if he hadn't left yet? In reality, what if he'd shot his wife?

Chapter Fifteen

At home once more, Caprice took Lady for a walk, and on the way back to the house realized there was one more thing she had to do before she could settle down to work. Yes, she had houses to stage and clients to make appointments with, and even a few virtual consultations to set up. But first there was something else she had to do.

Lady yipped at Sophia, asking for a chase. After a good long stretch, Sophia waved her tail, hopped down from the back of the sofa onto the seat, and then onto the coffee table. She looked at Caprice as if to ask, "Did you write down your affirmation for today?"

Caprice kept them in the silent butler on the coffee table. And no, she hadn't, but she did have to prioritize.

"Come talk to me about it in the office after you and Lady have a run," she told her feline, unbuttoned her coat, and hung it on the antique oak stand in the foyer.

As Sophia hopped to the floor, and Lady chased after her, Caprice headed in the other direction around the circle to her office. Once there, she took her phone from

her pocket as she awakened her computer. Calling
Marianne Brisbane for a favor wasn't something she did
often, but when solving a murder, the reporter could
help her. Caprice hoped she'd catch her in her office.
The odds were about fifty-fifty.

Marianne answered, sounding out of breath. "Hold
on, Caprice. I was trying to get an interview with the
mayor but he slipped into his car and drove away before
I could. I wanted to find out more about that new
member of the town council."

"And you think the mayor will give you anything but
a PR release?"

Marianne chuckled. "Probably not, but I was giving
him the benefit of the doubt by getting his take first.
What's up with you?"

"You mean, what do I want?"

"You rarely call me for a social visit though we really
should have lunch sometime."

That wasn't out of the realm of possibility. Caprice
was beginning to trust Marianne more and more, and
she did like her. "Maybe when things calm down a bit."

"They never calm down," Marianne admitted.

"How good are you with out-of-state databases?"

"They're harder to access sometimes. It just depends
if they're public records or not. What do you need?"

"I'm playing a hunch but I'm not sure what else to do."

"All right. I suppose this has something to do with
Louise Downing's murder?"

"Yes, it does. I think she might have had some secrets
no one around here knew about."

"Have you talked to her husband?"

"Let's just say that keeping those secrets hidden

could be in his best interest. So I'd rather go to him with some leverage. Do you know what I mean?"

"Oh, I know what you mean. What kind of leverage?"

"That's what I'm not sure about. But there's the possibility that Louise had a Texas connection, a very strong possibility. I think she might have lived near Austin. I've Googled her maiden name until I'm blue. I can't find anything. Can you see what you can find in Texas for a Louise Benton? B-E-N-T-O-N."

"That sounds easy enough. But I'm not going back to the office until this afternoon."

"That's fine. I have a lot of work to catch up on, and I'm going to be packing it in until Ace Richland's party tonight. Were you by any chance invited? I'd think he'd want the media there."

"Actually, I was. Not much media, though, from what I've heard. He's keeping this party small and as intimate as a rock star can. Do you want to connect there and I'll tell you what I've found?"

"That sounds like a plan."

The music was loud. However, the crowd assembled in Ace Richland's huge house wasn't wild. The group was simply enjoying themselves.

Caprice stood by a zebra-striped love seat. When she'd staged this estate, she'd done it in a wild kingdom theme. Ace had kept most of the furnishings and decorations, except for his daughter Trista's room and the pool area. Although February winds were blowing over the covered pool, the pool house itself was a bar for

anyone who wanted to venture outside. Caprice knew
Ace had to keep up his wild and crazy, on-the-road rock
persona now and then. But basically he was Al Rizzo
from Scranton, Pennsylvania, when he was around
people he was comfortable with and didn't have to
impress.

Right now he was jamming with his band for everyone's enjoyment. Rows of chairs had been added to the
immense living room along with a dais at one end for
Ace and his band. Ace kept glancing toward a pretty
blonde and gave her a wink. Caprice had heard he'd
begun regularly dating a rich widow in Kismet.

Thoughts of Ace's personal life aside, Caprice listened to the jam session, enjoying it. She had his music
on her playlist—"Zingy Chick"; "Gotta Keep Her
Yours"; "Swinging for a Future" and "Wrestling the
World." She enjoyed his music from the eighties and
was curious to hear what he'd come up with now. She
knew he was thinking about starting his own record
label.

As Ace swung his guitar to the left and then the
right, and tapped on it, belting out an old hit, she
watched his band members, none of them the original
bunch. This was a new band he'd put together that was
eclectic in age. She could tell the keyboard player, who
looked to be in his late twenties, had an eye for the
women. He flirted as much as he played. With his long
blond hair and blue eyes, lean build and broad shoulders, this guy was one to watch. Caprice bet he was
aiming for a solo gig.

Ace's immediate family—his parents, two brothers,
and their wives—were seated in an area arranged just

for them. The keyboard player seemed to have his eye on Ace's sister-in-law. She looked to be in her thirties, with spiked high-heel boots, skinny black jeans, and a tight red sweater that could have been an emblem for Valentine's Day. She was clapping along with the song and smiling back at the keyboard player. Her husband at her side didn't look any too happy. Was Ace's brother the jealous type?

As Ace and his band finished a song and took a break, Ace's manager gave him a thumbs-up from the back of the room. The reporters were easy to spot with their electronic tablets or their cameras, or both. Caprice spied Marianne and gave a wave. But before she and Marianne could meet up, Ace brought his mother over to her. They'd met last summer but hadn't had much time to talk.

"Mom wants that recipe for minestrone soup you were telling me about."

"Nana's minestrone. Sure, I can give it to you. Would you like me to send it in the mail, or do you have an e-mail address?"

"Oh, my sons and grandkids keep me updated. I have an e-mail address. It's MamaRizzo at—" She rattled off the server name.

"Makes sense," Caprice said with a laugh. "I'll e-mail it to you. Nana e-mails, too. Maybe you can let her know how you like it. I'll send you her address with the recipe. How do you like the party?"

Ace's mom clapped her son on the shoulder. "He has great parties. Now his friends aren't so bad either. They used to be an unruly bunch."

"You know what Father Paul always says," Ace

chimed in with her. "Bad friends, bad actions, bad con-
sequences. Got it, Mom. I think I've learned."

And Ace had seemed to learn. His life was about
music and spending time with his daughter.

Ace leaned down to Caprice. "Trista texted me that I
might see her tonight. She told me to hold off on the
new song until last if I could."

"That sounds as if she had something planned."

"That's what I'm afraid of."

When Marianne Brisbane came over to join them,
Ace wrapped his arm around his mom's shoulders. "Let
Dad get you one of those strawberry daiquiris you like
so much. Real strawberries."

Caprice could hear his mom laugh, a deep raucous
laugh that she imagined filled a house with lots of
love. But as she looked that way, toward where Ace's
dad was seated, she saw the keyboard player and
Ace's sister-in-law with their heads together, talking.
Ace's brother was nowhere around. Hmmm. But Caprice knew it was none of her business. That didn't
mean she'd stop wondering about it though.

Marianne nudged Caprice's elbow. "We could try to
get a date with that keyboard player. He came on to me
when I arrived."

"You're not serious."

"I could take that as an insult."

"I didn't mean it as one. You know that. Tell me what
you found out." There was excitement in Caprice's voice,
and a sense that something was about to break wide open.

"I'm almost as intrigued by this investigation as you
are. I found out that a Lucy Russell Mathers changed
her name to Louise Benton. Benton had been her

mother's maiden name. Her driver's license and social security information were modified to reflect the name change. I even saw a copy of the change order. It's amazing what scanning will do these days."

"Who scanned it for you?"

"Someone in the public records office in Austin."

"What else was on the change order? Anything good?"

"The reason listed for the name change was news coverage and dangerous disruption of life because of it. Lucy wanted a brand-new start. There's a whole story behind this, Caprice."

Suddenly the main doors to Ace's house burst wide open. Trista came running in, her mother trailing more slowly behind. Trista looked ecstatic. Her mother looked as if this were a prison and everybody in it were crazy inmates.

The party, which had been loud with conversation, suddenly went silent.

Ace hurried to his daughter and gave her a huge rocking hug.

Still, his ex-wife stood there with a frown and her arms crossed over her chest, her suede coat skimming the tops of her leather boots. "I didn't want to come. I didn't want Trista to come. You know how I feel about these kinds of parties."

She wasn't even attempting to keep her voice low. She wasn't even attempting to keep this argument private.

Marianne tapped Caprice's shoulder, and said into her ear, "I e-mailed you the info I found right before I came. You can study it after you leave. But I'll tell you right now, there's a woman involved in this story who could have wanted revenge. Give me a call after you look it all over."

Then Marianne slipped away into the crowd, joining another journalist she knew. She lifted her camera and actually caught a photo of Ace's sister-in-law and the keyboard player. She was staying away from Ace and his ex-wife and Trista. That's why she could be trusted.

So somebody in Louise's past life wanted revenge.

Caprice thought about that as Ace and his wife argued in front of his daughter.

"Trista made a monumental fuss about wanting to come," Marsha was saying. "She said she wouldn't go to school next week if I didn't bring her. I wasn't about to send her up here all alone with some chauffeur. I also didn't trust leaving her here overnight."

"You've left her here overnight this summer, and before Christmas."

"You weren't having a wild party then."

Ace waved at all his guests. "These friends, colleagues, family, and press aren't wild. They're just enjoying my music, which is something you could do if you gave it half a chance. You never did."

"I don't want to argue, Ace. I just want to get this night over."

"And that's a positive attitude if I ever heard one," he muttered.

"Maybe I'd have a more positive attitude if you hadn't been such a jerk when we were married."

That quietness rolled over the crowd again, and Caprice decided it wasn't a good idea to let this go on, especially with Trista hearing all of it. She was beginning to idolize her dad, and Caprice didn't want to see a monkey wrench thrown into that. Marsha was obviously putting her own feelings before the feelings of her daughter.

Standing only about ten feet away, Caprice walked up to the group when no one else had dared. Trista came right into her arms and hugged her hard.

"How are you, honey?" she asked.

"I miss Brindle. Mom wouldn't let me bring her. I can't believe how they're arguing."

Caprice and Trista had bonded when they'd decorated her room. They'd learned to speak plainly to each other. Ace's wife, however, didn't know that. She looked at Caprice disdainfully, her long lashes going up and down as she studied Caprice, from her short boots, up her bell-bottoms, to her fringed Stevie-Nicks-like top.

"Are you Ace's latest?" she asked with an edge to her voice.

But Ace cut her off, not even addressing her comment. "If you want to discuss anything, we can go to my office. If you came so Trista could hear my new song, I'm ready to play it."

Seeing that Caprice had entered the lion's den so to speak, Ace's family came over now. They all greeted Trista as if they'd missed her, and wanted her to be part of this celebration tonight. Marsha backed off, and she looked quite lonely, standing all alone, gazing up at Ace as if she might still have feelings for him. Could that be possible?

Caprice felt sorry for a family torn by divorce. She was grateful Joe and Bella had been able to work on their marriage. Would it ever be as good as it once was? Maybe it could be better. The important thing was both partners wanting it to work, and being able to compromise. Would either Grant or Seth be able to do that? Could she?

Ace drew Trista up to the dais where the instruments stood while Caprice turned toward the kitchen where great smells were beginning to percolate out. Drew was helping Nikki with the catering tonight.

Feeling at loose ends, not having come with anyone, she headed into the kitchen to see if she could help. She'd stopped in there earlier and at first, Drew and Nikki had seemed to work well together. But now . . .

"I don't plate the salad like that," Nikki was saying. "There's no room on the dish for guests to place anything else. It's for hors d'oeuvres, too."

"They can pick up one of the smaller dishes for that."

"Those are the dessert dishes, Drew. We don't have enough extras for everyone to have two of those dishes."

"Why didn't you bring extras?" he asked.

"Because that's not the way I work. I work efficiently—packing up, serving, washing, taking home. That's the best way to run a business."

Uh oh. Rippling waters in the calm of hearts and flowers. Valentine's Day was indeed past.

Drew glared at Nikki. "You don't want a partner. You want your twin." And with that, he slammed a dish on the counter, spun around, and headed for one of the sliding glass doors that led to the patio and pool.

Nikki shook her head. "I don't know what's wrong with him tonight. He's just . . . off."

"Have you known him well enough to know that?"

"I knew his reputation. He's not a hothead."

"Maybe you're just annoying him."

Nikki plopped her hands on her hips. "And why would that be?"

"Maybe because he's attracted to you, and you are to him?"

Nikki's golden eyes grew wide, her mouth opened a little, and she looked startled by the idea.

"It makes sense, Nik. He might not like taking orders from a woman he's attracted to."

"He's the one who wanted the job," she murmured.

"Maybe so. I guess it depends if you want a business partner or if you want another kind of partner."

Nikki sighed. "I want a life."

"Tough call. Do you want me to talk to him?"

"No, I will, as soon as Ace plays his new song. We have to be ready to serve, and I have to know he'll be here and not mess things up."

"If you want him to serve tonight, you'd better not go out there with guns blazing."

"What do you want me to do, be coy?"

"Coy isn't in your repertoire. Just be honest, but be a kind honest."

"Kind and honest. I suppose they can go together. But if that doesn't work, you might see him hitchhiking back to town."

Caprice laughed, and made her way back to the living room to a front and center seat where she could listen the best to Ace's new song.

Her thumb was itching to pull her smartphone from her pocket and read what Marianne had sent her. However, it could be a while before she could give her full attention to it, which was what she needed to do. Dulcina was pup-sitting Lady tonight. Caprice would have to pick her up and settle Sophia in for the night before she could fish through info about Lucy Russell Mathers.

Dulcina was pup-sitting Lady at her house. Although all Caprice wanted to do was attach Lady's leash, take her for a final night tour of the yard, and then settle at her computer, she'd been taught better than to simply rush off with a brief thank-you.

Besides, Dulcina seemed to want to talk because she asked, "How about some hot chocolate?"

As Lady stood looking up at Caprice, she gave her pet a few strokes around her ears and said, "Sure. Hot chocolate on a night like this is perfect."

Dulcina led Caprice and Lady through her living room, furnished with a gray and blue comfortable-looking couch and armchair, into her kitchen that was color blocked in blue and white. She definitely liked blue!

"Have a seat," Dulcina suggested, waving to her white wooden table and chair set that could make room for four. "I have one of those coffeemakers that brew a cup at a time. But I have hot chocolate pods and cider ones, too."

"Nikki suggested I might like a brewer like that. But when my family comes over, we need a whole pot."

"I understand that. I didn't get a chance yet to make coffee for me and Rod."

"So that's his name," Caprice responded with a smile. Then remembering the Valentine's Day dance, she remarked, "I saw the two of you leave the dance."

Dulcina frowned. "We were having such a good time. But then his sitter called and told him his thirteen-year-old wanted to go to a friend's house. Rod didn't want his daughter going out so late and when he said no, his daughter started crying. He felt he had to go home and take care of the situation."

"Did you go with him?" Caprice asked gently.

Dulcina shook her head. "He brought me home first. I don't think he's ready to let me meet his daughters."

All too well, Caprice remembered dating Travis a good three months before she'd met his four-year-old. As soon as she had, Krista had stolen her heart. Their breakup had seemed all the worse because she'd had to sever her relationship with Krista, too. She wondered about Ace's relationship with his ex-wife. Was he still attracted to her? Did he still feel connected because of Trista?

"Did *you* feel it was too soon?" Caprice asked.

"Oh, I agreed. We have to get to know each other better before he introduces me to them. They don't seem to mind him dating, but he's told me he hasn't brought many women home."

"That means he puts his girls first."

"I suppose," Dulcina agreed reluctantly. "But I don't just want to be a ruffle in his life, either."

A ruffle in his life. Caprice liked that phrase. She realized she didn't want to be a ruffle in Seth's life either. She glanced at the charm bracelet she wore now almost every day.

"Did you ever date a man with children?" Dulcina asked as she took one mug away from the beverage brewer, and moved another into position, adding a new hot chocolate pod.

"I did. Krista won four and we became pals right away. But he and his ex got back together." Although she and Dulcina had been friendly neighbors since Caprice had moved in across the street, they hadn't shared this type of history before.

"Rod's wife walked out years ago. That's why he has custody. She doesn't even live in Pennsylvania anymore." The brewer made a squirting noise again and then dispensed a second mug of hot chocolate.

"You sound as if you've had some serious discussions."

"We have. But enough about me. I saw you sitting beside your brother's law partner. But then you were dancing with your doctor friend. Are you dating both?"

"Oh, no! I'm not dating Grant."

"I see," Dulcina said with an almost imperceptible smile.

Why did everyone think there was something between her and Grant besides . . . friendship?

Because they could see it?

Just as she'd seen the connection between Chet and Malina?

No. She and Grant had never even . . . touched. She and Grant had gone sleuthing together. Their minds sometimes worked along similar paths. He had protected her family . . . and he'd protected her.

She sighed. Concentrating on Chet and Louise's marriage as well as Louise's background would be a lot more advantageous than thinking about or discussing her own love life . . . or lack thereof.

Chapter Sixteen

Caprice understood about delayed gratification, and she could practice it when she had to. Her life sometimes seemed to be a list of priority making.

The temperature had dropped even more significantly just in the past half hour. When Caprice took Lady to her backyard for a last nightly potty trip, she wondered if she should buy one of those cute little coats for her dog. Doggie fashion was trending right now.

From the moment Lady went down the back porch steps, she acted differently than she usually did. Caprice suspected it was the cold. Her dog hung around the little porch for a while, which was unexpected behavior.

But then Caprice said, "Lady, go potty."

When Lady looked at her again, she repeated, "Go potty." Her dog went to the patch of yard Caprice had cleared.

As Caprice breathed in the night air, it practically burned her lungs. The temperature could drop into the teens tonight. She thought about cleaning up after Lady, but she'd just have to do it in the morning.

She found her scooper at the side of the porch, pulled a bag from a box inside the garage, and went down the steps to take care of the yard. Lady was snuffling around as she did. But as Caprice went to the doggie-doo trash keeper, Lady's snuffling increased to a low whine. She slid between the porch and the shrubs along the back of the house.

Uh oh. A creature of the night? A raccoon? A possum?

She called to Lady, but Lady didn't come. In fact, she looked over her shoulder at Caprice and then pointed her nose back into the shrubs. It was as if she was telling Caprice she wanted her to come look there, too.

Not knowing what she'd find, Caprice crossed the yard over to Lady's side of the porch. As she got closer to her dog, she heard the tiny sound.

Meee-ow, meee-ow.

Uh oh, what had Lady found? It was so cold out here. If it was a feral cat, it would run as soon as Caprice got near it. But if it was an animal who needed help—

Caprice couldn't not go look. Crouching down on the ground, she pushed the branches on the evergreen aside, and there she found a tiny, gray tabby that couldn't be more than six weeks old.

"Oh, baby." As she reached for the kitten, it tried to run deeper under the bush but Caprice was quick. She caught it in her glove and lifted it into her arms.

"You can't stay out here, little one. Oh my goodness, how did you get here?"

She glanced around at her fenced-in yard, the tall trees on either side of her house, and she didn't think about any of it too long. She had to get this baby inside and warm her up, feed her, take care of her.

Tomorrow would be time enough to figure out where she'd come from. Right now Caprice had to make sure she was okay.

As she hurried up the steps and tapped her hip for Lady to follow, commanding, "Come," her mind went a mile a minute. She had some milk substitute from when she'd taken care of kittens last summer. It was powder and she could mix it with warm water. She might still have a couple of cans of kitten food in her pantry, too. If not, Sophia's would have to do for now. She'd just make sure it was minced up really well and add a little water to it to make certain this little one wasn't dehydrated. That could happen in winter as well as in summer, with no water source for a stray animal to drink from.

Underlying all that, though, she knew she had to separate the kitten from her other animals. She could have fleas, ear mites, worms, or all of the above. The best place to keep the kitten was probably the downstairs bathroom. Everything in it could be washed and there was a heat vent beside the sink. A carton from her garage would make a good bed if she lined it with towels. She always had an extra litter box on hand because she never knew when a stray might come along.

At the bathroom door, she said to Lady, "Down." Lady reluctantly lay down. Still holding the kitten, heaping praise on her cocker, Caprice then said, "Stay." Lady didn't move.

Caprice went inside the bathroom and closed the door.

The kitten barely filled her hand. She quickly took off her gloves and held the little animal close to her chest, near her body heat. The kitten snuggled right up against her, obviously needing love, attention, and warmth. Caprice sat on the stool at the vanity table and just held the little fuzzy animal, stroking her chin, trying to assess if she was okay. Quickly she took the hand towel from the rack alongside the sink. After she laid it on the floor under the vanity, she placed the kitten on it.

"I'll be right back, I promise. I have to get you everything you need. Don't worry, I'll take care of you."

Tomorrow she'd call Marcus and take the kitten in to him for an examination. Valentine's Day was over. But when the kitten looked up at her, with its little heart-shaped face, Caprice smiled. "You're an unexpected belated Valentine's Day gift."

The kitten meowed, and Caprice lost her heart to an animal all over again.

Caprice poured litter into the litter box, mixed food with water, smashing it really well, and filled a hot water bottle, wrapping it in a towel. She tucked that into a box filled with more towels and with a little clock that ticked like a mom's beating heart.

The kitten fell asleep as Caprice stroked her. Rising from the floor, she looked down at the teeny, gray tabby and said, "I dub you Valentine. It only seems fitting. Maybe it is a few days after Valentine's Day, but you're a heart-tugger. Sleep well, baby. I'll check on you in a few hours."

Hopefully Marcus could fit in her and the kitten tomorrow. Tonight Valentine would be warm with her needs met. In the meantime, Caprice had a murder investigation to continue and some new information to study.

Sophia and Lady stood outside the door to the bathroom as Caprice let herself out. "No contact for you two. Even if all is well with Valentine, it will be at least a few days. So come on, I have to wash up and then we have work to do."

Lady followed Caprice to the kitchen and then her office. Sophia was a little slower but decided to go where the action was, too. A few minutes later, Caprice sat at her computer, Lady on the floor beside her, Sophia on the printer.

Marianne had sent her a splash of articles about Lucy Russell from thirty years ago and Caprice read the story with interest. It read like a novel.

Copying and pasting from what Marianne had e-mailed her, she moved related sentences into a word processing document so she could study them more thoroughly. Of primary concern was the fact that Lucy had been a young heiress of sorts.

Lucy's parents had died in a plane crash, and she had received the insurance money. A human interest story had been written in an Austin paper, and Caprice read it with avid interest.

At age twenty, missing her parents, Lucy had left a private college and lived in the family home, tending to the roses her mother dearly loved. She'd been bereft and lost in grief. But this human interest story wouldn't have been of much interest if it had stopped there. Oh, no, the paper had written this story for another reason entirely. The reporter had gone on to say that a few months after her loss, Miss Russell attended a seminar on gardening at the community college. The guest lecturer had been Troy Mathers, a landscape expert from Killeen, Texas. Lonely and grieving, Miss Russell fell in love with him and they were engaged.

Caprice had the distinct foreboding this wasn't going to be a happily-ever-after story.

Not only were Lucy and Troy engaged, but they married at a justice of the peace. Two months later—

Troy Mathers had drained Lucy Russell Mathers's bank account, stolen gold coins and jewelry she'd protected in a safe, and fled. Lucy called the police. The authorities caught him and the whole sorry tale came out.

At the end of that article, the reporter stated Mrs. Mathers refused to comment.

That had been that article, but in a follow-up a week later, the same reporter went on to fill in details. Apparently, Mathers had been living with a woman in Killeen and had a child with her. His nursery business had been failing. He'd courted Lucy for the express purpose of stealing her money. He saw Lucy's inheritance as a way to start a new life with a woman he really loved. Those were his words. Apparently, he hadn't been as reluctant as Lucy to tell his story now that he'd been caught. He'd been on his way to Mexico when he'd been apprehended. At that time, he'd confessed that his lover, Stacy Miller, had intended to pack up their child and meet him in a border town. However, the reporter added, the authorities couldn't prove that his lover had been his accomplice. Mathers accepted a plea agreement and was sent to prison. Stacy Miller had gone free.

Caprice quickly scrolled to the third article, three months later. Troy Mathers had been killed in prison.

Lucy again had no prepared comment, but her lawyer had spoken for her. He'd said that his client had been devastated over everything that had happened.

Marianne had also found another follow-up story with the headline, LOCAL RESIDENT RECEIVES DEATH THREATS, dated a few weeks later. Caprice quickly scanned it, cutting and pasting as she went. There had been a dead rat in Lucy's mailbox, with a *You Will Die* note. Nasty harassing phone calls had interrupted her days and nights. Of course, Stacy Miller had been the main suspect. She'd been questioned but not charged. There was a fuzzy paparazzi-style photo of Stacy exiting the police station. But she was hardly recognizable in the old clipping.

Caprice sat back on the chair and made it squeak. That woke up Sophia. She lifted her head, twitched an ear, and only opened one eye as if to ask, "You've got something for me?"

"I think I do," Caprice said. "Lucy Russell Mathers changes her name to Louise Benton. I'd bet your pint of cream that the death threat, and the harassing calls, were the inciting incidents that convinced Lucy to change her name and maybe even to move here and start a new life. Had the authorities recovered any of her inheritance? Even if they had, maybe Lucy hadn't wanted anyone to know she had money so she couldn't be taken advantage of again. Maybe that's why she'd gotten a job at The Pretzel Party."

Sophia meowed as if she didn't want her cream going anywhere.

"Don't you trust my powers of deduction?"

Lady bobbed her head up as if to say she did.

Staring at the screen once more, Caprice took the questions deeper. Was it possible that Stacy Miller, all these years later, had found Lucy and taken her revenge? If so, was she still in Kismet?

That idea gave Caprice chills. Which way to go from here? There was only one way to go, to her next best lead, the Texas connection. Tomorrow she'd talk to Don Rodriguez again. Since he was from Austin, he might know something about all these incidents firsthand from living there during that time. And if he didn't? He still might know the truth about Louise Benton Downing that no one else in Kismet knew.

Once during the night and then again early in the morning, Caprice checked on Valentine. After coffee, she called Marcus. He told her to bring the kitten in before his first appointment. He knew she was worrying about whether the kitten might have FIV, feline leukemia, or anything else they could test for. She was grateful that he understood her worries. She waited until eight o'clock and then she phoned around the neighborhood and couldn't find anyone who'd lost a kitten. She would put up flyers on trees, in the grocery stores, and the drugstore, but she had a feeling about this one.

The icy air singed Caprice's lungs as she carried the box with Valentine in it to her heated van. This carton had a lid with holes. She'd lined it with old towels and stuck the hot water bottle inside wrapped in an extra one. Valentine had been meowing and hungry this morning, very good signs. Caprice, however, was holding her breath until Marcus did an FIV and a feline leukemia diagnostic.

Furry Friends Veterinary Clinic was devoid of activity and the front parking lot empty when Caprice arrived. She had caught sight of Marcus's black SUV out back as well as a boxy compact. That belonged to one of the vet techs.

Not knowing if Marcus had opened the clinic yet, she left Valentine in her van as she ran to the door, her maxi-coat flapping around her seventies-style overalls. Her short boots crunched on the gray slush that had frozen again overnight on the macadam.

Marcus must have been watching for her. He opened the door and held it wide. "Go get her before I let all the heat escape."

"I think it's a 'her,'" Caprice tossed over her shoulder as she returned to her van, hoisted the box into her arms, and ran to the door.

"Careful on that ice," Marcus warned. "I'm going to sprinkle ice melter on it as soon as the temperature rises a bit."

"It might hit thirty-two degrees by noon," Caprice returned wryly, glad finally to be inside.

Marcus motioned her to follow him to one of the examination rooms. Once inside, he closed the door. "Hopefully your stray won't run when we take it out of the box, but you never know. Jenny's in the back, ready to help if we need her."

After Caprice unbuttoned her coat, she draped it over one of the two vinyl chairs. "I'm already getting attached."

Narrowing his gaze, his brown eyes almost black, he remarked pointedly, "You always do."

He took the lid from the box and smiled. "What have we here?" Carefully, he lifted Valentine in his large palm. His smile grew broader. "Definitely a gray tabby. You were right about that."

Caprice knew he was teasing her, trying to lighten the mood before he did bloodwork that would tell her what she needed to know.

Ten minutes later Marcus was continuing his examination while they waited for the results of the FIV and feline leukemia tests Jenny was supervising.

"She seems healthy," Marcus said after looking into Valentine's ears and mouth. "This flea treatment will take care of the ear mites, too."

He took his stethoscope from his pocket and listened to her heart. When he'd finished, he nodded. "Robust little thing. She only weighs a pound and a half. She couldn't have gotten far with the snow and ice on the ground. My guess is someone dropped her near your house because they didn't want her. I can't believe the cold hearts some people have."

He glanced at Caprice. "Unlike you. She's lucky you found her. She wouldn't have lasted the night in this weather."

Valentine meowed several times and Marcus stroked her. "So how is your investigation going?"

"What makes you think I'm investigating anything?"

"Wasn't Louise Downing a friend of your family's?"

"Yes, she was."

"As soon as I heard she was murdered, I knew you'd be looking into it."

Marcus's analytical mind had helped her figure out a lead in the last murder she'd solved. "It's complicated."

"Murder always is."

The test results they were waiting for took about twenty minutes and Caprice realized Marcus was attempting to distract her. "Louise had a past life in Texas—before she came to Kismet."

"I see. And you think it had something to do with her murder?"

"Possibly. It was a love-gone-wrong story. Her first husband conned her and took her money. She pressed charges and he went to prison. But he was killed there."

"And that came back to bite Louise somehow?"

"Not the murder, but the guy's *real* girlfriend."

"Uh oh. A woman's revenge can be the cruelest."

"As if you'd know," Caprice joked.

"I've had my share of love-gone-wrong stories."

Caprice supposed everyone had.

"So what's your next step?" Marcus asked.

"Do you know Don Rodriguez?"

"The car mechanic who owns the body shop?"

Caprice nodded.

"I've taken my vehicles to him now and then."

"Do you think he's honest?"

"In business dealings I've found him to be so. Why?"

"Because he's from Austin, where Louise once lived. I've spoken with him once but I think I need to do it again and poke a little more."

"Don't poke so much that he pokes back."

"It's hard to know if I'm crossing a line."

"Take someone with you," Marcus advised.

"I thought about that but I don't think he'll open up if I do. I took Lady along last time."

"How did that go?"

"He liked her."

"What's not to like? She's a sweetie. But that's the thing, Caprice. Lady is *not* a watchdog. If she senses you're in danger, she might try to help you. But I don't believe she'd ever be aggressive. Still, warning you to be careful is like whispering into the wind."

"I'm careful," she protested.

He gave her a very long piercing look and she turned her attention to Valentine who'd curled up on the towel on the table and was almost asleep.

With a shake of his head, Marcus checked his watch. "I'll get those results."

Five minutes later, Marcus was smiling again as he returned to the exam room. "You're all clear. Bring her back in two weeks for rabies and distemper injections, if you don't find her a home until then."

Caprice would look for a home for Valentine . . . right after she interviewed Don Rodriguez once more.

Once she was home, Caprice put music on in the bathroom and made sure Valentine was cozy and contented. The flea treatment would take a few days to work. Then she'd have to give her a bath. She fed the kitten again, played with her with a shoelace, and then rubbed her little ears and neck and chin. She fell asleep once more. When Caprice exited the bathroom, Sophia and Lady sat right outside the door.

"She can't come out to play yet. Not for a few days," Caprice explained. After all, animals understood much more than humans gave them credit for.

Sophia gave a knowing blink. Lady gave a small bark.

She spoke directly to her cat again. "You can sit there and listen for her or take a nap. Lady and I are going to take a little jaunt. We won't be long."

As Caprice drove to Rodriguez's shop a short while later, she tapped her fingers on the steering wheel. Yeah, she was a little bit nervous because what happened if they got into the sticky questions? Lady would be with her, but would she stand up for her? That was hard to know until it was necessary. She told herself, *Keep cool, keep even, and above all, don't show Rodriguez you're nervous*. With all that in her head, she parked at the body shop, let Lady out of her crate, attached the leash, and guided her to the door where they'd been once before.

When Rodriguez looked up, he was at the desk again. He *was* surprised. Did he look a bit worried, too?

Thoughts began running through Caprice's mind. Maybe Don Rodriguez wanted Louise to leave Chet and be with him. When she wouldn't—he got angry enough to kill her.

Somehow that didn't quite ring true. But she did have to find out what *would* ring true.

"Do you mind talking to me again?" she asked.

"Would it make any difference if I would?"

"No, not this time."

He gave a resigned sigh. "Do you think you know who did it?"

"I think I'm on the trail of the person who did it. What do you know about Lucy Russell Mathers from Austin?"

"That was a big story a long time ago." Rodriguez thought about it. "I knew the same thing everybody else did. Some guy from Killeen hornswoggled her. He took her for all her money, but she got revenge like most people don't. He was killed in prison a few weeks after he was sent up there. She received death threats and everyone thought they came from the guy's live-in." He gave a shrug. "All of it was big news back then, when there wasn't something new every minute like now. There wasn't a twenty-four-hour news cycle. I had heard Lucy had left Austin, and her house was sold."

"Do you know if Stacy Miller, the man's mistress, was ever heard from again?"

Don leaned back on his stool. "Big Brother wasn't watching then like he is now. Stacy Miller wasn't important enough for anyone to take notice of."

Caprice wondered if killing Louise was a way for her to make everyone take notice now.

"Did Louise ever mention Lucy?"

He looked genuinely surprised. "We talked about the story once in passing. But I can't remember that Louise showed any particular interest. Why?"

"Because I think Louise was Lucy."

Now he seemed shocked. "You're kidding."

"Not even a little bit. Are you saying Louise confided nothing about her past?"

"I really didn't care about her past or how she ended up in Kismet. After all, I landed here, too."

"How did *you* find the town?"

"Friends took a trip up the East Coast. They visited lots of small towns. They had photos of Kismet. I took a look at the Chamber of Commerce Web site online, then came for a visit myself. I had nothing to keep me in Texas so I started over here."

"People usually talk about starting-over stories."

He thought about that, then responded, "Louise never did."

Because she was hiding heartache? Because she never wanted to think again about a past that could search her out and bite her?

Caprice spent a few more minutes with Don Rodriguez and realized she wasn't going to learn anything else here today.

She had barely stepped outside into the cold February wind when her cell phone played. Fumbling under her outside coat into the pocket of her retro overalls, she pulled her phone out and saw Nana's face.

She suspected what this call was about, and Nana confirmed it when she asked, "So how was the party? Maybe you should take me along sometime. I'd like to meet a rock star."

Caprice laughed as she walked to her car, and told Nana all about it. She also told her about going home and finding the kitten.

Nana was silent a few moments, then asked, "And what are you going to do with this kitten?"

"I'm not sure. Lady and Sophia keep me busy enough. I'm trying to find out if someone lost Valentine. If no one comes forward, I'll try to find her a good home."

"Valentine," Nana said quietly, and Caprice heard something in her voice. She waited.

"That's a special name, don't you think?"

"She's a special kitten."

Nana laughed. "You think they're all special."

Again she was quiet for a few seconds, and Caprice stopped at her van with Lady and waited again.

"Do you think I'm too old to have a kitten?" Nana asked.

"No one's ever too old to have a kitten. Not as long as they can stoop over, clean out a litter box, and feed a pet several times a day."

"I can do all that," Nana said confidently. "I haven't had a pet since I was a small girl."

Nana still seemed to be thinking about it, so Caprice asked, "Do you want a constant companion? I think Valentine's the type that will like to be close. It's hard to tell at this stage, but she likes to cuddle."

"A constant companion. You know, I think I'd like that, too."

"Do you want to think about it a couple of days? She can't go anywhere until her flea treatment takes effect."

But Nana wasn't an indecisive woman. Once she made up her mind, she made up her mind. "I don't need a couple of days. I'd like to have a furry friend. They seem to make you happy. What do I have to do to get ready?"

"You don't have to do anything. I'll stop in at Perky Paws and supply you with everything you need. When Valentine's ready for a home, I'll bring her and all of it over. I'll get you set up."

"In the meantime, I'll crochet a little blanket for her," Nana decided, obviously eager to do something.

"I'm sure she'll like that. They like to knead afghans and blankets with their claws. It reminds them of their mom. This little one must have been taken from her mom early."

"I'll make her feel as if she has one again. Thank you, Caprice. Valentine could be just what I need to make this winter not seem quite so long."

Nana loved to nurture and care for, and now she'd have a little being of her own to do that for. Nana and Valentine would be a perfect fit.

Chapter Seventeen

Lady was always welcome at Perky Paws Pet Shop. That was the fun aspect of this store along with baked treats for canines that looked and smelled fabulous enough for humans to want to eat them. The manager of the store—Gretta Hansen—made some of them herself and imported others from a dog treat maker in York.

As Caprice went inside with Lady, her mind wasn't merely on the list of supplies Nana needed. It was also on everything Don Rodriguez had discussed with her—revenge, untimely death, a crime, and a former husband. That history was a far cry from Chet and his affair, from someone who wanted to rob Louise and the robbery had gone wrong. Was she headed in the right direction now with the Texas connection?

In the front case today, Caprice recognized several types of biscuits, from peanut butter nuggets, gingermen-sized ginger biscuits, pumpkin biscuits, and cheese and bacon biscuits. Colorful dog cookies also decorated the case and were adorned with yogurt icing.

Lady noticed them, too, and stood at the case as if she expected one to jump out at her and she could eat it.

On Caprice's way out, she'd purchase a few of them.

After waving to Gretta, she headed for the back of the shop and litter pans and supplies. Once there, however, she almost ran into Danny Flannery! The teenager was painting a mural on the back wall.

"Danny, how are you? I haven't seen you since fall. How's your senior year going?"

Danny had been an almost truant teenager until Caprice had noticed his artistic bent and introduced him to Ace Richland. Ace had hired Danny to paint a dolphin mural on his poolhouse wall as well as a horse mural in his daughter's room. Danny had done such a terrific job on both that Ace had offered to cover his art school training after he graduated.

In the meantime, Ace had helped him set up a Web site from which he sold custom hand-painted T-shirts and sweatshirts.

"I've gotten my grades up," he announced proudly, crouching down to Lady and offering his hand for a sniff. "Mom framed my first-term honor roll card. She hasn't had one of those since I was a kid."

Lady sniffed his hand thoroughly. He grinned and petted her. Caprice chuckled. "Good for you on the honor roll. Have you picked out an art school?"

"Ace says I can go anywhere I want. But I don't want to travel too far that I can't get home on weekends. Mom could need me."

With a mother who'd worked hard for years to keep a roof over their heads, Danny was protective of his mom and had become a suspect in a murder investigation because of it.

Now he went on. "I talked to Ace about art institutes in Philadelphia."

"My sister Bella went to a fashion institute in Philly."

"Ace said he'd loan us his chauffeur so we can visit a couple in April. Then Mom doesn't have to worry about her car breaking down."

Underneath the rock star façade, Ace was a great guy. If only he and his ex-wife could work out their differences. Was that her Pollyanna complex at work again?

Danny rose to his feet once more and Lady sniffed around his sneakers. "Mom's working more hours at the Cupcake House so she could cut back cleaning houses. Now we're even home at the same time some nights."

"I send my friends to your Web site."

"Yeah, I noticed. They bought lots of T-shirts for Christmas presents."

"Everyone needs T-shirts," she said with a grin.

Suddenly Danny looked uncomfortable. "I don't know if I ever thanked you, Miss De Luca. For getting me that job with Ace. For believing I was more than a troublemaker."

Caprice patted his shoulder. "I think I related to you. When I was a teenager I felt a lot of defiance and rebelliousness but kept it inside. I learned to channel it in a positive direction and I hoped you could do the same. And you have."

She could see red start to creep up Danny's neck and she didn't want to embarrass him more. Moving away, she said, "I won't hold you up. I found a kitten and have to buy supplies for my nana who is going to take care of her and keep her if her owner doesn't come forward. In fact, I have a flyer for Gretta to post on her bulletin board."

"Gretta put out new pamphlets for dog and cat owners if you're interested."

She could see he was trying to back out of their conversation so she gave him help. "I'll check them out."

Touring the store, she picked up everything Nana would need for Valentine, from a kitty litter pan to litter, a nourishing kitten food, and a cute pink fleecy bed Nana could fit anywhere she liked. Caprice also chose a pink and black carrier to transfer Valentine to her new home. Nana could use it for veterinarian checkups.

Caprice had almost forgotten about the pamphlets Danny suggested until she settled the carrier on the checkout counter. At a glance, she noticed the heading on the pamphlet—**Plants Harmful to Cats and Dogs**. The list was broken down into two categories.

Toxic to Felines:

Amaryllis, Autumn Crocus, Azaleas and Rhododendrons, Bleeding Hearts, Castor Bean, Chrysanthemum, Cyclamen, English Ivy, Lilies, Oleander, Peace Lily, Spanish Thyme, Tulip and Narcissus bulbs, Yews

Toxic to Canines:

Castor Bean or Castor Oil Plant, Cyclamen, Dumb Cane, Hemlock, English Ivy, Mistletoe, Oleander, Thorn Apple, Yews

With spring coming, she'd be trimming and prettying up the yard. She'd never realized azaleas and bleeding hearts were poisonous to animals. She loved to see the azalea under her bay window bloom in the spring. But maybe it was time she dug it out and substituted a plant

that was more animal friendly. She knew about lilies
being toxic and had long ago cleared her yard of those.
Louise had filled her in on their poisonous properties.

Louise.

Caprice's thoughts often returned to Louise, her love
of flowers . . . and the awful way she'd died.

Ten minutes later, Caprice had turned onto her street
when her phone dinged that a text had come in. She
knew better than to text and drive, so she pulled over,
fitting into a parking space between snowbanks, and
checked her screen. It was Nikki.

Are you home?

She texted back. **Will be in five minutes.**

I'll be there.

Maybe Nikki wanted to talk about the Sherwood
Forest theme, and what she'd serve at the open house on
Saturday. Nikki always did her research. It would be
interesting to hear what she had in mind.

Another ten minutes later, Caprice was in the kitchen
cleaning up after feeding Lady, Sophia, and Valentine.

As soon as Nikki let herself in, she called to the
kitchen. "You should be keeping your door *locked*,
especially when you're snooping for suspects."

From the kitchen Caprice called back, "I knew you
were coming."

Appearing in the doorway between the dining room
and kitchen, Nikki waved her hand and headed for the

coffeepot that was already brewing. "It doesn't matter. Louise's killer could have gotten here before me."

A chill ran along Caprice's neck because she knew Nikki could be right. She should be more careful about something like that.

Nikki went on. "I hope that coffee is laced with chocolate because I need the endorphins."

"I might have chocolate chips to offer you," Caprice joked because she wanted to take her mind away from the idea of some stranger entering her house.

"Even chocolate chips sound good right now. They might melt into the coffee."

"I could make hot chocolate, too, as a chaser."

"Sounds good," Nikki decided, pulling four colorful mugs from the wooden tree on the counter.

Lady, who had been resting on a mat at the back door after her lunch, bounded over to Nikki as if she understood she needed consolation.

Nikki crouched down onto the floor with the cocker. Lady rolled over to have her belly rubbed and Nikki obliged.

"Is Drew the reason you need the chocolate?" Caprice asked, knowing Nikki's mood wasn't a laughing matter. Nikki was the steadfast sister, the one who didn't get ruffled, the one who always had a plan.

"Drew, the idea of a partnership, how a business decision on my part could affect what you and I do. I couldn't sleep last night, and that's not usually a problem."

Caprice considered Nikki's situation, and thought about the best thing to do. That was easy. "Would you like to meet Valentine?"

Immediately Nikki smiled. "Nana called me and told me all about the kitten you found. Sure, I want to meet her. I think it's a great idea for Nana to take her."

"She's a cuddle bunny and perfect for Nana. Marcus tested her and she doesn't have FIV or feline leukemia. By the end of the week, I'll take her to Nana."

Lady followed Caprice and Nikki to the bathroom door. "For now you have to stay out here, and Sophia does, too." Caprice hoped Lady, as well as her cat, would soon get the message.

"I didn't see Sophia when I came in," Nikki said.

"I think she went into my office. She's probably on my desk chair."

She opened the bathroom door and they both slipped inside to the sound of Lady's whine.

Valentine came right over to Caprice and meowed several times. Caprice scooped her up. "I just fed you."

She positioned Valentine in the crook of her arm and petted her gently. "This is Nikki. You'll be seeing a lot of her, too."

"Can I hold her?" Nikki asked eagerly.

Some of the worry had left Nikki's face. That's what animals did for humans.

"Sure, hold her close. I think she likes to hear your heartbeat."

After the transfer, they both sat on the floor. There was scratching at the door.

Caprice sighed.

After another minute or so, it stopped.

Caprice watched Nikki stroking the tiny kitten. Time to get to the issue at hand.

"How did you and Drew leave it after Ace's party? Did you talk?"

"We talked and—" She hesitated. "It doesn't matter what happened. He told me to call him when I made up my mind about the partnership. He's decided simply working for me isn't a good idea. He wants a partnership or nothing."

Caprice wondered exactly what *had* happened. But she wouldn't push Nikki to tell her now. "A man who deals in ultimatums. How do you feel about that?"

"I know you'd run in the other direction from an ultimatum, but it could be a sign of strength."

"Or a sign that he's a control freak."

"That is possible," Nikki agreed.

A control freak, Caprice thought. Just what her sister didn't need.

After their discussion in the bathroom, after Valentine had fallen asleep again, Caprice went to the pantry closet for cocoa and chocolate chips.

As she took a saucepan from the bottom cupboard, Nikki went to the mugs she'd pulled from the mug tree earlier.

"I want to get our menus settled for the Sherwood Forest staging," she said.

She'd dropped her tote bag near the table, and now she pulled out her electronic tablet. As she laid it on the table, she added, "I know what I want to do. I just need to see if you agree."

"Shoot," Caprice said, then realized that might be the

wrong choice of words as she thought about how Louise Downing had died.

Realizing the same thing, Nikki grimaced, then poured the coffee into two mugs.

"I'd like to start with an English pea soup. It's pretty much a standard pea soup but included in the recipe are crushed mint leaves. I can make it sinfully rich with a bit of cream."

"I like that idea. Would the soup be the appetizer?"

Nikki spooned sugar and poured milk into Caprice's mug and simply added milk to hers. "Exactly. An appetizer. One of them, anyway. I'd follow that with traditional English dishes. Did you ever hear of Toad in the Hole?"

Caprice laughed. "This is a recipe?"

"Sure is. It's similar to Yorkshire pudding. Instead, you place sausages in the batter before baking it."

Caprice stirred together cocoa, sugar, and salt. She mixed in water and cooked it until it bubbled. Then she added chocolate chips. "It sounds different, and hearty, and woodsy. I like that idea, too. You're on a roll."

Ignoring the compliment, Nikki took their mugs to the table. "For another appetizer, I'd add a dish called Angels on Horseback. They were a Victorian after-dinner snack—bacon-wrapped oysters. Supposedly the cooked bacon appears to be angels' wings."

When the chocolate chips melted, Caprice turned down the heat and stirred in the milk. "They sound unique, classy, and just what we need for this type of open house. What about your main courses?"

"How about roast beef with a white horseradish sauce, steak and kidney pie, and of course fish and chips! All of it very English. I researched a recipe for a dish called Bubble and Squeak—it's English fried potatoes and cabbage. I could also roast a vegetable, maybe Brussels sprouts, and dribble them with cheese sauce. We can serve mulled wine with everything."

"Mulled wine makes me think of England," Caprice agreed, adding vanilla to the hot chocolate and stirring it in. "The guests at the open house may not have even tasted some of these dishes, except for maybe the fish and chips. That white horseradish sauce will make the roast beef savory. I take it you have a list for desserts, too?"

"They were easy to come up with—orange marmalade cake, gingerbread cookies, plum crumble, bread pudding, and something called Eton Mess."

"Do I want to know what that is?" Caprice asked with a grin as she switched off the burner.

Nikki checked her notes. "It's a mixture of whipped cream, meringue, and berries."

"You have very sweet, semisweet, a little spicy, something heavier, and something very light. All the bases covered again."

"You really like the menu?"

"I do. Don't start doubting yourself because a man confused you a little."

"That's what men do, confuse me." She pointed to Caprice's bracelet. "I heard about *that*. Seth's trying to gain points, you know, because he's not here."

"I do know that, but I really like him."

"Hmm," Nikki said. "I can see we're not going to get anywhere with that."

Sophia ambled into the kitchen now to join the party,

took a look at Lady who'd settled under the table, and hopped up onto one of the chairs. After she kneaded the yellow braided seat covering, she turned around twice and curled up, her head on her paws, her golden eyes blinking up at Nikki.

As Caprice poured her hot chocolate concoction into two more mugs, Nikki rubbed her hands together. "Let's talk about your investigation. I need a good distraction, and that's it."

"Maybe you can help me see it more clearly."

Caprice had consolidated it so many times in her mind, that it was easy for her to click it off fact by fact. She began with the crime scene and what she remembered about the candies, the box being opened, the two candies on the floor, the fact that they looked like peanut butter creams that Louise liked, and why Louise might have them there. Candy for breakfast?

"Louise liked her chocolate-covered peanut butter creams."

"I think those candies have to be considered an anomaly," Caprice theorized. "Now let's go over all the suspects. There's Don Rodriguez who could have had a jealous nature. Maybe Louise wouldn't leave her husband, and he'd been asking her to. Maybe he resented her for it."

"What did you feel about him?" Nikki asked, knowing Caprice used her sixth sense just as Nana did, even though she might not admit it.

"I liked him."

"In what way?"

"He seemed courtly to me, like he cared about Louise. He wasn't going to interfere in her life, and he

hadn't all these years. He seemed as if he cared, and that
he was a real . . . gentleman."

"You weren't having the wool pulled over your eyes
with the Texas drawl, were you?"

"I don't think so. I think he was really trying to be
honest with me."

"Next suspect."

"Pearl Mellencamp still might hold a grudge. She
isn't living in the best of circumstances. Running a
cleaning service might not be that profitable. So settlement or not, I'm not sure she's in a better place."

"And then, though I hate to say it, you have an obvious suspect, don't you? The husband."

Caprice told Nikki what she'd done in phoning the
resort and pretending to be Malina Lamont. "It's pretty
certain Chet was having an affair."

"And it probably wasn't his first," Nikki said sarcas-
tically. "And you can't stop with Chet as a suspect. What
about Malina Lamont? What if she wanted him to ask
for a divorce and marry her?"

"What if he asked Louise for a divorce and she said
no?" Caprice offered.

"Murder is usually about passionate feelings and
relationships, and this one doesn't seem to be any different."

"Murder can also be about money, but I haven't told
you about my latest and best suspect, Stacy Miller."

Nikki's brows drew together as she looked down at
her hot chocolate and then at her coffee. She took a sip
of the coffee, then quickly took one of the hot chocolate.
"Now that I'm fortified, tell me who Stacy Miller is."

Following Nikki's example, Caprice took a few sips

of her coffee, then her hot chocolate. Not bad. Chocolate chasers could become a trend.

Focusing again, she said, "Louise had a past. I'm not even sure Chet knew about it. I'm going to visit with him next and delve a little more."

"A past with enemies?"

"Possibly one very important enemy—a woman who blamed Louise for her lover's death."

Caprice quickly told Nikki the whole story, thinking about Louise's change of name, the incidents that had led up to it, the betrayal she must have felt. Nikki switched from the coffee to the chocolate permanently. Then the two sisters gazed at each other.

"What did you say Stacy's job was?" Nikki asked.

"She worked for her lover who owned a nursery."

"So she worked with plants?"

Caprice nodded and suddenly remembered the pamphlet she'd picked up at Perky Paws. Rising, she crossed to the refrigerator where she'd attached it with a magnet. Slipping it free, she handed it to Nikki. "That's a list of plants that are toxic to cats and dogs."

Nikki read the list, then looked up at Caprice.

"What are you thinking?" Nikki asked.

"I'm thinking that there are plants toxic to humans. I'm thinking about Louise's trip to the hospital. She got sick after eating an organic chicken wrap, all natural ingredients supposedly. Just what were those ingredients?"

"But Louise was shot," Nikki protested.

"Yes, she was. But maybe a gun wasn't the first weapon of choice. I know it's a long shot, but I keep considering those chocolate-covered creams at the crime scene. Why were they in the greenhouse? It was a full box except for the two on the floor. I don't think Louise would have had them for breakfast."

"You never had chocolates for breakfast?" Nikki asked with a wry smile.

But Caprice suddenly remembered something else. "Not while I was working with plants. Louise's hands were all dirty from the ground she'd been using to transplant."

"I see your point. You think something lethal was in those chocolates?"

Caprice hopped up so fast, even Sophia and Lady glanced up at her. She reached for her cell phone charging on the counter.

"Who are you calling?" Nikki asked.

"Grant. I'm going to ask him to do me a favor."

Caprice just hoped he was still speaking to her. Well, why wouldn't he be? He was the one who hadn't asked her to dance. He was the one who'd left.

The bracelet Seth had given her jingled on her wrist as she picked up her phone.

Chapter Eighteen

When Caprice dialed Grant's number, she really didn't know what to expect. He usually had his phone with him. He usually answered right away. However, today, his phone rang three times, and she was beginning to give up. He could be walking Patches. He could be deep in work. He could see her number and ignore the call.

But he didn't ignore her call. He picked up.

"Hello?" The word was clipped as if he were busy . . . or something.

"Grant, its Caprice."

"I have caller ID."

All right, so maybe he had been thinking about ignoring her call, but then decided to pick up.

"I know you do. I mean—" Just what did she mean? That she'd known this conversation was going to be awkward? And just why was it going to be awkward? Because he hadn't asked her to dance?

Keeping her thoughts focused, she said honestly, "I need a favor."

Silence met that declaration until he asked, "A favor? From me? You have a brother who's a lawyer. You have a boyfriend who's a doctor. What could you possibly need from me?"

Whoa. He sounded angry, and just why hadn't she called Vince? Because Vince didn't seem to have the contacts in the D.A.'s office that Grant had. Because Grant had dealt with Detective Jones when Joe had needed a lawyer. Because . . . There were lots of becauses.

She said truthfully, "I thought you were the one who could do the best job with this."

"Just what job do you want done, Caprice?"

"I was going over Louise's murder with Nikki. I think we might have come up with a lead the police could have missed."

"The forensics team as well as Jones are thorough."

"I know they are, but just listen, okay?"

After about three heartbeats, Grant said, "I'm listening."

"Remember when Louise ended up in the hospital the week before she was killed?"

"I remember."

"I don't think she had food poisoning. I think she might have been poisoned. She had lunch with someone that day, an organic chicken wrap, according to Rachel. Half of it was left in the refrigerator, but of course she threw it away after Louise was taken to the hospital."

"Who did she have lunch with?"

"We don't know."

"You want me to call Jones and tell him that? That you

don't know who she had lunch with, and the chicken wrap was thrown away so it can't be tested?"

"No, I don't want you to tell Detective Jones that. I'm just trying to explain my theory."

She heard a sigh of frustration.

"All right, explain."

She told him Louise's story, about Stacy Miller, about the threats, about Louise's name change.

"I don't know if Jones has dug into all that. How did you find out about the name change?" Grant wanted to know.

"Marianne Brisbane investigated for me."

"That makes sense. So what's the favor? You just want me to tell Jones all this because he probably wouldn't listen to you?"

"No. It's about the chocolates I saw at the crime scene. Louise had no reason to have an open box of chocolates on her potting bench, not with all the dirt and grime and seeds and plants. I think the murderer brought those chocolates to her. I think the murderer might have wanted her to eat them, right then, because they were laced with something. Either the same something or a different something that was in the organic chicken wrap. The box was on the potting bench. There were a couple of chocolates that had fallen on the floor. I'm sure the forensics team gathered all that up. Could you ask them if they were tested? Can you tell him to look for a plant-based substance that might have been lethal?"

"And if there *is* something wrong with the chocolates, you think Jones should be looking for Stacy Miller?"

"Yes, I think he should be."

"Why would Louise have had lunch with this person?"

"Maybe Stacy was offering an olive branch. Maybe she told Louise she wanted to let bygones be bygones. I don't know. I haven't gotten farther than the chocolates. That's why we need the forensics team and Detective Jones."

"We? Because I'm your go-between?"

"No. *We* . . . because I know you want to see this solved as much as I do."

"Maybe not quite as much," he muttered. "But I do think your mom needs closure, and if this helps, I'll call Jones."

"Thank you, Grant."

"No thanks necessary."

She hesitated, but then said, "Maybe when the weather warms up a little, we can walk Patches and Lady together."

"My caseload hasn't lessened just because I'm working from home. It could be spring before I have time for that kind of outing."

Or it could be summer or winter or fall. She got the message. Grant was perturbed with her, but he wouldn't talk about why. He wouldn't talk about anything with her right now except the Louise Downing murder case.

"Will you call me if you learn anything from Detective Jones?"

"I'll call you if I learn anything from anybody."

At least that was something. But as she said goodbye and ended the call, she felt deflated, even though she might be on her way to solving Louise Downing's murder.

Caprice had no sooner put down her phone, when her

doorbell rang and she heard yipping outside her front door. Another stray?

Nikki must have been thinking the same thing because she rolled her eyes and shook her head as if to say, *Just what you need*. Instead she asked, "Is Grant going to help?"

"He says he'll talk to Detective Jones. We'll see what happens next."

Crossing to the door, Caprice opened it and her day turned a whole lot brighter. Roz was standing there and Dylan was the one yipping and hopping up and down.

Caprice missed the little dog and now she opened her door wide.

Roz held out a bag labeled with the Cupcake House. "I have the best chocolate cupcakes topped with cream cheese icing in all of Kismet. Do you have time for coffee?"

Roz watched her weight judiciously. She only bought cupcakes when she was stressed. She must be stressed about something and Caprice guessed what.

She waved toward the living room. "Nikki's here, too."

"I have more than enough," Roz said, coming inside after Dylan. "And two De Luca sisters might be just what I need in order to sleep at night again."

Dylan and Lady circled each other twice, touched noses, then ran off to the kitchen where Lady's dish still had a few crunchies. Dylan remembered that's where his food had been dished out, too.

"I'm glad they get along," Roz said as she sat on the sofa next to Nikki.

Caprice asked, "Talk first, coffee later? Or both at the same time?"

"I could eat a dozen of those cupcakes right now. Let's talk and eat," Roz said in the same tone she used for business negotiations. She must really be stressed.

As always, her friend looked like a model. She'd taken her coat off and thrown it over the oak mirrored bench in the foyer. Underneath the cream long wool coat, she wore an impeccably beautiful pale blue cashmere sweater and pale blue wool slacks. Sapphire studs in her ears were understated, but definitely expensive as was the matching ring on her finger. Her leather shoe boots were probably Italian made, and her purse was Prada. Roz had wonderful taste and Caprice admired that. It was so different from her own.

"I already have a pot of coffee on."

Nikki and Roz were discussing the latest issue of *Marie Claire* magazine when Caprice brought in all of their filled mugs.

Mug in hand, Roz looked first to Caprice and then at Nikki. "I need more than a little advice about your brother."

Exactly what Caprice had suspected. She exchanged a look with Nikki. "And you think we're qualified to give it?"

Roz gave a small chuckle. "As well as any two sisters are. You know him much better than I do."

"Some days," Nikki contributed, in an amused tone. "Neither Caprice nor I seem to understand men very well right now. They're an enigma, and that includes Vince. But we'll help any way we can."

Sophia, who had climbed her cat tree, jumped from the highest platform to the second highest to the lowest, and then sauntered over to the sofa as if to join in the conversation. She jumped up onto the back atop the afghan Nana had crocheted and stretched out behind Nikki.

Nikki gave the cat a chin rub. "Just what do you want to know?"

Dylan and Lady suddenly dashed through the living room, heading around the circle to Caprice's office. Obviously they'd finished the crunchies and were now looking for entertainment.

"I want to know what's in his head."

Caprice nodded to the cupcakes. "You'd better have a couple of those. No one's ever mapped Vince's head, and if you think Nikki and I have a GPS through it, you're wrong."

"I thought he was dating Lonnie Hippensteel," Roz blurted out.

"He brought her to Mom's birthday party at the beginning of the summer, and he dated her a couple of times," Caprice admitted. "But I saw Lonnie when I was Christmas shopping in December, and she gave me the impression they'd parted ways and weren't connecting again. Truthfully, Roz, over the past year, Vince's dating habits have slowed down. Nana used to tease him that he dated a different woman every weekend. I don't think that's true anymore. What do you think, Nik?"

"Like most men, Vince doesn't give much away," Nikki remarked. "But like Caprice, I don't see him dating as much. He joined Shape Up, but I really think it's to work out, not to hit on women. He seems quieter at our family dinners. He told me he felt honored that Joe and Bella asked him to be Benny's godfather."

"Did you have a good time at the Valentine's Day dance?" Caprice asked.

"We had a great time. And afterward . . . when he walked me to my door . . . he kissed me! That's why I'm so confused."

"I guess Vince had a good time, too," Nikki said with a shrug.

"He called last night and asked me out again."

"Oh," Nikki intoned, as if she understood it all now. "You want to know if this is going someplace."

"I want to know if it *should* go someplace," Roz returned. "It hasn't been a year since Ted died."

Long before Ted's death, he and Roz had been having problems. Not merely problems, but he'd been having an affair. Wondering if this was a trust issue, rather than a grief issue that was bothering her friend, she asked, "What do you want advice about? Whether or not you should see Vince? Do you want him to be serious? Do *you* want to be serious?"

Roz shook her head and reached for a cupcake. "I don't know. I thought he just asked me to the dance so we'd have a good time."

"And you did," Nikki reminded her.

"But you kissed," Caprice added. "And that's what changed everything."

"Vince asking me out again is what changed everything."

Nikki reached for a cupcake, too. "What kind of date?"

"He wants to take me on a tour of a winery, and then go out to dinner."

Lady and Dylan dashed through the living room

again, this time the bigger dog chasing the smaller dog. They ruffled the throw rug and it went sliding across the hardwood floor. But Caprice was used to such antics. What she wasn't used to was her brother possibly being serious about her friend.

"I could talk to him," she offered.

But Roz's response was immediate. "No, don't do that. If I have questions, I'll have to ask him myself. I guess I just have to be clear about what I want."

"And that is?" Nikki and Caprice asked at the same time.

"I don't want to get hurt. I want to know that Vince and I are on the same page. I never want to fall for a man like Ted again."

"Vince isn't like Ted," Caprice assured her. "He has a good heart."

"But we're prejudiced," Nikki chimed in. "He's our brother."

Caprice reached over and patted Roz's hand. "And you're our friend. If you and Vince have fun at the winery tour, then you need to have a long talk at dinner and figure out what both of you want."

As Roz nodded, Caprice realized she should be taking her own advice. Maybe she and Grant should have one of those long talks, too.

Caprice loved the rawness of the inside of the Sherwood Forest-themed house as she stood in its great room on Saturday. The owners had chosen not to be here for the open house, and she understood that. Although the list of guests was impressive, from a few millionaires from New York to a celebrity home shopping Idol to anyone who inveigled themselves onto a real estate agent's list to acquire an invitation, Caprice knew it was difficult for homeowners to see their house toured by strangers. Especially after it was staged, it was then no longer really theirs.

Nikki was setting up in the kitchen with her wait-staff who looked like actors from a Robin Hood movie. Caprice always liked these moments when she was relatively alone in the staged house, simply admiring its beauty. In this case, the main eye-catching draw was the exposed eight-inch round beams lining the slanted ceiling two stories above. The stone fireplace was two stories high and automatically took an onlooker's gaze to those beams. She'd taken advantage of the ceiling appeal and added two foot-long lighting fixtures that resembled old-time lanterns. They added drama. The cavernous living room consisted mostly of wood, from the knotty-pine paneled walls to the distressed plank flooring.

The homeowners' furnishings had been modern comfortable and hadn't gone with the ambiance of the place at all. She'd mostly removed those, adding a twelve-by-twelve-foot woven rug in brown and taupe, its fringes extending a foot on either side. The swing chairs were unusual and conversation starters. No two accent tables matched, which was the idea of their lodge-pole pine, rough-hewn allure. One of the lights was actually fashioned of copper, two others carved from logs. Rawhide shades enhanced them both. This house could easily be a retreat, away from the hustle and bustle of city life. That was a selling point she'd wanted to accent.

Nikki came into the living room and looked up at the ceiling with a sigh. "This is the kind of place I'd love to have someday. You really transformed it."

Nikki had seen the photos Caprice had taken when she'd first accepted this house as a staged makeover.

"It looks rustic yet has all the conveniences," Caprice agreed. "Denise should be here any minute, and two of the other real estate agents are bringing clients. I'm glad the weather cooperated or we would have had to eat all your steak and kidney pie ourselves."

"Food's almost ready."

"I noticed Drew wasn't with you today."

A shadow crossed Nikki's face. "I told him no partnership. I just didn't think we'd work together. Not as partners, at least. And he wouldn't try it the other way."

"I'm sorry."

"Nothing to be sorry about."

"Maybe you could have been more than partners."

"And maybe we couldn't have if he was that way about business. Goodness knows how he'd be about a romantic relationship. No, I think I escaped Cupid with my business acumen intact."

Caprice had to smile.

"Is anybody puppy-sitting this afternoon?" Nikki asked.

"No. I left Lady in the kitchen with her Kong toy and the ball that rolls around dispensing kibble. That should keep her busy for about an hour and tire her out. Hopefully she'll nap until I get home. I put Sophia in my bedroom so she doesn't tease her."

"You really miss her when she's not with you."

"I do. The first few months were like taking care of a

baby. A trainer once said the few feet around me should be the safest and most fun place for my dog to be. And if that's true, she'll never want to leave my side. Well, that's kind of true for me, too."

Caprice's cell phone played just as Marianne Brisbane walked in the front door.

Caprice checked the screen. It was Grant. As Marianne approached, she said, "I'll just be a minute. Can you explore the food?"

"How do you know I didn't come to report on the food? I haven't done a piece on Nikki's catering yet. I thought this might be a good time, with news being slow."

Caprice nodded as she took a few steps away from the two women in order to take Grant's call. "Hi, Grant. Did you talk to Detective Jones?"

"I did. He's not giving much away. I told him what you said about the chocolates and he wondered why you didn't call him yourself."

"Because I didn't think he'd want to hear from me."

"I told him that, too."

"Grant, you didn't!"

"I'm honest with my police contacts, Caprice. That's the only way we can have any give-and-take. He's looking into whether or not the candy was analyzed. In the meantime, I did find out one thing."

"What?"

"Chet Downing *does* own a gun. But it's not the caliber that killed Louise," he added.

"That's good news," she murmured, remembering Pearl had told her about Chet's gun.

"Of sorts. But if he was planning to kill his wife, he wouldn't have used his own gun. He's not a stupid man."

"No, Chet wouldn't have gotten as far as he had in business if he wasn't intelligent and maybe a little ruthless. Thanks for letting me know."

"What are you going to do next?" Grant asked.

"I'm not sure. I'm at an open house now and that's what my mind should be on."

"*Should* be?" he asked.

Impulsively she said, "You should see this place. I think it's the kind of house you would like—lots of wood, a rustic atmosphere, a huge fireplace."

"And a price tag that's way out of my budget, I imagine."

"You could look for a smaller version."

"Do you think there is one?"

"I have contacts."

"I have to go, Caprice. Patches is barking at the door. You know what that means."

"You really could teach him to ring a bell. I intend to do that with Lady once she's a little older."

"Then I'd have bells ringing in my head. I prefer the barking. Go sell a house."

Caprice ended the call before she reminded him that she wasn't the one who sold the houses.

She pocketed her phone in her long, maxi-length burgundy wool skirt. The soft material of her cream-colored blouse with its wide bell sleeves flowed around her arms as she approached Marianne, who was standing at the pedestal table in the dining room taking photos of the food in the warmers on the sideboard. She said to Caprice, "The only thing I've heard of here is the fish and chips."

"Nikki's done a fantastic job again of preparing foods that complement the theme."

Dropping her camera so that it hung on the leather band around her neck, Marianne asked, "So have you uncovered anything new about Louise's murder?"

"No, I haven't. Sometimes I think the whole thing is a wild-goose chase and I should leave it alone, leave it to Detective Jones. But then I remember Mom's face and her plea for me to uncover whoever did it. I remember Louise was her good friend, maybe her best friend. I really need to figure it out, and there's only one avenue I haven't pursued enough yet."

"What's that?" Marianne asked curiously.

"I need to talk to Chet Downing again."

Chapter Nineteen

Caprice took Lady with her. Really, it was a no-brainer. She wasn't going to leave her alone again after she had left her at home for three hours. Besides, Chet liked Lady. Having her cocker along could help him relax, too. If he was relaxed, he might tell her more. Right?

Would Chet be honest with her? Would he admit he was having an affair?

She needed to confront him and find out. After all, he might have had an affair. He might have thought Louise was having one with Don Rodriguez. But deep down, Caprice didn't believe he was a murderer. She simply couldn't see him buying a gun on the street or shooting his wife in the greenhouse he had built for her.

Although snow wasn't in the air, the temperatures would be dropping to around ten tonight. Snow that had melted had slicked up, and Caprice was careful to avoid icy spots. Black ice was as bad as regular ice. Remembering driving this same route the night she'd met with Nikki and Louise, her heart felt weighted with sadness. That was one of the reasons why she had to figure out who had done this, one of the reasons why she had to ask Chet serious questions.

As she turned into the Downings' driveway, she didn't expect to see what she saw. At eight o'clock on a Saturday evening, what was a beat-up truck doing sitting there? She thought she remembered seeing that truck somewhere before. It was green with an open bed, somewhat filled with snow. There were a few scrapes along the side and rusted marks, too. It was as if the owner couldn't afford to have it painted. Where had she seen that truck?

After she parked beside it, she switched off the ignition and climbed out of her van. At least the wind wasn't blowing.

She opened the back door, released Lady from her crate, praised her, and petted her a few moments so her cocker wouldn't barrel out and jump down off the van too quickly. Lady was always ready to give a kiss or receive a pet.

When Caprice gave the command to sit, Lady sat, and Caprice gave her a treat from her coat pocket. Then she attached her leash and they strolled together up the walk to the back door, hoping Rachel was nearby. Maybe the truck was a second vehicle that belonged to her.

Caprice rang the doorbell. She couldn't help glancing over to the greenhouse. Louise had spent so many happy times there, but that wasn't what that structure would be remembered for now.

After a few moments, the door was flung open. Rachel had answered it quickly but she wasn't looking like herself. She appeared so pale and very . . . green.

Lady was ready to walk right in, but Caprice said, "Stay," and Lady obeyed. One of the reasons was probably that Rachel was holding on to the door as if it were holding her up.

"Are you all right?" Caprice asked, worried now.

"No, I'm not. My stomach's really queasy, and I've been to the bathroom. My heart feels . . . funny. I had one of those peanut butter creams that Jamie brought. They looked and smelled so good—"

Rachel had become even paler by the moment. She tossed over her shoulder, "Bathroom again," and ran off to the downstairs powder room, which was closer than her apartment.

That truck. Caprice had seen that truck in the parking lot at Garden Glory. She'd just never associated it with Jamie because Jamie used the Garden Glory van to make deliveries. She suddenly remembered the truck that had sped away from the snowy driveway the night she'd met with Nikki and Louise.

Standing stock-still beside Lady, Caprice thought about Jamie, plants, chicken wraps, and the peanut butter creams at the crime scene. She considered Louise's heart condition—atrial fibrillation and her tachycardia episodes. What had been in those peanut butter creams? What had made Rachel sick—gastric symptoms, her heart feeling "funny"?

As Lady looked up at her with questions about why they weren't moving forward, Caprice's mind calculated the events. Louise could have had lunch with Jamie Bergman the day she got sick. They'd been friends because of the Garden Club. Jamie had only moved to

Kismet about a year ago. She didn't have a Texas accent, but more of a Midwest one. Still . . .

Suddenly Caprice heard her name being called. She said to Lady, "Let's go," and patted her hip.

Rachel called her name again, and she was indeed in the powder room about five feet from the kitchen. She was on the floor near the toilet, looking whiter than death, holding her hand over her heart.

"I think that candy had something odd in it," she gasped.

"You said Jamie gave it to you?"

"Yes. She's with Chet. She was going to give some to him, remind him how much Louise liked them—"

If Jamie was with Chet, and if Jamie was the murderer, Chet could be eating that candy right now, headed to death's door.

Taking out her cell phone, Caprice jabbed in 9-1-1.

When the dispatcher came on the line, she said, "I need an ambulance at 1642 Middlebrook. It might be poisoning. I think Louise Downing's murderer is in the house. Send police backup, too. This is Caprice De Luca. Detective Jones knows me. I can't stay on the line."

Though Caprice left the line open, she slipped the phone into her pocket. She had to see what was going on with Chet and do it right now.

Thank goodness Lady had learned how to heel. Caprice was tempted to tell her to stay in the kitchen and her dog might do it . . . but she might not either. The last thing she wanted was Lady running around, with a murderer in the house. Her gut was telling her, with each second that passed, that Jamie Bergman was probably that murderer. Puzzle pieces were falling into place.

Caprice's footsteps and Lady's pawsteps were muffled by the hall carpet. The door to Chet's den was ajar.

Jamie must have already started in on her story because Caprice heard Chet ask Jamie, "So you changed your name and after thirty years you thought no one would recognize you?"

"No one did."

Caprice recognized Jamie Bergman's voice. But she wasn't a woman named Jamie Bergman.

The nursery clerk went on to say, "No good photograph of me ever was printed. With a haircut and dye job and thirty years on me— It's not hard to buy a new identity. After my daughter died, I saved for a year to do it. It took me another year to find Lucy. I couldn't hire no fancy private detective like *you* would have done." There was bitterness in her voice, enough for Caprice to know that this was Stacy Miller, Troy Mathers's lover. And she was set on more revenge.

Chet must have wanted answers or wanted to keep her talking. Did he think Rachel would save him?

"But why revenge after all these years?"

Now even more venom was obvious as Stacy spoke. "Your *wife* was the reason Troy got killed. Your *wife* was the reason I lost my daughter to drugs three years ago. Troy and Shandra and I could have been living a good life in Mexico. I was going to meet him there. But after he was sent to prison and was killed, I could hardly put food on the table."

Stacy's voice was rising with each sentence. Her outrage could be heard down the hall, and Lady was getting restless. She'd sat at the door when she'd heard Chet's voice, but now she stood, nosing closer to that partially open door.

Caprice used her hand to try and wave her back.

Lady did take a few steps back but was agitated. Caprice wasn't sure what she was going to do about Lady, about herself, about Rachel, about Chet . . . about Stacy Miller.

However, she listened as Stacy went on. "Shandra had to wear thrift store clothes. She always felt like an outcast. She started on drugs early and couldn't get clean. You bet I have to get revenge for all of it."

"But why kill *me*?" Chet's voice cracked, and Caprice wondered if Stacy had more than candy in that room.

Apparently Stacy was tired of keeping the whole story bottled up, tired of being someone else, tired of the life she'd led.

Her words spilled out with as much force as fury. "You gave Louise everything," she almost shouted like the mentally unhinged woman that Caprice realized she was. "From fine cars to jewels to this house, she had everything. I found that out when I traced her down. You gave her anything she could have ever wanted," she said again.

Apparently remembering Chet's question, she answered him. "Why kill you? Because she loved you. Because now you can identify me. Your housekeeper can, too. But soon you'll both be so sick you won't be able to move. I want both of you retching on the floor, your hearts crazy, then slowing down to nothing. I'm going to collect everything of value I can in this house and fence it all—the sterling, the artwork, the jewelry.

I overheard Louise telling Frau De Luca at a Garden Club meeting that she was going to wear the emerald necklace she stored in a fake book on the bookshelf in her bedroom. She had no right to have everything a woman dreams of with you."

Caprice held her breath and prayed for Lady to be still.

Obviously Stacy was proud of what she'd learned and the plan she'd thought up. She didn't hesitate to explain it all to Chet. "The first time I tried to kill Louise with the shaved oleander leaves in the chicken wrap, I messed up. There weren't enough to kill her. But when I came back to the greenhouse, if she would have eaten just one of the peanut butter creams with the tincture of oleander injected in it, she would have died without anyone knowing it was murder. Her heart would have just gone crazy, and the symptoms would have been the same as a digoxin overdose."

"What happened the day she was murdered?" Chet asked hoarsely, as if he was short of breath.

"She wouldn't eat even *one* candy! So I shot her. The day I killed her, I couldn't take the chance of collecting any valuables. I knew the open house people could arrive anytime. But I knew tonight, if I could just get in, I'd be home free. If the oleander doesn't kill you by the time I leave, I'll shoot you and Rachel just like I shot Lucy."

"I think I'm going to be sick," Chet said.

When he did, Caprice knew he'd eaten at least one of those candies, too.

Caprice tried to wave Lady away from the den, but she wouldn't go. In fact, she suddenly pulled hard on her leash, and it fell from Caprice's hand as her dog raced straight into the den.

Caprice rushed after her and saw exactly what she'd feared. Stacy was holding a gun on Chet.

Caprice froze. The problem was, Lady didn't.

As Caprice dove for her pet, she wasn't quick enough. Lady ran toward Chet, the leash wrapping around a tall, metal waste can. It fell over with a clang.

Caprice wished she'd taken that self-defense refresher course that Grant had wanted her to take, but she'd never forgotten how to pitch the way Vince had taught her. She tossed her heavy, fringed purse at Stacy's wrist and knocked the gun from her hand.

Apparently Chet wasn't too sick yet because in a last energetic lunge, he fell on top of Stacy.

Now Caprice used *more* than her purse.

"Lady, come," she called, and the cocker came to her side immediately. She unfastened her leash and jumped on top of Stacy along with Chet. Somehow they both managed to roll the woman over and Caprice used Lady's leash to tie her hands in back of her.

Sirens screamed now, and Caprice hoped the paramedics would be rushing in first. She just hoped they weren't too late to save Rachel . . . or Chet.

Epilogue

Two weeks later

Saint Francis of Assisi Catholic Church held many memories for the De Luca family. Caprice knew today they'd be making another one here.

The church was about a hundred years old and had that innate holiness about it. The painting of angels on the high ceiling in the sanctuary, the arched stained-glass windows depicting the nativity, St. Francis, as well as the archangels, all added to the hushed sacredness of the place. Afternoon sunlight streamed in the windows now. Father Gregory had performed Benedict's baptism in conjunction with the last Mass. Caprice, Nikki, and Vince had taken turns holding him, and he'd been the best baby ever.

Now as they all gathered at the back of the church, Joe and Bella looked so proud. Friends of the family had gathered there, too—Bella and Joe's neighbor who often babysat the children, a few of her mom and dad's friends, Roz and also . . . Grant.

Nikki, her mom, and Nana were the first to leave. Nikki had prepared trays of lasagna, sausage bread, salad, and an assortment of cookies for dessert. They'd decided to have the gathering at the De Lucas' home since Joe and Bella's house was smaller. It just made sense.

Caprice hadn't spoken with Grant since the debacle at the Downing estate had gone down. Caprice knew she'd walked right into it, not knowing what she was walking into. Thank goodness the paramedics had rushed Chet and Rachel to the hospital quickly enough to save them from the effects of the tincture. Thank goodness for modern medicine—activated charcoal, gastric lavage, and breathing support. Thank goodness Stacy Miller had been caught. In a bit of rage, she'd confessed to everything, even to Detective Jones after she had been Mirandized. She'd been charged and arraigned for first-degree murder, two counts of attempted murder, and aggravated assault. Since she seemed willing to plead guilty, her sentence could be life imprisonment instead of the death penalty.

Joe and Bella tucked Ben into his bunting and then into his car seat. Bella said to Caprice, "We'll see you at Mom and Dad's."

"I'll be right behind you," Caprice assured her.

She heard Vince ask Grant, "You're coming to dinner, aren't you?"

Grant glanced at Caprice. "I'll be along."

Vince exchanged a look with Roz, with whom he was spending more time, and then nodded, guiding her out of the church with his hand at the small of her back.

Grant approached Caprice, and she felt a bit jittery.

"They seem to be getting along," he said as an opener.

"They are. The Valentine's Day dance could have started something."

Grant looked uncomfortable at the mention of the dance, and Caprice hadn't wanted to make him feel uncomfortable, so she quickly rushed ahead. "The christening went well, don't you think?"

"I think you and Nikki and Vince will make terrific godparents."

"We'll certainly try."

Avoiding eye contact, Grant looked up the aisle at the inside of the church, along the pews, his gaze settling on the altar. "I haven't been in a church for a long time."

Caprice thought that was as personal a statement as Grant had ever made to her because it spoke deeply about what he'd been through, about dark days, about his attending the christening anyway in spite of what he might be feeling.

She waited, having no idea what he'd say next.

"It's a day I wanted to be here, not just for Joe and Bella and your family, but because I have a lot to be grateful for. You being here, for instance."

Now he did look at her, really look at her, and she couldn't look away.

She swallowed hard. "I'm okay, Grant. I can't tell you I wasn't in any danger . . . because we all were. But I didn't go to the Downings' looking for what I found. I just wanted to talk to Chet."

"I know. Vince told me that, along with how you saved Chet's and Rachel's lives."

"Lady did that," she said with a smile, hoping to lighten their conversation.

"I don't know if I want Lady being your partner in snooping."

"I would have caught on to Stacy more quickly if she'd originally been from Texas and had an accent, but she was raised in Kansas. Her family moved to Texas when she was a teenager."

"And if you had caught on more quickly?"

"I would have gone to Detective Jones, of course."

Grant was quiet for a few moments, and then he asked, "Have you taken a refresher course in self-defense yet?"

She felt herself blushing, because she was embarrassed she hadn't. "With the pups, raising and training Lady, and then the holidays . . ." She trailed off.

Grant stepped a little closer. She smelled his woodsy cologne and liked the crags on his face. She liked so many things about Grant Weatherford.

Shoulder to shoulder with her now, he said, "You can't rely on the pitching arm Vince helped you develop if you're going to continue to investigate murders. You've got to take that refresher course. I'll be glad to pup-sit for you."

Her heart beat faster. She quickly agreed. "I'd like that."

Together they left the church, looking forward to the christening celebration at the De Luca family home.

Original Recipes

Fran's
Baked Macaroni and Cheeses

Preheat oven to 350°.

- 2 cups elbow macaroni
- 3 ½ tablespoons butter
- 1 small clove garlic, grated
- ¼ cup finely chopped onion
- 3 ½ tablespoons flour
- ½ teaspoon salt
- ¼ teaspoon pepper
- 2 ½ cups whole milk
- 12 ounces Cooper Brand CV Sharp Pasteurized Process American cheese cut into small cubes (I use this cheese because it melts smoothly and doesn't separate.)
- ½ cup Monterey Jack cheese, grated
- A sprinkle of smoked paprika

Bring four quarts salted (2 teaspoons) water to a boil. Pour in macaroni and stir. Boil according to package directions—about ten minutes. Drain well and pour into a three-quart ungreased casserole.

Melt butter in 3-quart saucepan. I use a stainless-steel pot on medium heat. Add onion and garlic and stir for about one minute. Do NOT brown. Blend in flour, salt, and pepper. Cook, stirring constantly on medium heat until smooth. Slowly stir in milk. Allow mixture to come to a boil (I turn to high-medium heat—if heat is too high, you will get lumps!), stirring continuously so it doesn't stick to the bottom of the pan. Let bubble until thickened—about two minutes. Lower heat and add cubed American cheese and grated Monterey Jack, stirring often. Once cheeses are melted, stir the cheese sauce into the macaroni. Cover and bake for thirty minutes. Uncover and bake an additional ten minutes.

Remove from the oven and sprinkle with smoked paprika.

Caprice's
Pepperoni and Cheddar Bread

Preheat oven to 350°.
Grease and flour a 9"x5" bread pan.

    5 eggs
    ½ cup 2% milk
    2 cups flour
    3 teaspoons baking powder
    1 teaspoon ground mustard
    ½ teaspoon salt
    2 ounces turkey pepperoni, torn or cut into small pieces
    8 ounces shredded cheddar cheese

Beat eggs until they are frothy. Add milk, flour, baking powder, ground mustard, and salt. Beat until smooth. Stir in pepperoni and cheddar cheese. Pour into prepared 9"x5" pan. Spread evenly. Bake at 350° for 45–50 minutes until golden brown. Cake tester should come out clean. Remove from pan after 10 minutes. Enjoy warm. Refrigerate remainder when cool.

Caprice's
Cran-Orange,
White-Choco Cookies

Preheat oven to 375°.

½ cup margarine (softened)
½ cup butter (softened)
½ cup granulated sugar
2 large eggs
2 teaspoons baking powder
½ teaspoon baking soda
¼ teaspoon salt
1 teaspoon vanilla extract
2 cups flour
2 tablespoon grated orange peel (I use one tablespoon
    fresh—about 2 navel oranges grated—and 1 table-
    spoon dried. (Adjust for your taste!)
½ cup Rice Krispies®
1 cup dried cranberries (I use Ocean Spray Craisins®)
1 cup white chocolate chips

Mix softened margarine and butter. Cream with sugar. Add eggs and mix well. Add baking powder, baking soda, salt, and vanilla extract. Mix well. Add flour ½ cup at a time. Mix in orange peel. Stir in Rice Krispies®, dried cranberries, and white chocolate chips.

Drop by rounded tablespoonful onto lightly greased cookie sheet. Bake about 12–13 minutes until golden brown and set. Peek at the bottom of one to make sure it's golden brown. Remove from cookie sheet immediately.

Makes about 33 melt-in-your-mouth cookies.

Please turn the page for an exciting sneak peek at
Karen Rose Smith's next
Caprice De Luca Home-Staging Mystery

DRAPE EXPECTATIONS

coming in August 2015!

Chapter One

Caprice De Luca's cocker spaniel bounded up the wide staircase beside her.

"Why do you think Ace wants to see us?" she asked Lady, her golden-colored, seven-month-old pup.

Lady gave a bark and Caprice stopped midstaircase to smile and ear-ruffle her dog. Lady was a lower pack, stay-close dog who responded easily to praise, attention, and conversation. Caprice was about to engage in more conversation when—

Suddenly she heard Ace Richland's baritone call to her from his mansion's second-floor hall. "We're in the secure room."

Ace was a rock star legend making a comeback. He'd bought this estate in Kismet, Pennsylvania, after Caprice had staged it to sell with a wild kingdom theme. He'd wanted a place to relax away from glitz, glamour, and glare to reconnect with his twelve-year-old daughter. Her mother enjoyed sole custody and Trista spent the odd weekend with him.

Caprice wondered who was with Ace. He'd said,

"*We're in the secure room.*" Was his daughter here this weekend? When Ace had phoned her, he hadn't told her why he wanted to meet with her. Maybe he had another room he wanted her to redecorate.

But certainly not the secure room, with its climate control and digitally coded locking mechanism.

Ace had told her she could bring Lady, but she didn't know if he wanted her dog in *that* room. The previous owner had stored expensive artwork in there. Upon Caprice's suggestion, Ace used the room for his vast collection of guitars.

When she reached the room with Lady, Caprice said, "Stay," giving her dog a hand motion for the command. At seven months old, Lady still had a lot of pup in her.

Lady whined a moment. She liked Ace and had probably already caught his scent.

Caprice's straight, long, dark-brown hair fell forward as she pulled a treat from the little pouch belt she wore and stooped to reward Lady. Though praise usually did the trick, every now and then Caprice still liked to give the pup something extra.

"She can come in," Ace called. "All the guitars are hanging on racks, and she certainly can't hurt this rubber floor."

Caprice walked into the room, letting Lady wait a moment so she didn't receive confusing signals. Ace *wasn't* alone. A blond woman stood there, her shoulder-length waved hair perfectly coifed, her jeweled necklace and earrings screaming, *Lots of money here*. Her perfectly matched cranberry-colored sweater and slacks, evidently bought from a designer rack, shouted sophistication. Manolo Blahnik shoes accentuated her long legs.

Although Caprice knew fashion, she indulged in her own fashion sense, mostly wearing vintage and retro. On this March day, with the wind blowing, she'd opted for her red bell bottoms, one of her favorite Beatle T-shirts in red and black, and a crocheted yellow vest. After all, this wasn't a professional visit, she didn't think. Ace was sort of a friend.

Now he gave her one of his wicked grins. "Let Lady come inside and I'll introduce you."

Caprice turned toward Lady, patted her hip, and said, "Come, girl."

Lady bounded toward her, wiggled at her feet for a few minutes, and then ran right over to Ace.

Immediately he crouched and petted the dog's head. "You're such a good girl. Just like Brindle."

Ace's daughter had taken another one of the pups in the litter that Caprice had helped deliver and named her Brindle.

The blonde cleared her throat and Ace got to his feet. Caprice watched Lady for her opinion of Ace's guest.

Her dog stayed close to Ace with wary eyes on the blonde.

Lady was a good judge of character, but Caprice should at least have a conversation with the woman before she sized her up too quickly.

"Caprice, meet Alanna Goodwin. Alanna, Caprice De Luca, home-stager extraordinaire. After all, if it weren't for her staging, I never would have bought this place."

So *this* was Alanna Goodwin. Caprice had heard

gossip about Ace and the Southern-born-and-bred Alanna. Supposedly he'd met the widow at a black tie function in Harrisburg over the Christmas holidays and had been dating her ever since. Now that Caprice had a good look at her, she remembered this woman attending an at-home concert Ace had given for the drop of his new single last month.

Caprice extended her hand to shake Alanna's. Alanna gave her outfit a look, somewhat like the look her sister Bella often gave her when she criticized her fashion sense.

But then the Southern beauty smiled winningly. "Hello, Caprice, it's so good to meet you. Ace speaks highly of you."

"Well, good," Caprice said with a smile. "I speak highly of him."

Ace gave a chuckle. "As I told you, Caprice says her mind. But she's usually right on the mark with staging and decorating."

Caprice wondered what Ace was up to. Drumming up business for her?

"Do you need my professional services with something?" she asked Alanna.

"Ace insists you're the best." Alanna looked toward Ace adoringly. "Do you want to ask her or should I?"

Ace's boyish look and a twinkle in his eye told Caprice he wanted a favor.

As he moved closer to Alanna, Lady came to stand with Caprice.

He said, "Alanna's going to sell her Kismet house and move in with me. I'd like you to stage it to sell. You can fit her in, can't you?"

He gave Caprice a little wink, and she knew what that meant. He was playing the friend favor card. After all, he'd done a couple of favors for her that had included leading a teenager on the right track in life. Ace was a good guy under the razzamatazz rock legend exterior, and she would help if she could.

She mentally reviewed her professional commit-ments. She hadn't intended to schedule a new client for another two months.

"Ace said you do your best work under pressure, al-though I don't know how he knows that," Alanna com-mented with a probing glance.

If she was honest with herself, and she usually was, Caprice had already sized up Alanna just as Lady had. She sensed there was an edge of steel in the Southern beauty, and she wondered if they'd clash or mesh on the best staging course to take if she accepted her as a client.

Alanna sweetly but cuttingly asked, "Have you been in Ace's guitar room often?"

Maybe Alanna just wanted to know if she was a threat. There had never been anything romantic between her and Ace.

Caprice explained, "I've been in here before when I was staging the house. I'm the one who suggested that he use it for his guitars."

"Caprice has been in my home more than most people," Ace added. "She redecorated Trista's room before she came to stay for the first weekend, and then redesigned it again when I got it all wrong."

"All wrong?" Alanna asked with a perfectly shaped eyebrow quirking up.

"I wanted it in pink and ruffles, trying to keep Trista a little girl. She hated it. But she and Caprice put their heads together and came up with exactly what Trista liked. Caprice will do a good job for you, Alanna. I know she will."

The best course to take was to see Alanna's house as soon as possible. So much for having a free Sunday afternoon.

She asked Alanna, "How does tomorrow afternoon suit? I can take a look at your house and you can decide if you'd like me to stage it."

After Alanna gave Caprice a once-over again, including Lady in the assessment, she nodded. "I'll pencil you in. But just so you know, I have a cat. You'll probably want to leave your dog at home."

A stiff March breeze whisked past Caprice's restored yellow Camaro on Sunday afternoon as she drove toward Alanna Goodwin's house a few miles outside of Kismet. Winter had been long and harsh this year. That sometimes happened in Pennsylvania. She'd spent many nights curled up on her sofa in front of a blazing fire, Lady on the floor beside her, her cat Sophia on the afghan on the back of the sofa as she worked on home-staging designs. But today, the promise of spring was faintly in the air.

As she turned down one rural road after another, she appreciated the bucolic setting with its rolling hills, groves of maples, sweet gum, and sycamores. She considered the older neighborhood where she lived in a 1950s Cape Cod that was just perfect for her and her animals. She was five minutes away from everything in Kismet, yet close enough to Harrisburg, York, D.C., and Baltimore to draw clients from there.

Her Camaro made a vroom as she took the last turn leading to Alanna's house. She drove her work van more than she used to when she had Lady along so her dog could be housed in her crate in the back. It was safer for her pup that way. Today she appreciated the responsiveness of her Camaro, and the exhilaration she felt when she drove it.

Lady was home alone this afternoon on another trial run. Her training was going well, and instead of penning her in the kitchen, Caprice had been giving her the run of the downstairs when she wasn't going to be away more than an hour or two. Lady and Sophia were buddies now. Toys that, when batted about released food crunchies, also kept Lady busy and out of trouble.

Alanna Goodwin's house, White Pillars, was easy to spot. Caprice had Googled Alanna after meeting her. The widow's deceased husband, Barton Goodwin, a self-made multimillionaire, had built the edifice for them twelve years ago when he'd moved them from Mississippi to Kismet. He'd died about a year ago. Apparently Alanna wasn't still in mourning and was ready to move on with her life.

Caprice tried not to be judgmental. She didn't like anybody judging her. Alanna and Ace? They just didn't seem to fit together quite right.

Alanna's home resembled a plantation mansion. Tall white pillars that had given the estate its name surrounded two sides of the house. Along the east side of the mansion stretched a screened-in veranda that

Caprice imagined might also stretch along the back. As
she parked in the driveway, pulled her patent-leather
purse with her electronic tablet from the seat beside her,
and climbed out of her car, she stared up at the mansion.
The entrance somehow managed to be both formidable
and southerly inviting. She felt as if she was traveling
through the old South and had come upon an historical
showplace.

A multi-toned chime sounded when Caprice pressed
the bell. Alanna herself opened the huge white door,
smiled easily, and after a "hello" invited Caprice inside.

Today Caprice had dressed in loose-legged khaki
slacks with a military-cut jacket reminiscent of one the
Beatles wore at their landmark Shea Stadium concert.
Her low navy patent pumps coordinated with her purse.
As she stepped into the house, her long hair swished
over her shoulder. She was ready for this meeting. She
just hoped Alanna Goodwin was too.

"What do you want to do first?" Alanna asked.

"Let me have a look around. A theme is already
presenting itself, but I want to make sure. I'll run it by
you after I take a look at everything."

Right away, Caprice could see Alanna's furnishings
were all Southern hospitality with traditional appeal. A
crystal chandelier in the foyer, large prisms dangling
from it, hung directly above a round, pedestal table with
a three-foot-tall flower arrangement. Lilies projected a
sweet scent that probably permeated the adjoining
rooms. If Alanna had a cat, she shouldn't have lilies anywhere in the house. They were toxic to felines.

As Caprice moved forward, she could see early to
mid-nineteenth century style landscape paintings deco-

rated the walls in the living room. She was pretty sure
the mid-nineteenth century antiques were *not* reproduc-
tions. High-backed, floral upholstery-trimmed chairs in
dark wood complemented two velvet settees.

As Caprice stepped into the dining room, admiring
the dark wood table with its solid wood chairs, made
unique by ornamental backs and arms, a beautiful white
Persian cat suddenly appeared. It blinked at Caprice and
meowed.

"Well, hello there! Just who are you?"

The cat gave another meow then walked slowly
toward Caprice, ending up beside her and rubbing
against her leg. Without hesitation, Caprice automatically dropped down and held out her hand.

The animal sniffed it and butted her head against
Caprice's palm. Caprice laughed, touching the soft-
as-cotton long hair. "You're a beauty."

"And she knows it," Alanna said. "That's Mirabelle.
She's declawed. You don't have to worry about her
scratching you."

Declawed—so she wouldn't mar any of Alanna's
furniture, carpet, or heavy drapes. Caprice tried not to
look too aghast. When trained correctly, a cat didn't
have to damage anything. Apparently Alanna hadn't
wanted to put the effort into teaching her to use a
scratching post.

Mirabelle kept by Caprice's side as she rounded the
long dining room table with its green eyelet runner and
ornate stand in the center that held a display of fruit and
nuts. In the kitchen, pie safes, glass-fronted cabinets
and hutches provided additional storage to display decorative plates and large tureens.

As Caprice made a thorough tour of the rest of the house, Mirabelle followed her the whole way. Every once in a while, Caprice stooped and petted her, and the cat responded affectionately as if she was starved for the attention. That really wasn't fair. Caprice didn't know what kind of a pet owner Alanna was.

At one point Alanna said, "I can tuck her away so she doesn't bother you."

Caprice wasn't exactly sure what Alanna meant by that. But she already liked the cat who just seemed to want company. "She's fine with me."

However, pets aside, by the time she returned downstairs, she wasn't sure how Alanna and Ace were going to combine their very different styles. She didn't think Ace would particularly like heavy armoires and four-poster beds, pie safes, and ornate sculptures. Yet, maybe it was Alanna's Southern charm that had attracted Ace to her. Who knew?

In the living room with Alanna once more, Caprice sat on a settee, Alanna on a chair beside it.

Mirabelle stood at Caprice's feet and looked up at her lap.

But Alanna shook her finger at the cat. "Oh, no. You go over there and sit on your bed."

Caprice took one look at the ornate, shiny brass cat bed low to the floor, not placed in any direct sunlight, and wondered why any cat would like to sleep on it. Cats she knew preferred high places, windows, sunshine in as many forms as they could get it. But Mirabelle must have been used to listening to her owner because she went to the bed, folded her paws under her, and didn't look particularly happy.

Caprice told herself If she wanted Alanna as a client, even only as a favor to Ace, she really should bite her tongue and be pleasant.

So she tried to be. "I think it's easy to see what the theme for your staging should be—Antebellum Ecstasy. We'll play up all the best parts of Southern hospitality and emphasize the charm of living in a Southern mansion. You really should be able to keep most of your furnishings here, but one of the first rules of staging is to declutter."

"Declutter? I don't understand."

"Even though I plan staging themes, I have to make sure a prospective home buyer can imagine moving in their possessions too. Besides that, too many pieces of furniture take away from the beauty of each one. Many of my clients rent a storage shed or begin selling the furniture they don't intend to take with them when they move."

"I'm not exactly sure what I'd be moving into Ace's," Alanna said with a pensive look. "We haven't discussed that."

"You should make a list," Caprice advised her. "There are also advantages to incorporating a few more inviting colors rather than the deep browns and dark greens in most of these rooms."

"I'm not changing my color schemes."

Ah hah. The resistance she'd expected with this woman. "I'm not suggesting you change them. I'm suggesting you incorporate lighter colors with them."

She motioned to the draperies in the living room, the heavy tie-backs with the fringe. "For instance, just think about removing those draperies, hanging sheers, letting in more daylight. That will make the room more inviting."

"I am not taking down my draperies. They go with the house. They're part of its character."

Caprice swallowed a retort and reminded herself Alanna could be the love of Ace's life. "Mrs. Goodwin, would you like to sell the house quickly?"

Alanna looked trapped. "Yes, I want to sell the house quickly. That's the whole point of hiring you. I'm ready to make a home for me and Ace."

Caprice nodded, seeing that in her statement Alanna seemed sincere. "Why don't I make a list of suggestions of pieces of furniture you can remove. Instead of removing the draperies entirely, maybe we could take away the tiebacks and the dark semi-sheers and use something more see-through. I'll compromise with you, Mrs. Goodwin. But you have to remember, whatever I suggest will aid in selling the house. For example, I would never remove your Oriental carpet. But I might add a shawl over the back of one of the dark chairs to complement the lighter blue in the rug. I might take away the dark velvet throw pillows and use a pale green that might match the sheers. Do you see the changes I'm talking about?"

Today Alanna was dressed in a pale gray cashmere sweater and deeper gray slacks. The pearls and earrings she wore were classically beautiful. This woman should be able to understand easily what Caprice wanted to do.

Alanna cast a glance around the first floor of her home. "It will be hard to leave this," she said. "But I'm ready."

Knowing Ace wasn't alone in this new romantic

adventure and his daughter Trista would be along for the
ride, Caprice couldn't help but ask, "Have you and
Trista spent time together?"

At that question, Alanna's face took on a look almost
the same as when she talked about her cat. Shuttered.
"I'm not concerned about Trista. We've met, but she
doesn't live with Ace. She's simply a now and then
weekend daughter. That's a shame, of course, but that's
just how it's going to be."

That seemed to be a line drawn in the sand for
Alanna. However, as she finished with her conclusion,
a shadow passed over her face. Alanna was about five
years older than Caprice, maybe in her late thirties. It
was hard to tell. From her background research, Caprice
had learned Alanna had begun her professional life as
a journalist in Mississippi. She'd met Barton Goodwin
when she'd interviewed him for a story and they'd
married a few months later. Apparently Barton had in-
vented a new kind of scaffolding for construction sites,
and his company had established enterprises worldwide.
He'd moved them to Kismet to be closer to Washington,
Baltimore, and New York. With his sudden heart attack,
he'd left everything to Alanna, including his company.

From her research Caprice had surmised Alanna
didn't seem to have much to do with the day to day
running of the company, but she did sit on the board
of directors. Maybe she wished she and Barton had had
children. Often when women reached their late thirties,
they thought about that more. However, Caprice was
just guessing. She didn't know Alanna and doubted
she'd get to know her. The widow seemed to be the type

of woman who usually kept her guard up—a mint julep
with more bite than sweetness.

Caprice took her electronic tablet from her purse. "If
you don't mind, I'm going to go upstairs again and
make that list for you of the pieces you can remove. That
is, if you're interested in hiring me."

"Ace would be disappointed if I didn't."

"I can e-mail you a proposal tonight."

After considering Caprice's services once more,
Alanna nodded and gave Caprice a fake smile. "Make
your list. I promise I'll consider each item seriously."

Caprice doubted that she would. But if they could
compromise, they could make this house staging a real
success.

When Caprice returned to the living room twenty
minutes later, she found Alanna seated at a roll-top desk
in the side parlor adjacent to the larger room. Mirabelle
was no longer in sight and she wondered if Alanna had
"tucked" her away.

This room possibly served as Alanna's office. She
didn't mean to sneak up on Alanna, but the woman
seemed focused on something at her desk. As Caprice
looked over Alanna's shoulder, she spied a photo of a
little girl who looked to be about six.

The charm bracelet Caprice wore almost every day
now must have jingled as she shifted her tablet in her
hand because Alanna started, then quickly slipped the
photo back into the desk drawer. Caprice wondered who
the child was.

That was none of her business.

She asked Alanna, "Do you have an e-mail address
where I can send the proposal and my list of notes?"

Alanna rattled off her address. As she did, the white porcelain and gold decorative phone on her desk jangled. Alanna said, "Could you excuse me a minute? I'm expecting a call."

"I can see myself out."

Alanna shook her head. "There is something else I'd like to ask you."

As Caprice wondered what that could be, she moved away from the parlor into the living room to give Alanna privacy.

Still, she could hear bits of the conversation, although Alanna kept her voice low.

"It worked. That's what matters," Alanna said. After she listened a few moments, she murmured, "It's not sabotage when it's for his own good. Keep me up to date."

Without even a goodbye, she set the handset on the receiver. Glancing at Caprice, Alanna manufactured a smile and joined her in the living room.

Wanting to get back home to her animals, thinking about taking Lady to the dog park before she put together Alanna's proposal, Caprice said, "You wanted to ask me something?"

Alanna studied her. "Are you and Ace good friends?"

Caprice picked up her purse from the settee where she'd left it and made eye contact with Alanna. "I don't know if we're *good* friends. We've talked to each other about some things that matter. I like his daughter a lot. Last summer, I found a stray dog who was pregnant. When she had her litter, Ace said Trista could have one of her pups. Trista and I've talked a lot about the dogs and training them, and Ace has been around for that too."

"I care about him deeply," Alanna said firmly, as if that was in doubt.

Caprice wasn't exactly sure what to say to that. If Ace was in love and had found a soul mate, she was all for it. But had Ace dated Alanna long enough to really know her?

"I wish you two all the best," Caprice responded sincerely.

But after Caprice left, after she climbed into her Camaro and headed for home, she wasn't sure what that "best" would be.